WHISKERS IN THE DARK

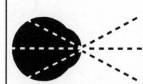

This Large Print Book carries the
Seal of Approval of N.A.V.H.

A MRS. MURPHY MYSTERY

WHISKERS IN THE DARK

RITA MAE BROWN
AND SNEAKY PIE BROWN

Illustrated by Michael Gellatly

THORNDIKE PRESS
A part of Gale, a Cengage Company

Farmington Hills, Mich • San Francisco • New York • Waterville, Maine
Meriden, Conn • Mason, Ohio • Chicago

Copyright © 2019 by American Artists, Inc.
Illustrations copyright © 2019 by Michael Gellatly.
Thorndike Press, a part of Gale, a Cengage Company.

Thorndike Press® Large Print Basic.
The text of this Large Print edition is unabridged.
Other aspects of the book may vary from the original edition.
Set in 16 pt. Plantin.

LIBRARY OF CONGRESS CIP DATA ON FILE.
CATALOGUING IN PUBLICATION FOR THIS BOOK
IS AVAILABLE FROM THE LIBRARY OF CONGRESS

ISBN-13: 978-1-4328-6720-1 (hardcover alk. paper)

Published in 2019 by arrangement with Bantam Books, an imprint of Random House, a division of Penguin Random House LLC

Printed in Mexico
1 2 3 4 5 6 7 23 22 21 20 19

For Professor Iris Love
She has held the past in her hands
Therefore she knows the future.

THE CAST OF CHARACTERS

THE PRESENT

Mary Minor Haristeen, "Harry" — She's loyal, logical, loves her husband, her animals, her friends. She farms on her old family farm. Her weakness is her curiosity. Her husband is Pharamond Haristeen, DVM, "Fair," an equine vet specializing in reproduction. More sensitive than Harry, he provides ballast.

Susan Tucker — She's known Harry all her life; they are now forty-two. She tries to keep Harry out of trouble, rarely succeeding. Ned Tucker, her husband, is a first-time representative to the Virginia House of Delegates. Susan's grandfather was a former governor of the state, who owned Big Rawly Estate.

The Very Reverend Herbert Jones — As the pastor of St. Luke's Church, he knows his flock and is a central part of the community. Widowed, he has three Lutheran

9

cats: Lucy Fur, Cazenovia, and Elocution.

Arlene Billeaud — Master of Blastoff Beagles, she was wounded in the Middle East while in the Army. She has a prosthetic leg and moves around easily. This year she is in charge of the Hounds F4R Heroes fundraiser for veterans held at the Institute at Aldie, Virginia.

Jason Holzknect — Retired from the foreign service where he built a fine career in communications, he is Master of Chesapeake Beagles. He's made bundles of money through his car dealership.

Clare Lazo Holzknect — Joint Master with her husband, she was a Navy captain, having met Jason overseas.

THE EIGHTEENTH CENTURY

CLOVERFIELDS

Catherine Schuyler — Highly intelligent, she assists her father in his business. Her passion is breeding and training horses. Impossibly beautiful, she is married to Major John Schuyler, a hero of the Revolutionary War. It is a good marriage.

Rachel West — A warmer personality than her older sister, by two years, the twenty-year-old Rachel is married to a former POW, a British captain, captured by

Catherine's husband at the Battle of Saratoga. Both are involved in building St. Luke's Lutheran Church, which Charles designed, thereby finding his passion apart from his wonderful wife.

Ewing Garth — The owner of Cloverfields, the father of the above sisters, he is a sound businessman. He pays attention to the economy, nascent, as well as Europe's. He is a warm, kind man who greatly misses his deceased wife.

Maureen Selisse Holloway — Rich beyond imagination, she owns Big Rawly, still in the Holloway family today. Susan Tucker's maiden name is Holloway. Maureen's younger second husband, Jeffrey Holloway, not well born, works with his hands and is divinely handsome, which overcomes the above. Maureen has a sharp business sense, is farsighted, and can be brutal and ruthless when she needs to be.

Yancy Grant — Infuriated more than anyone by the above hasty marriage, he hates Jeffrey. Being challenged to a duel by Jeffrey wounded both men, yet a respect resulted from this.

THE SLAVES: CLOVERFIELDS

Bettina — A cook of magical abilities, she is also head slave woman on the estate.

When Ewing's wife was dying, Bettina nursed her and stayed with her. When Isabelle died, Bettina promised her mistress she would take care of Catherine and Rachel. She kept her promise.

Jeddie Rice — With good hands and a light seat, he has a sure touch with horses and soaks up everything Catherine teaches him. At nineteen he's a man but evidences no interest in anything but the horses. He is ambitious without being obnoxious, for a horseman can rise in the world, slave or free.

Ralston — Seethes with competitive anger at Jeddie. He's not a bad hand with the horses, but he lacks Jeddie's marvelous gifts. At sixteen he thinks he knows everything. He has discovered women and is making a mess of it.

Tulli — He might be eleven but he looks about nine. Such a sweet little fellow, he works at the stables and tries very hard.

Barker O — Runs the stables, drives the horses, is splendid on the seat of the carriages. He enjoys a big reputation among horsemen, much deserved.

Roger — Being butler, his is a powerful position. He must know most of the people who call on Ewing, as well as how to treat them according to their station.

He's a good, reticent man.

Weymouth — Roger's son, in his twenties. He does a good job but he lacks his father's drive.

Bumbee — She's in charge of the weaving, buying yarns and fabrics. She's an artist, truly, and the ladies who work with her do as they are told.

THE SLAVES: BIG RAWLY

DoRe — Runs the stables, is Barker O's counterpart. As Jeffrey Holloway now builds sumptuous carriages, DoRe shows them off to buyers. He has been courting Bettina.

Elizabetta — As Maureen's replacement lady's maid since Sheba vanished with a fortune in pearls set amidst diamonds, hers is a nonstop position. She's lazy when Maureen is away. She's a decent sort.

William — Worked in the stables but escaped Big Rawly riding a neighbor's blooded horse. He has sneaked back, foolish, but he's come to steal more things and he's come for Sulli.

Sulli — Pretty, in her teens, she believes she and William can run away together and live happily ever after. Not only will they be free; they will be free and rich. She thinks she's in love.

THE ANIMALS

Mrs. Murphy — Harry's tiger cat, who often evidences more brains than her human.

Pewter — A fat gray cat with an inflated opinion of herself. She believes the world began when she entered it.

Tee Tucker — An intrepid corgi bred years ago by Susan Tucker, the sensible dog watches out for Harry and endures Pewter.

Pirate — A half-grown Irish wolfhound who came to Harry and Fair when his owner died. He is very sweet and learning the ropes from Tucker. Rule One: Never believe anything Pewter says.

Tomahawk — Harry's retired gray Thoroughbred.

Shortro — A gift from Joan Hamilton of Kalarama Farm, this young Saddlebred is adjusting to hunt seat. He's smart.

Ruffy — A beagle ghost living at the Institute.

THE EIGHTEENTH-CENTURY ANIMALS

Piglet — The corgi that started the corgi line still at Big Rawly. He endured the war and captivity with Charles West.

Reynaldo — A blooded horse, terrific conformation and fast. He's young, full of fire.

14

Crown Prince — The above's half brother, calmer.

Black Knight — Thoroughbred stolen by William, he has come to Cloverfields, where he has been restored to health and happiness.

Chief — A bombproof horse who takes care of Ewing Garth.

Sweet Potato — A saucy pony for the children.

1

April 5, 2018
Thursday

"Did you kill anybody?" Harry asked as the firelight flickered on her face.

"Do you think I'm going to answer that question?" Arlene Billeaud laughed at her.

Harry Haristeen, her best friend, Susan Tucker, Arlene Billeaud, Jason Holzknect, and his wife, Clare Lazo Holzknect, sat by the fireplace in the large stone building known as the Institute in Aldie, Virginia. Built in the 1850s as the Loudoun Agricultural and Chemical Institute, it had weathered many a storm. In 1855 an advertisement claimed that courses would benefit the farmer, the merchant, the engineer, certainly a broad student base. But the panic of 1857, a damaging depression for so many, ended the Institute. Next came the war. Still it persevered, today being the home of the National Beagle Club of America.

The people in the inviting room had come from Maryland and Virginia to clean up paths, move downed trees, and repair the kennels, as violent storms had swept through Loudoun County and much of Northern Virginia.

They were there to prepare for the annual competition hosted by Hounds F4R Heroes at the end of the month. Anyone could enter two pairs of beagles — four hounds — to hunt, prizes being given to the top couples.

The purpose, to raise money for veterans, drew many spectators and competitors. The funds were used to provide veterans with fishing and hunting events. This was done in other states as well and was growing nationally.

The small group arrived early for tomorrow's work. Others would drive in the next morning. Harry and Susan stayed in one of the cabins, the first ones built in 1917 when the Institute was just up and running. Other cabins were added later, tight, warm if you kept the fire going, with enough windows to let in the light. Harry's two cats, Mrs. Murphy and Pewter, along with her two dogs, Tucker, a corgi, and Pirate, a half-grown Irish wolfhound, were back at the cabin. No dirty paws at the Institute.

"Another drink?" Jason, tall, maybe mid-fifties, offered, pointing to the opened bottle of wine.

"No thanks," Harry, not a drinker, replied.

"A smidge." Susan raised her glass as did the other two women.

Apart from the work they expected to face tomorrow, they talked about packs of hounds, both bassets and beagles; their hunting season, which had just ended; friends in common.

"Oh, come on." Harry tweaked Arlene. "We know you had a dangerous job before you retired."

"Not as dangerous as you might think. I was not an undercover agent."

Arlene had recently retired from the Central Intelligence Agency.

"Rats." Harry pretended to pout. "I want good stories."

"Well, this isn't a good story, but my area was Russia, so I was responsible for absorbing and digesting information from that area."

"From undercover agents there?" Harry was fascinated.

"I would never say we have agents there, but I can promise you we have their agents here." Arlene smiled.

Clare, a former Navy captain, sipped her white wine. "Not only does Russia have agents here but so do our allies. Everyone spies on everyone and yes, Harry, we, too, have agents everywhere. One must."

"The best way to look at this is that power is amoral." Jason settled into his chair, having poured himself another glass of wine.

"I know what you're saying is true, but it drives me crazy," Susan said. "All that money to sift through people's computers, hacking this and hacking that. Following people, and I suppose killing some. Harry isn't far wrong."

"So the question is if one must kill, say, a Nigerian undercover agent who is funneling American funds to a terrorist group, thousands are dying, is the murder justified?" Arlene asked a question back.

"Well, if we aren't being killed, no." Harry was firm.

"What about the terrorists, at least I think of them as terrorists, who kidnapped the girls in Nigeria? It doesn't affect us, but you don't kidnap hundreds of children." Susan tried to think this out.

"But sending operatives over there costs a lot of money, sending troops outright even more," Jason said. "When I was in the diplomatic corps, depending on where I was assigned, we were always told and trained, 'Hands off!' "

Clare spoke again. "The theory is that every state has sovereign rights. They may treat their people quite differently than we treat ours, but we have no right to interfere in internal issues, no matter how repugnant. Hence agencies like the CIA, which does not necessarily interfere, but provides information to shape our foreign policy that a diplomat going through normal channels may not be able to provide."

"Jason, did you ever feel you were in a tight spot?" Harry's curiosity kept her questioning.

"Not physically. As you know, my longest posting was in Ankara, Turkey. I speak fluent Turkish, know the culture, and have a smattering of some languages of countries near Turkey. Enough to be able to read, say, a Russian headline. But Turkey's geographic position guarantees it will forever be a trade and political crossroads. Any violence in surrounding countries, such as Greece — remember they've had riots — could spill over into Turkey."

"Greece would invade Turkey?" Harry was incredulous.

"Not today." Jason smiled. "But riots in Greece or in the Crimea, for instance, might set off the disaffected in Turkey. Every nation has a pool of disaffected people who can take to the streets with or without much provocation. This includes us."

"Unfortunately, it does. Which is why Hounds for Heroes is important." Arlene put her feet up on a hassock. "Those men and women, many of them, have seen service in miserable spots. But if you've worn our country's uniform, you deserve some recognition. I'm thrilled we can provide sport."

Harry knew that Arlene had lost a leg in the Middle East. She had a good false limb masked by well-tailored slacks and socks. She'd served in the Army before being recruited, not a word that Arlene used, for the CIA. Her analytical skills and her IQ made her particularly valuable. Not that she wasn't valuable in the Army, but while she was recuperating in a Veterans Hospital she was wooed. Turned out to be a wonderful job for her. She liked the Army but she loved the Agency. Then again, she was in no danger of losing her other leg in Washington.

"I predict Ashland Bassets will win the basset day. Beagles, maybe Sandanona or Ben Venue." Jason sounded authoritative.

"Why aren't we going to win?" His wife raised her eyebrows.

"What do you think?" Jason asked Arlene.

"Since I'm the director of the event for this year, I plead neutral. I'm hoping for good weather, whoever wins."

"Ashland Bassets, Waldingfield Beagles." Harry gave her favorites.

"Can't do that, Harry. We know those hunts. Of course, we want them to win, but who knows?" Susan looked at her watch. "You know what, I'm turning in. We should be up and out at first light tomorrow, especially since we don't know how much damage there is. We have five hundred and twelve acres to canvas."

"Glad as I am that the founders of the National Beagle Club had the foresight to buy all this, it is a lot to maintain," Clare posited.

"Is, but there's no place like it." Harry stood up with Susan. "Cold though, isn't it?"

"Going to be a late spring." Arlene knew she should rouse herself, but she was ready to fall asleep where she was.

Harry and Susan left the building, hurrying to their cabin, smoke curling out of the chimney since Harry had built a solid fire before they joined the others. As the humans opened the door, the dogs awakened, hurried up, tails wagging.

"Oh, I missed you." Tucker, the corgi, licked Harry's hand.

"Me, too," the growing giant, Pirate, agreed.

One eye now open, fat, gray Pewter, grumbled, *"Suck-ups."*

Mrs. Murphy, sprawled on the comforter on the narrow bed with Pewter, flicked the tip of her tail. *"We can at least purr."*

Harry carefully placed two more logs on the fire, adjusting the grate cover. "That should see us through the night."

"You build good fires. I kind of think there's going to be a lot to do."

"Yeah." Harry agreed with Susan. "Wasn't Clare in the Navy?"

"She speaks fluent Russian. She was, according to her, mostly on a giant ship out in the Gulf of Finland, listening to the Russians, not far away."

"I wouldn't have the patience for that. Would you?"

"I suppose I could do it, but I wouldn't like it. Well, I wouldn't mind being on a ship for months at a time." Susan took off her shoes and socks, stripped off her clothes, quickly jumped into bed. "I'd think of it as a long respite from housework."

The room was warm but the bed would be warmer.

"I am not moving," Pewter announced as Harry also stripped down, turned back a corner of the covers.

"Pewter, I need to get into bed."

"I was here first."

"Come on, move over." Harry pushed the large cat a bit away from where the covers were turned back.

"Abused. I am being abused!"

"Shut up," Tucker, in front of the fire, called out.

"Lickspittle!" Pewter replied.

"Come on, you two. I need to sleep," Mrs. Murphy suggested.

"Here we are in this cabin, in the middle of nowhere. Nothing ever happens here. I feel boredom already. I am a saint to come along. Really," Pewter whined.

"I would hardly call being in Loudoun County the middle of nowhere." Mrs. Murphy felt a pair of feet slide under her.

"Isn't it the most populous county in Virginia?" Tucker questioned.

"If it isn't, it soon will be," Mrs. Murphy replied. She listened to everything Fair, Harry's husband, read aloud from the *Richmond Times-Dispatch*.

"Night, Harry."

"Night, Susan. Night babies."

"Night," came the chorus.

25

2

April 6, 2018
Friday

"Wish the buds would open. You can see the color, but so far, nothing," Harry remarked to Susan.

"We have a few warmish days and then bam, cold again." Susan cleared a tree limb from a footpath far from the Institute building.

The earth, hard underneath, wore out one's legs after a time, made one's feet hurt. The two had been at their labors all day. Their bodies were beginning to talk back to them.

"Jeez, that's a big one." Harry exhaled.

Susan stood and looked over the massive uprooted tree from which the limb had been torn. "I thought *we* suffered horrible windstorms. Had to be worse up here."

"Northern Virginia's weather is different from ours. What are we, an hour and a half away, and yet it really is different. Well, girl, let's start at the thinnest end and do this in small sections. That way, we can pull them to the side of the path as we go."

"Okay."

They worked six feet from each other, fired up their chain saws, wisely placing them under the tree limb, cutting up at an angle, stopping as they neared the top. Then each woman slipped the chain saw down and cut from the top, thereby lessening the chances of it slicing through the limb faster than they anticipated and cutting a thigh. Happened all the time to people not accustomed to operating chain saws. As these were two country girls, they handled equipment — chain saws, posthole diggers, tractors — with ease.

These old friends had been in the cradle together, and primary and high school, then Harry went to Smith and Susan went to William and Mary. For vacations they'd team up together, sometimes traveling to other countries. They adored each other's husbands, shared friends and some passions, especially gardening. Susan was the better gardener, Harry the better farmer.

Cutting off their chain saws, they each moved a hunk of tree limb to the side.

"What do you think?" Susan asked.

"Well, beagles and bassets can pass. People, too, if they look where they're going." Harry studied the opening they were cutting through the trees. "You know, the competitions are only two weeks away. There will be dozens more people here than on a regular trials weekend. Basset trials on Friday, beagle trials on Saturday, cocktail parties both nights, and a dance party and pig roast. It'll be quite a party, but no one anticipated so much damage could happen in the month since the Triple Challenge. The trails will be ready, but it will take many hands. It's so important." Harry hastened to add, "We all want the event to go well."

The Triple Challenge, sponsored by the National Beagle Club, a three-day event, tested both hounds and humans. Three phases included the hunting talent of the individual hound, the ability to contribute to the working pack, and the qualities of conformation, movement, condition, and temperament.

Hounds F4R Heroes, a competition later in April, not only showed off the beagle's versatility but also the basset's. The competitions hunted on different days since one didn't hunt bassets and beagles together. Last year Hounds F4R Heroes contributed twenty thousand dollars to veterans.

Each year the event grew as more people learned about it. All the beagle and basset hunters wanted to contribute however they could.

Beagle packs and basset packs had foot followers. People stayed in good shape as they walked the hounds in the off-season, ran after them during the season. Both types of hounds chased rabbits. Anyone who had ever called a rabbit a "dumb bunny" hadn't chased one. Bunnies managed to elude the hounds, but sometimes the run might go on for an hour or even longer. What a thrill that was for the huntsman, the whippers-in, and the people running their butts off behind the hounds.

Harry and Susan followed the Waldingfield Beagles, the oldest pack in America, having been founded in 1885. Harry and her husband also foxhunted, but Susan and her husband weren't much for riding so Harry started running along with her friend and found that she loved it. She never could jog — bored her to tears — but following a flying pack enlivened her. Being in good shape anyway, she was now in even better shape.

"How far are we from the cabin?" Harry wondered.

"I don't know. Maybe fifteen minutes,"

Susan guessed. She looked up at the sky. "Doesn't look good, does it?"

"What was it Satchel Paige said, 'Don't look, something might be gaining on you'?"

Susan laughed. "Don't look back. Well, girl, I'm about done. Bet the other work parties are, too. Let's head back."

"Sounds good." Harry put her fingers between her lips, emitting a loud whistle.

Tucker, Harry's corgi, and Pirate, who Harry and Fair had taken in when his owner was killed, lifted their heads.

"Time to go," the obedient corgi announced.

"Oh, this smells really good." The already large dog waffled.

Tucker ambled over, put her nose to the ground, inhaled. *"Yes, it does smell good, but you don't want to meet this guy. A bear. Even bigger than you when you're full-grown."*

Pirate's lovely brown eyes widened. *"A bear. Like we see on TV sometimes?"*

"Yeah. Mom watches those nature shows. Black bears don't want trouble but best to keep your distance. Actually, it's even best to keep your distance from some deer. Not every animal likes dogs." Tucker turned, trotting in the direction of the whistle. *"Come on. If we show up late, she'll fret."*

Taking a brief breather, the two friends

30

sat on an old fallen tree off the road.

"I'm feeling my age." Susan shook her head.

"At forty-three?"

"Forty-two!" Susan squinted at Harry.

"Just wanted to see if your mind was going." Harry giggled.

"Better be careful. I know how to get even." Susan punched Harry's arm lightly.

"Oh, but Susan, you're such a good Christian."

"You're pushing it." Susan laughed as she noticed the two dogs, smiles on their faces, coming toward them.

"I smelled a bear," the puppy enthused.

Tucker added, *"And a mess of turkeys. I don't know how many rabbits there are here, but you could sure hunt turkeys."*

Harry dropped her hand on Pirate's head as Susan petted Tucker. "Isn't this the ridge near where the First Massachusetts Cavalry was slaughtered? Is that what I'm looking at over there?" She pointed in the direction of the bend in the old road west of the farmhouse. Neither the Union forces nor the Confederate expected to encounter one another that seventeenth of June 1863, but encounter they did, and the First Massachusetts was cut to ribbons.

"That's supposed to be it." Susan loved

31

history, having been a history major at college. "People don't realize that sixty percent of that war was fought in Virginia. There was a reason we didn't want to secede. We knew those soldiers would cross the Potomac long before they'd get into Georgia or other parts." She sighed. "But this engagement was fought piecemeal. Brigadier General Judson Kilpatrick, in command of the Massachusetts Brigade, never sent scouts ahead. None of the Union commanders did. And let us never forget, we grew up riding. Those New England boys did not."

"How many men are in a brigade?"

"Varies. A lot of times, the papers reported bigger numbers than there were to try to scare the enemy. Didn't work. But maybe a thousand. Anyway. There was a curve — we'll pass it once we hit the rise where the Confederates held their position. The Federals never had a chance."

Harry rubbed Pirate. "There's no such thing as a good war."

Susan nodded. "No, but there are necessary wars. Got my wind back." She stood up.

"There's our little red wagon, waiting for us up ahead. I'll be glad to dump my chain saw. It gets heavy after a while."

Overhead the birds started to head home

as the women placed their tools in the wagon. Harry took first turn pulling while the dogs tagged along.

They reached the kennels, wooden structures for the different packs, well built, but a tree limb had smashed right through the roof of one kennel, knocking down the fence as well.

"Guess they'll get to that tomorrow," Susan noted.

Harry paused a moment. "The main stone building really is impressive. It was a hospital during the war. It seems as good as the day it was built. The white porch and railing set off the stone. Like I said, impressive."

"Stone lasts," Susan replied.

"Does." Then Harry said, "Yet I feel this tug of sorrow when I look at it."

"What's strange is that so many died when it was a hospital, and no one is sure where they are buried. But the limbs, the amputated limbs, are supposed to be over there." Susan pointed to a long, low mound.

"Odd." Harry grimaced.

They trudged to their cabin, eager to reach it.

As they reached the cabin, sitting on the front porch were Mrs. Murphy and Pewter.

"Killed a platoon of mice. We set a world

record!" Pewter puffed up.

As she was given to overstatement, the dogs looked to the far more reasonable tiger cat.

"Barn is full of them." Mrs. Murphy verified Pewter's bragging.

The mouse infestation was the reason the cats had been allowed to visit. Of course, none of the house pets could come to the fundraiser, but they were useful right now and happy to be along despite Pewter's complaining.

Once cleaned up, food put down for the animals, a fire renewed in the fireplace, for it was really getting cold, Harry and Susan walked over to the stone house for supper. The food was always wonderful. Everyone had worked up an appetite.

About twenty people sat at the tables, all talking at once about respective work parties.

Harry, next to Amy Burke Walker, a member of the board of directors and a whipper-in for the Waldingfield Beagles hunted by Dr. Arie Rijke, mentioned the mound.

Amy agreed. "Right, no one knows where the bodies are but people say they've seen ghosts out and about. Some have been seen in this building."

Liz Kelly, a young archivist, leaned toward them from the opposite side of the table. "For over one hundred years people here have claimed to see Civil War ghosts."

Liz Reeser, the assistant treasurer, piped up. "I swear I saw one. A young man who walked right by me in the middle of the night. But I wasn't afraid. I don't know why."

Betsy Park, from Sandanona Hounds in New York, smiled. "Oh, people always say that about a war hospital."

Mary Reed, Master of Bassets for Ashland Bassets, agreed. "They do, don't they? Still?" She raised her eyebrows.

Jason Holzknect smiled. "When I was in Turkey, every part of any city or little town hosted ghosts. There were ghosts from the fifth century B.C., ghosts from Justinian's time, ghosts from Atatürk's takeover. More ghosts than the living. I never saw one." He laughed.

Arlene tweaked him. "Maybe you scared them off."

He laughed back. "Could be."

Jason rose high in his profession, got good postings, finally ending his career in Paris, owned a car dealership outside of D.C. in Maryland. He'd made a great deal of money. Of course, Clare helped.

35

"Well, I wasn't in Turkey like you, but I did see Istanbul," Arlene said to Jason. "It is exciting. The Russians still lust after it. Always will."

"We have everything in this country," Mary Reed added. "Deepwater ports on both the Atlantic and Pacific Oceans. Great rivers. Good soil. When you travel, you realize Mother Nature made us rich."

"True," Susan agreed, then turned to Arlene. "Did you ever see ghosts in your travels?"

A long pause followed this.

"I'm not sure. Once I thought I saw something but" — she shrugged — "who knows?"

As the humans chatted away, the two cats and two dogs sat on the porch of the cabin, fur fluffed out to ward off the cold, although Pewter was ready to go inside and sit by the fire. Miss Pewter liked her creature comforts.

"Who's that?" Tucker noticed a beagle in front of the stone house.

"I thought we were the only animals here." Pewter sat up for a better look as the beagle moved toward them.

The little dog stopped. The four friends could see its tricolor, its handsome head,

36

but somehow the animal appeared insubstantial.

Mrs. Murphy, whiskers forward, called out. *"Who are you?"*

The dog stared at them, did not answer, and turned, heading for the tree line behind the kennels.

Pirate, puzzled, remarked, *"I can see through that dog."*

All four, now on their feet, watched the disappearing beagle.

Tucker, voice low, declared, *"That's a ghost."*

3

April 7, 2018
Saturday

Rich Shaw, sheriff of Albemarle County, thought golf would help him stop smoking. How he arrived at this conclusion remained a mystery. He was out on Farmington Country Club's golf course puffing on his Shepheard's Hotel like a chimney. That was the other problem. He smoked only expensive foreign cigarettes, Dunhill being his other favorite.

Playing with him on a notoriously cool day were Cindy Chandler, Nelson Yarbrough, D.D.S., and Catherine Hanlon, M.D., a physician visiting from New Jersey. None of these people said a word about Rick, who did exhale downwind of everyone.

The greens, tended even throughout winter, proved better than expected. The maintenance of any golf course costs a bundle. An old grand course like Farmington really cost. Like all golfing places, it had been added to over time: driving ranges, more parking, and another back course. Poor people did not play at Farmington, but then, in general, poor people did not play golf.

Despite the cold, all four were glad to be outside. There's something in the back of a golfer's mind that if you get out at the first hint of spring, winter will be behind you.

Nelson made par a lot, as did Cindy, whose putter was golden this Saturday. Catherine, a beginner, broke 90, to her excitement and that of the others. A natural athlete, she was determined to master this notoriously difficult game.

Grateful for their sweaters and heavy socks, they finished their game in good humor. Dropping their two carts at the small parking area, the cart garage, they were soon seated at the nineteenth hole, shedding their sweaters, glad for indoor warmth.

They replayed every hole until Nelson changed the subject, asking Rick, "You never found out about the body in St. Luke's graveyard, did you? The one where I looked at the teeth."

"A body?" Catherine's antennae picked

up. "In a graveyard, of course."

Cindy, a hot cup of tea warming her innards, which she needed, told her, "St. Luke's is the Lutheran church, first one here, and it was built, finally finished, in 1787. You've driven by it. It's the lovely fieldstone with the church in the center, steeple on top, white, and then an arcade on each side with white simple pillars, Doric, I think. And at each end there are two duplicate two-story square buildings that were originally used one side for men's meetings, another for the women's. The pastor's big office is in the men's. The courtyards are beautiful. There's the one between the arcades and then there are descending levels and each level is a rectangular courtyard finally ending in the graveyard, surrounded by a stone wall, same stone as the buildings. It's a sort of terraced effect, but flat with steps between levels. People built things to last back then. It's in remarkable shape and was the design of a British war prisoner who stayed and married here." She smiled, looking to Nelson. "Did I get that right?"

"Always do." He adored Cindy. Everybody did.

"Really? A Lutheran church? I thought they were up in Pennsylvania," Catherine

41

wondered.

"Well, ours was and remains special, but we even had a Catholic church then and that was very unusual, for the prejudice ran so deep, except in Maryland, of course." Cindy paused. "I am always curious about these things because I'm Catholic."

"Me, too." Catherine felt a kinship with the good golfer.

"Then there was Jefferson. You know I read the Jefferson Bible. Interesting." Nelson had been the quarterback at UVA in 1959 and a good student to boot. "When you go to Mr. Jefferson's university, you pay attention to things that might otherwise elude you."

"Curious." Rick leaned back in his chair. "Back to the body. Catherine, it is that of an African American woman. She was laid, no casket, on the caskets of Sara and Michael Taylor, the first people to be buried at St. Luke's. We think, according to the notation in the Bible at church, they perished of tuberculosis. They were buried October 15, 1786, before the church was totally finished. Someone last year kept knocking over their tombstone. And really, that's about all we know."

"Vandalism?" Catherine's eyebrows raised.

"At first that's what the Reverend, actually the Very Reverend Herbert Jones thought. He's usually in his office at the church, so he believed this had been done in the night. Really cold nights, I add." Rick filled her in.

"But Harry, you've met Harry," Cindy added. "She's in charge of building and grounds. She noticed and she told her husband, the big guy, six foot four, an equine vet. So Fair, her husband, and Ned Tucker, a friend who's also a member of the church, muscled the tombstone upright. All seemed to be well. It snowed. More snow. No problems. The snow melted and boom, tombstone over again. This time Harry noticed incursions like stabbing marks had been made into the earth. Not true digging but stabbing. That's the word she used."

"How strange." Catherine was intrigued.

"And it was stabbing," Rick chimed in. "Finally, after fulsome discussion, the grave was opened. Those caskets were as good as the day they were built, but on top, no effort to cross her hands over her chest, had been what I think was dumped, but at any rate, there was a woman's body. Bones, a scrap of mustard silk fabric. What was shocking was she wore a pearl necklace. Large, large pearls, two long strands, and earrings to match with diamonds surrounding the pearls. We had Keller and George appraise it." He looked at his audience. "Six hundred thousand dollars if a penny. Can you believe it?"

Keller and George, in operation since 1875, could be relied upon to carefully study antique jewelry. They cleaned it, took photographs from every angle. Called in an expert from the Virginia Museum of Fine Arts who came to the same conclusion they had concerning value and approximate age based on design.

"Who was she apart from being rich?" Catherine asked.

"We have no idea. The medical examiner's office thought she died in the late 1780s. Probably near the time the Taylors were laid to rest. But she didn't die. Her neck had been snapped cleanly by someone who was powerful and knew what he or she was doing."

"I checked her teeth." Nelson looked up as his hamburger arrived. "Little decay. She had eaten some refined sugar but her teeth were better than a lot of what I see today. I'd estimate her age, based on wear, maybe early thirties at the most."

"The medical examiner came to the same conclusion concerning her age." Rick smiled as his lunch arrived.

They were all hungry.

"That's one of the strangest stories I've ever heard." Catherine dug into her Cobb salad, a cool lunch but filling.

"And she was African American." Cindy, too, thought this quite strange. "Granted, there were rich African Americans as there were rich tribal individuals who owned slaves, too. But wouldn't you think someone that wealthy would have been reported missing?"

"You'd think," Catherine responded.

Rick cut his sandwich in half. "We have good records from that time. The constable did his job and with clear handwriting, too. No mention at all."

"Why didn't the killer take her jewelry? That could have set someone up for life." Nelson couldn't understand that at all.

"No records at St. Luke's?" Catherine inquired.

"No, and St. Luke's has fine records kept in a temperature-controlled vault. Every year's offerings and expenses are noted to the penny. All illnesses are recorded. All deaths and probable causes of death. Births are recorded, as are baptisms. Nothing. Not one iota." Rick shook his head.

"Well, if she was a businesswoman, someone would have noticed. If she was local or even from as far as Richmond." Cindy, having seen those pearls at Keller and George in the vault, imagined the wealth that purchased them.

"Herb canvassed the congregation. No one came forward regarding disturbing the grave. Obviously, whoever was fooling around at the Taylors' grave had some kind of suspicion about the body's whereabouts and maybe even about the pearls." Nelson waved to a club member leaving the nineteenth hole. "If they found out, why can't we?"

"What if she was kept by a wealthy man?" Cindy was practical.

"With six hundred thousand dollars' worth of pearls plus the diamonds around the earrings! What did she know that we don't?" Catherine queried and the others laughed.

"There were people of enormous wealth at that time. The Garths, the Selisses. She became a Holloway after her husband was murdered. And there were people like Yancy Grant who had a lot of money but ultimately lost it. Still, I can think of no one who would buy that kind of jewelry for a mistress. We'd know. You can't hide something like that." Rick was firm about that. "I mean even

Jefferson couldn't hide, you know?"

"They all tried." Cindy bit into her sandwich.

"Still do." Nelson laughed.

"Maybe I should retire from medicine and go into detective work. This is really fascinating."

"Well, I know one thing," Rick stated. "She was hated. You don't kill like that, hide the body, and leave great wealth if you don't completely hate the victim."

"Maybe she deserved to be a victim. My mother used to say, 'Some people need killing.' Maybe she did something horrible. Women can be bad guys, too," Cindy stated.

"Equal rights." Catherine winked.

"I make one prediction." Rick shrugged. "This is close to home."

4

April 9, 2018
Monday

Harry, Susan, and the animals awoke to 43°F, gray skies, light winds. Bright embers glowed in the fireplace as Harry had awakened in the middle of the night to put more logs on the fire. She added more to keep the cabin warm as the windows rattled a bit in the wind. Both women pulled on extra layers of clothing.

"What's your weather app say?" Harry peered at her phone.

Susan stared at hers. "Spring snowstorm. Predicted to start early evening."

"Didn't say that yesterday. Mine says the same thing as yours. Certainly looks threatening."

Susan wrapped a scarf around her neck. "Supposed to snow from Maine to North Carolina. A nor'easter. Those are hateful and my phone says it's already snowing in

New England. Moving down." She looked around for heavier gloves than yesterday's light work gloves.

"The changing seasons. You never know but usually by April fifteenth we've seen our last hard frost. By then the forsythia's in bloom. Guess not this year." Harry zipped up her lightweight down jacket, which did keep her warm. "Let's make a run for the bathroom. Got your toothbrush?"

"Do."

They charged out of the cabin, sprinting up to the stone house, where running water was actually running and hot. There was no bathroom or kitchen in their cabin. Their items, even towels, were at the stone house.

After brushing their teeth and tidying up their hair, they put their items in bags, a Dopp kit for Harry, a baby blue bag with a ribbon for Susan. Harry usually bought men's things because they were better made, lasted longer. She always bought men's work boots.

"Let's leave our bags here. No one will care." Susan slipped her blue bag on a shelf. Harry did likewise.

They clambered upstairs for breakfast.

"Susan, I'll be right back. I need to make sure I closed the door to the cabin. Tucker will push it open if I didn't."

"Okay." Susan sat next to Jason Holzknect, set to talk about his Chesapeake Beagles in Maryland, while Harry dashed back to the cabin.

"We want to go with you," Tucker announced.

"All right, you all. Stay inside. It's cold outside, the barn will be cold, too. You've got your food and water." She put two more large logs on the fire, checked the fire screen. "I think we'll probably leave early today and I don't want to go on a search and annoy mission. I search, you annoy."

"Not me," Pirate protested.

"Perfect." Pewter flopped on the bed.

Harry had brought her comforter and Susan brought her heavy sleeping bag, so the kitties snuggled into them while the dogs sat in front of the crackling fire.

"I should go with you. You need protection," Tucker grumbled.

Harry walked to the door, looked back. "Be good. I'll see you soon enough." She opened the door and closed it firmly behind her.

Once in the dining hall, muffins on the tables, the president announced that those who had come from the North, north of the Mason-Dixon Line, should leave now as the storm, according to her app, was sweeping

50

down and would be in New York and Pennsylvania by noon. They just had almost enough time to outrun it — some snowflakes but the worst would be later.

Jason leaned toward Harry. "Heard you've got a lot of miles on your Volvo station wagon. Let me sell you a Highlander. Great car for snow. I'll give you a preacher's price."

Harry's eyebrows raised. "What denomination?"

Those around her laughed, then Arlene smiled. "He would sell you one, too. Actually, I think Jason could sell ice to Eskimos."

None of the people from the northern hunts rebelled. Everyone had endured a tough winter and knew what was coming: yet another storm to dump inches of snow everywhere.

Jason remarked, "Well, I can work for maybe two hours. Maryland will be later. I am so tired of winter."

"We all are," Liz Reeser said, and everyone agreed. "Okay, those who are staying. Two groups. Work until about noon. Clear what you can and then let's all pack up and go. We aren't going to get lucky with this storm."

Jason folded his arms across his chest. He looked out the windows. "It's the wind I worry about. Well, ladies, let's go."

51

Susan, Liz, Jason, Harry, and Mary Reed comprised one work party. Clare, the other Liz, Mag Walker — all from Hermit's Hollow Beagles, who had driven down early this morning — made up another with Arlene and Jessica Anderson. They headed toward the first creek crossing, which wasn't far from the stone building. Branches were down; some had fallen into the creek.

The mound could be seen to their right.

"The mound looks clear." Susan pulled a branch out of the water. "You'd think because it's higher, the winds would have done more damage there than here."

Mary said, "Well, sometimes the wind almost funnels down here. I think it's worse."

"Maybe the wind wants to leave the arms and legs alone." Jason half smiled. "Every now and then some historian from a university wants to dig up there. What good does it do to find arm and leg bones? You don't know who they once belonged to. Just let everything be."

"I agree." Harry slipped a pair of sharp clippers into a leather pouch on her belt.

Jason, cut branch in hand, said to Harry, "Highlander's perfect in snow, mud, sleet, rain. Think about it. Preacher's price."

She smiled at him. "I will."

The two groups labored intensely and by noon returned to the stone building.

Arlene Billeaud and Jessica Anderson, from the other group, came into view. Jessica hailed from New York, a northern hunt, but was staying with Mary Reed in Warrenton. The two groups waved at one another.

"How'd you do?" Arlene asked.

"Pretty good. Got the big stuff off the trails. Most of the limbs, too, but the wind is really picking up. We've quit in time," Susan offered.

"We've done all we can do but we'll have to come back and lop off the hanging branches." Mary noted a necessary chore. A branch coming down during a hunt couldn't be risked.

The sky was darkening. Amy Burke Walker looked up. "Maybe this is starting early. We'd all better pack up."

When Harry and Susan reached their cabin and opened the door, the two dogs shot out, ran around in circles.

Pewter, on the bed, rolled over. *"Dogs are stupid."*

The dogs, free, didn't hear it. Not that her opinion would change anything.

As the two women packed up Susan's station wagon, Harry left to retrieve their kits from the bathroom in the stone building, where she ran into Jason in the hall.

"I guess I'll see you next weekend. We'll need to come back."

"We will." He stepped outside, Harry beside him.

A sapling was bent over the mound area.

Harry inquired, "How many died?"

"There's a cenotaph on the road, not in the direction you're going. If I remember, it was placed there by the First Massachusetts Cavalry twenty-eight years after their defeat. Out of two hundred and ninety-four troopers in combat, one hundred ninety-eight were counted as casualties, many wounded but enough killed for it to be infamous."

"That many?"

"If I remember it correctly, yes. Out here, far from much help, no wonder they were carried to this stone building, and I guess surgeons were commandeered from the Confederate men. Probably local women came in to help, too."

"You know what I think about? How seeing what metal does to the human body — grapeshot, stuff like that — seeing that, how it affected those women who came in to nurse. I remember reading how many sat by bedsides to write letters home for the wounded. Those women must have gotten close, gotten to care about the men, whether they were Yankees or our boys. When you think of it, really they were kids."

Jason nodded. "What's the saying: Old men make the wars, young men fight them? That's why we have Hounds for Heroes. Nothing changes. All right, gear's in the truck. You and Susan have a safe journey." He climbed up, as Clare was already in the truck, turned the key, a satisfying rumble announcing a true eight-cylinder engine. Driving off, they both waved.

Susan slid in her bedroll, followed by the comforter. It's one thing to work outside in the cold; it's another thing to be cold inside.

"Drinks?" Harry asked.

"In the cooler in the front. You can put your feet on it."

"Okay. Ran into Jason when I was picking up my Dopp kit."

"Saw you two talking at his truck." Susan wiggled her fingers in her gloves.

"Like you, an amateur historian, I guess. But we were talking about how civilians must have felt as they nursed the wounded, the wounded of both sides."

Susan breathed in, the air tingling in her lungs. "I guess if you read about that terrible war when you're in school in Montana, it might not affect you. We live with it. See battlefields every day. What astonishes me is that the estimate of those enlisted was seven hundred and fifty thousand. Harry, if we had that percent of men in combat with our current population, that would number about eight million, give or take. It's incomprehensible."

"Is. I always thought the state should have funded former governor Doug Wilder's museum of slavery. Didn't."

"Yeah, well, Ned" — she named her husband, a representative in the House of Delegates — "can talk about that. For one thing, it wasn't a good time financially. Biz is picking up."

"Depends on the biz." Harry walked back into the cabin for her PLP, paranoid last peek.

Nothing left, everything tidied up, the fire put out, she closed the door. "Remind me to bring a picture to hang on the wall. A beagle or a basset, I know." She grinned.

Both women leaned on the wagon for a moment, looking around. "Didn't get to the tree branch that crashed right through that kennel roof." Susan pointed it out.

"Next weekend. I'm assuming we'll be back next weekend, kennel repairs and lopping off the low hangers. We're running out of time." She peered at the kennel maybe one hundred fifty yards away. "Can you think of the force? That branch crashed straight through the roof."

"Where are the cats?" Harry asked.

"On the seat where you folded up your comforter. You didn't think they'd stay in the back, did you?"

"Well, I do have everything fixed up, plus they can look out your back station wagon window, which is big."

Susan smiled. "When are you going to figure out that your animals do exactly as they please? No one has ever accused you of being a disciplinarian."

"Well —" Harry whistled for the dogs, who were seemingly in conversation by the front door to the stone house.

The beagle had walked toward them.

Pirate whispered, *"It's that dog we can see through."*

Tucker called out, *"Who are you?"*

"Ruffy." The dog came near, then sat down.

"Do you have a safe place to bunk up?" Tucker was curious.

"I can go anywhere I want. In the kennels, in the cabins. All of Aldie is mine."

"How come I can see through you?" Pirate asked.

"I live in a different dimension."

"I don't know what that means." The big puppy was confused.

"Just accept it, Pirate," Tucker commanded. *"Ruffy, I believe you're a ghost. Why are you here?"*

"I'm here to stay with my friend," Ruffy replied.

"Is your friend dead?" Tucker was blunt.

"Yes," came the reply.

"Come on, you two bums," Harry hollered.

Tucker turned her head, then turned it back. *"Ruffy, I'm sorry."*

"That's okay. Will you all be back?"

"Next weekend, I hope," Tucker answered.

"That would be nice." Then Ruffy walked away, fading with each step.

Once in the station wagon, doors locked because Pewter knew how to open them, Susan steered down the long driveway. "Look at that sky."

"Why is it that spring snowstorms are the worst?" Harry peered out through the passenger-side window. "I think we'll just make it. Then again, I don't know. Looks ominous."

"Spring snowstorms are the worst because we all want winter to be over. Maybe we let our defenses down." Susan reached the paved state road.

They drove in silence along winding roads until they reached Route 50, called the

Little River Turnpike at the time of the Battle of Aldie, where Susan turned left, east, then turned right at the circle. She'd hit Route 29 above Warrenton. They drove in companionable silence, the animals now asleep.

Harry broke the silence. "Don't know what it is about that mound, but it kind of makes me shiver."

"Well, arms and legs are one thing, but I think it's creepy that no one knows where the bodies are buried. I mean, how could you forget that?"

"Beats me." Harry swore she saw a tiny snowflake fall. "Maybe when there are that many wounded in a hospital, you lose track. You're so busy trying to keep men alive, you don't fret over where someone has put the dead. I expect all of our battlefields are full of unknown burial spots. I mean, it isn't like Manassas or Gettysburg, which are shrines. And who really knows where all their dead are there?"

Susan thought, then replied, "But they had burial details."

"Depends on the battle, doesn't it? First Manassas the Federals ran, leaving behind their dead, their wounded, and their dancing clothes. They thought they'd be dancing in Richmond. Can you imagine just leaving your wounded screaming on the ground? We took them to our hospital tents."

"No. Then again, with the exception of those men who had fought in the Mexican-American War, no one had seen wounded, heard the guns, moved forward in clouds of gun smoke, blinded. The smells and the noise alone would be terrifying and there you are, an eighteen-year-old farm boy from Iowa or a kid off a fishing boat in the Chesapeake Bay. Chaos. So I expect it was chaos in the field hospitals, too, and then the wounded were transferred to anyplace that could hold them. All transferred south. The North just ignored them."

"You're the history student. But I swear I feel something at Aldie and it's concentrated sorrow."

Susan nodded. "Yes, being there, I could almost believe in ghosts." She leaned over to turn up the heat on her side. "Actually, I do believe in ghosts."

"For thousands of years people have sworn they've seen spirits. I'm not arguing with thousands of years. I'm not saying I want to see one." Harry saw another snowflake.

"Me neither. What I'd like to see is sunshine."

"Forget that. I have seen two little snow-flakes."

"Well, Harry, let's hope they stay little because if the heavens open up, we'll have a devil of a time getting home. You know Southerners can't drive in the snow."

"Hey, we're Southerners." Harry sat up straight.

"We're the exception that proves the rule." Susan smiled. "Like Northerners not knowing how to pass and repass. It's kind of equal, driving versus talking."

"They don't." Harry pronounced this as though it was an edict from the Supreme Court.

Passing and repassing means when you run errands or encounter someone, known or unknown, you bid them hello or good day or whatever. If it's someone you know, you must ask about their day, their health, their family, all that stuff. They reply, the repass. This is why any errand takes twice or three times as long as it does north of the Mason-Dixon Line.

"They are in too much of a hurry," Susan said, then laughed. "Although sometimes when Big Mim" — she mentioned a rich citizen of their little town, Crozet — "goes on a tear, I rather envy them. I can actually get wistful about Massachusetts."

"Ha. But think how much we learn every time we step out the door. Anyway, I think they're hinckty. They should learn to do it our way."

"Hinckty" meant a snob, the worst kind of snob. So Harry sat there in the glow of having said something awful about someone or someones. But happily, it didn't sound awful. Even better, the people from the North wouldn't recognize the word.

"Harry, you're being ugly." Susan sounded prim.

"I may be ugly but I'm your best friend and you love me, love me, love me." She paused. "Don't you?"

They both laughed, rolling along, happy to be together, happy for the tiniest break from being wives.

Susan returned to the buried. "You know, maybe ten years ago, archaeologists or historians or someone with a shovel found Varus's lost legions, three legions that left from the camp at Koblenz during the reign of Caesar Augustus, in A.D. 9, and never returned. And they finally found them in Teutoburg Forest. We now know they were ambushed by Germanic tribesmen two thousand years ago."

"Well, maybe in two thousand years, we'll know where some of the dead at Aldie are buried."

They wouldn't have to wait that long.

5

"Looks like swaying skirts," Catherine Schuyler, twenty-two, observed to her sister, Rachel, two years her junior.

Surveying the hundreds of acres of mature hay, Rachel said, "Waves like water, golden waves. Father will be happy. Our third cutting. Usually we get only two. A bountiful year."

"So far. We've got to cut it, turn it, dry it out, then get it up and into the hay barns. The easier route is to put the hay in hayricks but, Rachel, I don't care what they say, hayricks don't shed enough water. Better to take the time, load it on wagons, haul it into the big shed. It will stay dry there. Good hay means happy horses." She scanned the beautiful fields again. "John is fretting about a storm. I told him so far so good. A thunderstorm can come up in a minute, but

I think we're okay to cut this. We've got to do it before it goes to seed."

"No one will ever accuse your husband of being lazy."

"Nor yours," Catherine replied.

They stared at the hay, bending, swaying, the sound of wind sliding through the tall thin blades.

"Charles" — Rachel named her blond husband — "has been buoyant lately. The organ is nearly installed at St. Luke's. And he received a letter from his brother, who said he expected to receive the funds from Maureen Selisse before month's end."

Calling Maureen Selisse Holloway by her newly married name, Holloway, proved difficult to those who had known her late, unlamented husband, Francisco. Maureen, the middle-aged daughter of a now deceased Caribbean banker, was rich, very rich. She stashed money in accounts in the new United States, in the Caribbean where her father hid much of his ill-gotten gains, and also at the Bank of England on Threadneedle Street. Rumor had it she had transferred her funds out of Paris when the King called the Assembly of Notables. But rumors about tremendously wealthy people always fly about.

Charles's older brother, Hugh, was

crushed by the debts their father, the Baron West, left when he died. A man of potent charm and good cheer, the late Baron, freed from middle-class skills, spent money. He never made it. Maureen wanted a title for her much younger, divinely handsome husband, Jeffrey Holloway, who had been a cabinetmaker who worked with his father until she snapped him up.

Maureen wanted a pedigree. No matter that titles didn't exist in America. They existed everywhere else. The thought of people addressing Jeffrey as "My Lord" when husband and wife traveled pleased her greatly. Now, for a handsome price, the penniless Baron would adopt the handsome cabinetmaker, pleasing everyone.

"What will Charles do?" Catherine wondered as Rachel's husband, the younger son, stood to gain nothing from the arrangement he had engineered. But then, younger sons tended to be a burden in England and were farmed out to the Navy, Army, or Church. More enterprising younger sons might take a different route, practice law and, if inclined to study, even take up medicine, but most of these men were unsuited for such labor. The odd duck might become a Don at Oxford, but one thing that was certain was that younger sons would need to scramble. If their older brother, once having the title, chose, he could and often did provide his siblings with some form of allowance. Sisters needed more supervision than brothers and a beautiful sister could restore depleted finances in a heartbeat, literally.

"Charles will accept that Jeffrey has been adopted. He is free. That's the word he always uses. Free."

"So many rules, the Old World. Well, I guess we have a few of our own." Catherine smiled. "Father received another letter from Roger Davis. He said only forty-one men are left at the convention in Philadelphia, but it is drawing to a close."

"I should be interested. I know you and Father are, but I imagine men with paunches seated in that wicked heat, talking, talking, talking."

"Well, yes." Catherine threw her arm over her sister's shoulders. "Tell me about the organ."

Rachel brightened. "Oh, it's much larger than I anticipated. When I go there I hear them testing it, all speaking German. Charles knows a bit because of serving with the Hessians. And then there's the bellows. Who will keep that going? But truly, you and Father must come when we have our first service with music."

"You've become a believer."

"I've certainly learned about Martin Luther." Rachel laughed, then quieted. "I have. I do believe."

"You have always been more spiritual than myself. But what I have learned is we can no longer pray for the health of the King and we are no longer Church of England. I go because it's expected of me and truthfully it's good for business. I like the ritual but I don't believe. You believe. Maybe that's the difference between the Episcopal Church and the Lutheran Church. To me it's essentially the old religion but changed so Henry VIII could get his way. Somehow that doesn't seem very Christian, does it?"

"No, but Catherine, the popes often had more power than the kings. It was inevitable they should become corrupt."

"Father said something yesterday when we were working." Catherine watched the sun dip below the Blue Ridge Mountains, the blue now intense. "He said, 'Once our form of government is truly settled, and Madison's separation of church and state — which we have here in Virginia — is part of the nation, I predict, and mark my words, that all these watered-down faiths will pop up. We'll even have Presbyterians. There will be no end to this.' So I said, 'Father, aren't we watered-down Catholics?' He waved his hand. 'That doesn't count. We were forced out of the Church of Rome.' "

Rachel laughed. "I can just see him. Father is fond of pronouncements."

Hoofbeats caught their attention. They turned to view Jeddie Rice, slender, gifted with horses, riding toward them with Ralston. Ralston, sixteen, worked in the stables but lacked Jeddie's gifts, although he wasn't bad with horses. Jeddie, nineteen, disdained Ralston. The two were competitive and had completely differing personalities.

"Miss Catherine. Miss Rachel. Mr. Ewing says don't forget the Saltonstalls will be arriving today. He says wear your best for dinner."

"Thank you, Jeddie. We'll just wrap ourselves in silk and satin." Catherine emitted a long sigh.

Rachel smiled at her sister. "You can wear anything and look ravishing."

"Ugh." Catherine crossed her arms across her perfect bosoms, looking up at the two young slaves and their horses. "Those two will make good farm mounts. If Timmy is smooth, maybe we can train him for Father. Can't put Mr. Ewing on a blooded horse."

A blooded horse was bred using riding horse blood, as opposed to a draft horse blood, mixed with royal blood. The early ones had been imported from England and would become what we know now as Thoroughbreds.

"Yes, ma'am." Jeddie agreed, as he and Catherine worked closely together.

Ralston, puffing out his chest, bragged. "I put Crown Prince through his paces today. Give me enough time and I can make him for Mr. Ewing even though he is blooded."

Jeddie's lip curled. He began to speak, but Catherine headed him off. "Ralston, my father is slowing down a bit. We must look out for him. No blooded horses now or ever. You all go on back and Jeddie, tomorrow at sunrise."

The two young men turned the horses, riding back to the large, beautiful stable just visible in the distance.

"What an ass you are." Jeddie spat.

"At least I know what to do with my ass." Ralston dug at Jeddie, who ignored him.

The sisters walked back toward their respective houses.

"The men will talk about banking and the proceedings of the convention in Philadelphia." Rachel wrinkled her nose. "I dutifully try to look interested."

"I am interested but I can't say anything." Catherine thrust her hands into the pockets of her work skirt, made of strong, everyday cotton. "Father keeps returning to the law. He says if we don't respect the new laws, then we'll fall apart. He fears militias will be called out if people become disobedient. It's possible. No matter what they've come up with in Philadelphia, plenty of people will find fault with it."

"I don't understand it. Charles explains it to me but he contrasts it with Parliament and I don't understand Parliament either. Do you know a man can be elected or stand for Parliament and he doesn't even have to live in the place? How can they do that?"

"Money. Money buys everything in England. I think that's one of the reasons they made mistakes over here. Many of those officers bought their commissions. Didn't know a thing."

"Charles's father bought him his commission."

Catherine quickly replied, "He had to, but your husband studied. He is a most unusual man, Charles, and as for getting captured at Saratoga, John says Charles and his men fought hard and honorably and were basically left to fend for themselves. The British couldn't bring up their cannon. Anyway, that's what my husband says and you know the two of them are now two peas in a pod."

They laughed.

"Men get over things."

"Most do. That's what I hope about this convention. Father frets over the war debt. He's not so interested in the other issues, which I guess have had all those delegates in a temper. But Father wants to know how we are going to pay for the war and how a new government can bring the states to heel."

"You're smarter than I am." Rachel shrugged.

"No. I work with our father and he's uncommonly intelligent. He's taught me a lot about business. I enjoy it. And he's taught me how to use John and even Charles as a foil, I think that's the word. Better to say nothing, to be thought a beautiful woman but nothing more. Let men think all husbands are in charge. Father says I will wind up learning more than he ever could. And I do listen. I listen with both ears. I'm more than happy to work behind the scenes."

"Yes, I suppose. And what have I been hearing about?" Rachel's eyes rolled upward. "Bumbee and Mr. Percy. She's in a huge snit, has left him again and moved back to the weaving room this morning. I went down to sort yarns and fabrics with her." She paused. "Charles needs more shirts. Not his good ones, but he's torn most everything else down there working on the church. Anyway, no one knows these things better than Bumbee so I got an earful about her husband, but I know she didn't tell me everything."

"Do you think it will ever end?"

"No, of course not." Rachel watched a northern harrier fly over toward a marshy area. "They don't say much."

Catherine looked overhead. "They fly low. I like to watch them. Does this mean Bumbee will be up at the house asking Bettina" — the cook, a woman of power — "to intervene?"

"No. At least, I hope not," Rachel replied.

Bumbee, in charge of all weaving and spinning, organizer of yarns and fabrics, even dyeing some of them, was a forty-odd-year-old slave married to a man who had a wandering eye and a body that wandered with it. He happened to be a good gardener, a man of some skill, but he couldn't restrain himself when it came to the women, especially the younger women, at Cloverfields or elsewhere. They'd repair their relationship when the other woman tired of Percy. A period of calm would prevail, then Percy would see another woman, often at another estate. Given his skill with arranging plants, colors, knowing what could last the winter, he was often hired out when other plantation owners would ask Ewing for Percy's help. Then it would start all over again. This last time Bumbee had cracked a pot over his head.

Rachel gave Catherine the lurid details, especially about the pot.

"Why doesn't she just shoot him?" Catherine laughed.

"You have a point."

They parted ways but were soon reunited at the splendid dinner for the Saltonstalls of Connecticut. John, tall, broad-shouldered, muscular, was not a talkative man. He was a hero at Yorktown fighting under the Marquis de Lafayette, so fortunately other men didn't expect him to be a popinjay. Catherine would reach for his hand under the table, squeezing it. She was fascinated by the talk, John less so. Charles, on the other hand, fabulously well educated, Harrow then Oxford, delighted the men, and he could make the ladies laugh. Charles glowed each time he looked at his wife. Ewing, in his glory, was the consummate host.

Rachel excused herself for a moment to check on the food.

The summer kitchen was in full swing,

like a clock, literally, although Bettina didn't need a clock. She had the cooking times in her head. Large cast-iron pots hung over open fires in an open outdoor hearth. The meats were cooked on spits, with boys turning the meats every five minutes. The heat radiated outward from the two big outdoor fires. Bread warmed on an outdoor oven as well.

"Bettina," Rachel called to her. "They are beside themselves with your selection of dishes. Mrs. Saltonstall exclaimed when she cut open her small rolled pork to find little raspberries inside."

A big grin covered Bettina's face. "Oh, just a thought." She then turned. "Serena, not the oak. Have the boys put beech on the fire now." She turned back to Rachel. "I can't take my eyes off them. You never know but I am telling you, these younger people are dumb as a sack of hammers."

"You and Father." Before she returned to the dinner Rachel couldn't help from adding, "Bumbee talked to me but I know she didn't tell me everything. I bet you know."

"Ha," Bettina exploded. "You have no idea."

Rachel, reluctantly, returned to the elegant dining room, where she promised all that Bettina had invented a dessert that was out of this world and urged them to finish up. This was said somewhat in jest. But Rachel was dying to know what really happened with Bumbee and Percy, whom Bumbee always called Mr. Percy. Life could be so unfair.

6

April 9, 2018
Monday

St. Luke's, covered in snow, looked like peace itself. Light from Herb's office caught the falling snow and cast a pale glow across the white.

Cazenovia, Elocution, and Lucy Fur, the three Lutheran cats, looked on as Herb studied accounts. Bookkeeping, done by a parishioner, was always accurate, but he felt it his duty to check and double-check.

Upstairs, Herb could hear Harry's light step as she checked the ceiling. Before the frosts arrived, in fall, a patch of slate roof had been repaired and now she wanted to see if any leaks occurred. Flashlight in hand, she trained it in the ceiling corner. Tight as a tick. She liked being in charge of building and grounds.

Harry, practical and handy, contributed where she felt she could do the most good.

Not social, not a born organizer like Susan, this was her participation in the church where she had been baptized. However, she also pitched in on whatever Susan cooked up, usually doing something aesthetic as opposed to pragmatic.

Turning off the beam, she looked out the old hand-blown paneled windows. The large rectangular courtyards, white, were fading to pale gold, soon to pink, then gray as the sun was setting.

Mrs. Murphy and Pewter sat on the window ledge watching the snowflakes. Tucker and Pirate reposed on the floor awaiting Harry's next move. Usually the cats played with Herb's three Lutheran cats, but today they had followed Harry up the stairs. The cats knew the church better than most of the parishioners as they trailed Harry on her rounds. The view from the second story was always good. One could really see the birds in the trees and this always provoked a promise from Pewter to send them to the great bird in the sky. No one paid the least bit of attention.

Leaving the clean room, closing the door behind her to conserve heat, Harry descended the stairs. A large closet under the stairs gave the cats a hopeful moment. Communion wafers were stacked in the

closet along with red wine for communion. Years ago, when that door had been left slightly ajar, Mrs. Murphy and Pewter, along with Cazenovia, Elocution, and Lucy Fur, wedged in and pulled down communion wafers. Cat communion. What a glorious event. When Herb and Harry came upon them, Herb stopped, then burst out laughing. "I'd better confirm them," he said, and Harry laughed, too.

She knocked on the office door. "Hollywood calling."

A deep, deep voice rang out. "You need a phone for that. Come on in." Herb pushed his sums away, looked up as she entered, cats and two dogs in tow.

"Roof's good." She beamed.

"Praise the Lord." He smiled. "Caught it in time. Repairing a roof, especially a slate roof, isn't cheap, but at least I could plan for it with the budget. It's those unexpected bill bombs that get you." He looked outside the symmetrical paned-glass windows. "Ah, a spring snow. We're all waiting for daffodils, but it is very beautiful. When Charles West designed St. Luke's, including the grounds, I often wonder did he carry with him ideas from England? Ideas of small churches in glens? The cathedrals impress to this day, but it's the small churches wherein most of us gather. I never tire of St. Luke's."

"Nor do I," she agreed.

"Coffee? Tea? A libation?"

"Ah, well, maybe tea, a brisk afternoon tea as the light fades."

The office and small kitchen decorated at the turn of the last century by the Dorcas Guild retained its gracious atmosphere with modern conveniences. Those long-departed ladies felt the pastor should have a Chesterfield sofa and two matching chairs in dark brown leather in the center of the large room. The desk reposed near the corner window and probably hadn't been moved since the day it was placed there. It would take four men to move it. The Victorians did not believe in spindly furniture.

Herb walked to the kitchen, followed by Harry, as they caught up on church business and people business.

The cats leapt off the back of the leather sofa, pulling down the warm wool throw as they did. It slid onto the cushions. The cats all moved toward the kitchen, where they knew treats would be dropped.

"Come on, Pirate. The Rev is generous," Tucker instructed the puppy.

"Just ignore my beggars." Harry glared at her pets really working their sweet number.

"Ah, now Harry, the miracle of the fishes

81

and the loaves applies to animals as well." He pulled open a cupboard door. The doors were like little windows, glass-paned. "What do you think?" He showed her a tin of enticing fake fish as well as a bag of Greenies.

"You spoil them."

Herb tossed each animal a goodie. "What's the point of loving somebody if you don't spoil them a little?"

"I'm sure you're correct." Looking down, Harry advised her friends. "You are very lucky."

"We're worth it." Pewter happily snagged another fish.

As the pets enjoyed the treats, the people waited for the water to boil.

"So what have you all been doing? We've stayed inside. Boring, but I'm not going out there," Lucy Fur announced.

"I have been killing mice. Dozens of mice. I set a Virginia record." Pewter dropped a few crumbs from her mouth.

"There are that many mice at Harry's farm?" Elocution suspected Pewter's usual exaggerations.

"Aldie." Mrs. Murphy then informed them what Aldie was, the National Beagle Club, and the barn that truly was overrun with mice.

"We saw a ghost." Pirate, a little shy,

wanted to join in.

Cazenovia looked at Mrs. Murphy. *"You said there had been a battle there. A ghost from the hospital or someone killed on the field?"*

Tucker, content from her Greenie, said, *"No, it was a beagle."*

"He said he was there with a friend." Pewter wanted to return to her prodigious hunting skills. *"The barn will be filled with ghost mice."*

Harry's pets ignored this.

"So he was there with his cavalryman?" Elocution, having seen ghosts in the graveyard at off times, was not too surprised.

"He didn't say," Tucker responded.

"The world is full of spirits. Some are unquiet. Others want to watch over someone they loved." Elocution considered the reasons why a spirit would hang around.

"The unquiet worry me." Lucy Fur switched her tail.

"I wonder if we'll see the beagle again." Mrs. Murphy headed toward the living room, the sofa and chairs. *"We'll be back at Aldie again this coming weekend."*

Harry picked up the wool throw as she returned with her tea, placing it over the back of the sofa, then sat down. "What do you think of a St. Luke's homecoming? We could do it on the day the cornerstone was laid or the day the church was finished, organ inside."

"I never thought of that." Herb settled down, happy not to be looking at accounting sheets.

"Just think. The children you baptized. Those of us you taught catechism. Those you married. Those whose family members you buried. By now, Rev, it has to be so many people."

"Well" — he paused — "yes, I'm almost eighty."

"You're the youngest person I know." She meant it. "While we're at it, we can celebrate your eightieth birthday, which I think is close to the day the cornerstone was laid."

He waved his hand. "I forget."

"Bullpucky."

He laughed. "You know, given people's schedules, a late spring day or early summer might be better. You know, when colleges are out for the summer. If we announce this early, then people can plan for it." He brightened. "Harry, what a good idea."

"Sure. Susan, organizer extraordinaire, can send out RSVP forms or people can do it via email so we can plan for enough food. If we're going to do this, we better do it right. The fishes and the loaves."

They both laughed.

"Do you think we're losing it?" she then continued. "Churches, I mean? We used to be the nerve centers of the countryside, towns, and even big cities."

He folded his hands over his chest. "Well, we're losing congregants. Not so much here, but we are in a unique position. Same with St. Paul's Ivy." He mentioned a county Episcopal church. "People come together but there are so many competing messages now, families rarely are close to one another, not like in my childhood. I worry about it. I believe in the church."

"You make us believe in the church. You are a remarkable pastor."

This touched him. "Thank you. I never know if I've fulfilled my responsibilities as well as I should." He glanced outside. "This snow won't stop." He paused a moment. "It's April ninth."

"Well, we're in Virginia. I doubt anyone has really forgotten."

April 9, 1865, was when Lee surrendered at Appomattox.

"November eleventh is another one. Always sticks." He tapped his head.

"As near as I can tell, Reverend Jones, ending a war solves one set of problems and creates an entirely new set."

"April ninth is one of those days. Henry V was crowned king in 1413. Agincourt." He grinned. "Now there's a story. Here's another. The child king, Edward V, should have ascended the throne in 1483. I think this would have been the exact day much postponed, and then he and his brother disappeared forever. The princes in the tower. History spills over with unsolved crimes, odd events, and truly odd people." He shook his head. "Then again we have enough of that now."

She agreed. "I guess where I struggle is accepting that good can come from evil and evil can come from good. For instance, terrible wars and yet medicine advances due to war. Our ability to mobilize and organize advances. Well, if you win, I guess, but think of it. It seems like such a contradiction. Kind of like the #MeToo movement. Pain, frustration, and sorrow but something good will come of it. Not overnight but a reflecting, rethinking of how we treat women, or I should say how men treat women."

He nodded. "How those in power treat those who are weaker, or who are trying to hold on to a job. The one thing that strikes me about predators is how they identify their victims. It's not at all like war. That is clear and in many ways simple. Or at least it seemed so to me when I was in Vietnam."

"Do you think any good came from that?" Harry, at forty-two, was too young to have been involved in all that.

He sipped his tea, thought. "I'm not sure I'm the person to ask. It certainly caused us to question civilian leadership, whether the presidency or Congress. But then again, new military leadership began to develop. People, mostly men, of course, due to the times, who were more flexible, who realized we had to engage the local populations. The Vietcong were way ahead of us. General Giáp was an outstanding leader, even if on the wrong side. The other thing, and I turn this over in my mind a lot, I think the war helped break down racism."

"I never thought of that."

"Fighting next to a man who has your back, you forget about color even if it was once important to you. You forget about a lot of things. It's a hell of a way to learn. Harry, you ask the damnedest questions."

"Sorry." She paused. "From my reading, I think Vietnam's antiwar movement over-lapped the civil rights movement, which nudged along feminism. You lived it. I just read about it."

Pewter came up to pat Herb's leg.

"I think you're right. It was a volatile time.

I reckon 1968 was the bombshell year and then the counterculture took off. You know, Harry, Americans are a pretty tough people." Herb mused.

"Don't give her any more. She's too fat," Harry requested.

"I am not fat. I have big bones." Pewter sang her usual aria.

The other animals wisely kept their peace.

"Speaking of mysteries, old stories, we still don't know who was laid on the Taylors' caskets." Herb shifted in his seat. "I really think we have to give her a proper burial. After all, she was unearthed in November 2016. Obviously, no one is going to claim her, or they would have done so by now."

"You'd think they'd claim the pearls. People don't know Keller and George is keeping them in the vault, but I believe they are part of this attempted exhumation."

"I wonder about that," Herb said. "I believe whoever tried to disturb the Taylors' grave must have had some information, information that has lain dormant for over two hundred years."

"That's just it, Rev." She called him by her nickname for him. "Whoever did it is still out there and why now, well, in 2016?"

"I don't know. But back to the subject. She deserves a proper Christian burial."

"You can't bury her in the graveyard. She wasn't a parishioner. We'd know. That death would be in the records."

"I've thought about that. We know either she was in the way or hated. Her neck was snapped. The medical examiner said it was clean. One powerful snap and she was gone."

"I vote for hated. The pearls were left. I would think another reason other than hatred, even if the killer had to hide for years, would ultimately have brought him back to the grave to dig up the booty. And I expect it was a him because of her snapped neck."

"Yes, that, too, has occurred to me. I propose, and I will bring this up to the Dorcas Guild and St. Peter's Guild" — he named the men's guild — "that we fashion a wooden casket, something appropriate to her time on earth, and bury her under the red oak. It's lovely and not far from the cemetery."

"But what if she really was an awful person and that's why she was killed?"

"We all must ask for God's forgiveness. It is not our place to judge."

"You know I will support whatever you think best. I wonder if whoever was rooting around that grave will be drawn to the service."

"Chances are whoever did that isn't a Lutheran."

"No, but the paper will print this. It's too good not to make the news. What I'm trying to say is perhaps this is a very old crime that isn't over."

"We'll see."

"If she's vengeful, let's hope she knows we aren't the wrongdoers."

" 'Vengeance is mine, saith the Lord.' " Herb paused. "The ghosts at Aldie have made an impression."

"Oh, people there say they've seen them in what was the hospital. I don't know, I'm just running at the mouth. Then I think about what you've said, about the princes in the tower. Maybe they're still there, wandering the halls. I wonder."

"Trust in the Lord, Harry, trust in the Lord."

7

"Keep your hands off Reynaldo's bridle." Jeddie Rice stood two inches from Ralston's face.

"I'll do what I want." The tall young man nearly spit in Jeddie's face.

Jeddie worked the blooded horses at Cloverfields. The young man possessed good hands, a light, sure seat. Ralston had a long leg but not the sensitivity a good rider needed. Catherine, who worked well with Jeddie, had put the young man, nineteen, in charge of the blooded horses. The two of them would go over conditioning routines, food, turnout depending on season. She put Ralston in charge of the everyday farm horses but not the driving horses or the draft horses. Catherine had a soft spot for the big, gentle drafts.

Ralston resented Jeddie's authority. Both

young men took orders from Barker O, famed throughout Virginia for his uncanny ability to drive horses. No one looked as splendid as Barker O, in full regalia, the reins between his fingers, driving the exquisite Cloverfields coach. DoRe, who drove coaches for Maureen Selisse Holloway, ran Barker O a close second. The two men enjoyed a healthy competition, truly liked each other.

DoRe, a widower, had been quietly courting Bettina, a widow and Cloverfields gifted cook, for the last year. He'd find ways to slip away from Big Rawly. Maureen, difficult as she could be, pretended she knew nothing about the courtship for she needed DoRe. Jeffrey, her younger second husband, built expensive, beautiful coaches, brass lanterns beside the side doors, subtle pinstripes on the coach itself as well as the wheels, color coordinated with the coach body. Maureen had built a large workshop for Jeffrey. She overcame her aversion to trades because he was gorgeous, kind, and did what she told him. Also, his business was thriving and that did bring in money, not that she needed it. DoRe would drive those coaches for the prospective buyer or for the person who ordered the vehicle, taking the time to sit next to whoever their coachman was and give him pointers about the abilities of the coach.

Barker O heard the young men cussing each other, walking into the fancy blooded-horse stable just in time to see Jeddie throw a pail of water in Ralston's face. Fists flew. Barker O crossed his arms over his massive chest.

Let them settle it, he thought, even though he was tiring of Ralston's insubordination and sudden awakening to the delights of women, delights Ralston longed to sample.

Ralston made a fool out of himself daily, chasing every girl on Cloverfields and asking embarrassing questions about good-looking slave girls on other estates. So far not one young woman anywhere gave him a tumble, even though he wasn't bad-looking.

Jeddie, whose shoulder had been broken in a horse race, couldn't swing as hard as he would have liked on that left side, but his right was good. Ralston ducked low, grabbed Jeddie by the legs, and brought him down. The two rolled around in the aisle.

"Neither of you will ever make a penny as fighters." Barker O finally spoke.

Both jumped up. Ralston pointed at Jeddie. "He started it."

"The hell I did. He's not to touch Reynaldo's tack or Crown Prince's. I saw him pick it up."

Ralston opened his mouth, but before anything came out, Barker O rumbled, "Go on out to the north hayfield. Check the horses and unhitch them, take them down to the creek for water and a bit of shade."

"Percy can do that." Ralston pouted. "He's got the energy now that Bumbee left him again."

"Do what I tell you, Ralston. You, too, Jeddie. I'll beat your ass until you bleed."

They shut up, left the barn, trudging to the north hayfield, neither one speaking to the other.

Barker O watched them as Catherine came into the stable from the other end. She'd just left her husband, who had mentioned it was his commanding officer's thirtieth birthday. John admired Lafayette tremendously. As he rarely discussed the war, Catherine had lingered at the breakfast table.

"Another disputation? I could hear it walking down from Father's house."

"Chalk and cheese, those two." Barker O smiled at the Mistress. They were both horse people, which created a bond that could occasionally subvert the restraints of slavery. Also, Barker O's abilities brought luster to Cloverfields stable, and the horses were Catherine's domain.

"Barker O, I've looked at the cut hay, went over to the fields this morning. Good hay. With luck, we'll put up enough to get us through the winter. Our first cutting and then the second were outstanding. I thought this year would be so-so, but it's been such a wonderful year."

"Yes, Miss Catherine, it has."

"I wanted to talk to you about our oats."

"Good. Everything's good."

"Well, it is, but I'd like you to go with John" — she mentioned her husband — "to Yancy Grant's. Father has promised to buy all his oats. We don't really need them, but Yancy has fallen on hard times."

"Not all his fault," the large man quietly replied.

"Maureen." She thought a moment. "Obviously she never read the Bible. 'Vengeance is mine, saith the Lord.' "

Barker O nodded. "Her husband bears no grudge."

Jeffrey Holloway and Yancy Grant had engaged in an ill-advised duel after Yancy said some foolish things while drunk at a large party at Cloverfields. Everyone assumed Yancy would put a hole in Jeffrey, who was a cabinetmaker originally, not a countryman like Yancy. Turned out Jeffrey shot up Yancy's knee and Yancy grazed Jeffrey's arm. Then, once healed, the men made up. Maureen, however, sued Yancy, drove him nearly to the poorhouse with legal bills, then magnanimously dropped her suit. She even allowed Yancy on her place to visit her husband, to check her horses.

"Today?"

"No. You two can go over tomorrow. Take two wagons. He'll have everything in barrels. I expect you'll know how much is to be done once you get there. I hope we have enough room to store it all."

"I'll make room." Barker O looked out to see how far the two had gotten, just in time to see Ralston push Jeddie. "That boy needs a good whipping."

Catherine followed his gaze. "He's the type, Barker O, will only make him worse. To add to his list of misdeeds, he tried to kiss Serena and even pulled down the front of her dress."

"Great day." Barker O shook his head. "Her husband will kill him."

"Bettina prevailed upon Serena to forgive him and John and Charles had some kind of a talk with him about women. It should have been Ralston's own father."

"I haven't seen Hodge sober for three years."

"Nor have I, but he gets his work done." She smiled at the big fellow. "Never ends, does it?"

He laughed. "No, Miss Catherine. My momma used to say, 'People are no better than they have to be.' "

"She said a lot else as well."

They both laughed, for Barker O's mother, elderly when Catherine was a child, said exactly what she thought when she thought it. They gave Momma a wide berth. Catherine wondered if one of the reasons Barker O turned out to be a quiet, thoughtful man was he never got a word in edgewise.

"I'd better go on to the north field to check up on those boys." Barker O shook his head.

"If they made it in one piece."

8

April 14, 2018
Saturday

"Blastoff Beagles." Harry laughed at Arlene Billeaud, Master of Beagles. "How did you come up with that name?"

"Oh, I was dating a man who worked for NASA. Nearly married him, but that rocket never landed." She laughed. "By that time, I'd named my pack Blastoff Beagles."

Harry laughed, too. "No one will forget the name."

Harry and Arlene, dragged down by heavy mud on their boots, had been checking creek crossings as the others worked on more repairs at Aldie. Tucker and Pirate, also muddy, walked along. The cats, back on barn duty, were sure to be insufferable once Harry and Susan, who was with the kennel work party, returned.

"You no longer smoke? I remember when I first met you, you did."

Arlene, mid-fifties and in great shape, shook her head no. "The terrible truth is I miss it. Calmed me and I loved the taste. But I'd had enough friends die of lung cancer by the time I turned fifty. Granted, all were older, from that generation that smoked and drank sociably. Still."

"Know what you mean. I never smoked myself, but Mom and Dad did, as well as their friends. No one thought a thing about it. Tobacco certainly helped build our state."

"Imagine Aldie in the old days. People hunting with puffs of smoke trailing them." Arlene laughed.

Harry, right foot sinking deep into mud on the far side of a creek, the bank less stable than she had thought, picked her foot up with a sucking sound. "Dammit."

"The fundraiser draws ever closer. I sure hope this dries out. The one good thing is the moisture — even if there's more hard rain, it should help scent."

"Moisture is one thing. Snow another." Harry sighed.

"Ain't it the truth." Arlene also got a bit stuck, so Harry, now on firm ground, grabbed her hand and pulled her out.

"Thanks." Arlene looked down at her mud-covered work boot. "When I was in the Army I remember a saying, really stuck with me. 'If you're in trouble, it doesn't matter what color the hand is that reaches in to pull you out.' Makes it all so simple, doesn't it?"

"Does. Which brings me back to tobacco. I remember the big warehouses down by the James. I was in grade school, but we'd go down. Walking along those piles of cured tobacco was a white man with a black man at his shoulder. Those men knew tobacco. The white man was the big boss, the black man, maybe he didn't have a title but he was number two and had a lot of respect. All gone. All that knowledge gone and those men have no one to pass it along to. I guess what I'm coming back to is wherever you are, whatever time in which you live, you work it out the best you can."

"I certainly did." Arlene walked alongside Harry as they headed to check the last creek crossing. "I can't say women were welcomed in the Army, but they had to take us. We stepped up to the plate. That shut up a lot of naysayers."

"My father used to say, 'Do your job and shut up. Your work will speak for you.' "

"Smart man." Arlene walked without a hitch, her artificial leg so much better than those of the past. She paused. "Today Abraham Lincoln was shot at the theater and Alexander II escaped an attempted assassination in 1879."

"They finally got him, didn't they?"

Arlene nodded. "Why is it they always kill the person who is trying to help move things forward? What happened? Russia swung so hard after that, shutting down growing liberties and creating a secret police that would kill you as soon as look at you. Assassination never works. Look at Julius Caesar."

"One genius followed by another." Harry tested the bank where the water was reduced to a tiny little trickle. "How often did that happen in history?"

"Rarely, but sometimes genius is close. Or great change. I guess I'm thinking of Henry VIII, who caused more suffering than any king before or since, but his daughter made good on all of it and here we are in Virginia, named for the Virgin Queen."

"Did you learn that much on the job?" Harry smiled.

"Oh, I'm not that studious, but I was surrounded by bright people, knew history. I had a friend in the Agency, Paula Devlin, I swear she knew everything." The attractive woman smiled. "What do you think?"

Harry pressed down harder with her right toe. "Fortunately, this piddling stream we can jump over. If it were wider and everyone clambering over, the damn bank would just give way and then people would have to wade across. I hate getting my feet wet, don't you?"

"Worse in the cold and now I only have one." Arlene shrugged. "Well. Let's make a loop. Get down on the southernmost path and walk back. I don't think anything has come down since we've been here. The snow was three inches, not much wind. It's the wind that does the damage when there's been a lot of rain or snow."

"Sure does. How did you become interested in beagling?"

A big smile crossed Arlene's face. "I come from Michigan. No beagle or basset packs there. When I was accepted to the University of Kentucky, my roommate hunted with, as it was then called, Fincastle. So I went out with her and really liked it. Then when I was in the Army for five years I was stationed in England. Hunted with every beagle pack I could. Then with the Agency I was based in Washington and I discovered the Fouts, Orange County, hunted with them, and I'd drive up to Apple Grove Beagles in Unionville, Pennsylvania." She stopped a moment. "What I loved about Middleburg-Orange Beagles is that I had to bring a child to be admitted. I borrowed everyone's children I could think of and the parents were usually quite happy for me to take them and wear them out. I always thought the Fouts were so smart to do that, to allow the young up front."

They both laughed, finally reached the southern footpath, the dogs at their heels. As they approached a rise, the two dogs stopped. The ghost beagle, on the rise, watched them. As the humans passed, the fifteen-inch fellow fell in with Tucker and Pirate. He remained silent but kept up.

A long, low mound, mostly covered with bracken and some trees, hove up on their right.

"Isn't that where some of the limbs are supposed to be buried?" Harry inquired.

"So they say."

"God knows how many people are buried in this place."

Exactly.

9

April 15, 2018
Sunday
The second day at Aldie saw the Virginians and the Marylanders lopping off hanging branches and clearing the few large trees remaining on trails. A small work party focused on the kennels. When they built a new roof for the badly damaged kennel, they discovered two other kennels needing repair. It took four of them to cut up and pull out the large tree limb that pierced the roof.

Everyone kept at it. The trials would be April 27 to 29.

The ground, soggy, clung to work boots, making every step heavy. Apart from the kennel crew, two work parties moved through the grounds. The weather, still cool, would numb fingers if one pulled off gloves. Wisely, everyone wore layers.

The cats, patrolling the barn, kept out of

the slight wind, plus they had those luxurious fur coats. Still, Pewter would occasionally curl up in scattered straw while Mrs. Murphy hunted for mice.

"There's a chill." The gray cat draped her tail over her nose.

"If you'd hunt mice, you'd stay warmer." The tiger cat crouched by a mousehole, mouse not budging.

"I killed so many mice last week, there can't be many left." Pewter noticed an old cobweb, dead flies still imprisoned therein.

"There are enough left. The mule will be stabled here. No point in the mice eating her grain."

"If she would chew properly, like cats, she wouldn't spill much grain."

"Of course, you're right" — Mrs. Murphy uttered those golden words — *"but horses and mules can't help the way their teeth are made. They grind down sideways on grains and grasses. We tear and chew."*

"Quite right." Pewter was startled when a chickadee flew into the barn, perching overhead on a rafter.

"Whatcha doin'?" the little bird asked.

"Looking at you." Pewter narrowed her eyes to appear fearsome.

Didn't work.

Mrs. Murphy looked up at the black-

capped, white-throated bird, asking, *"Do the owls ever come in here? They're good hunters."*

"Not so much anymore. There are so many fancy barns in the area, lots of mice, leftover sandwiches, stuff like that. They're spoiled now. The owls don't want an old barn. Has to be new. And I suppose the new ones are better built, so their high nests are toastier."

"You live here? At the Institute?" Mrs. Murphy gave up on the mouse, and the minute she walked away, tiny black whiskers appeared at the mousehole.

Just checking. The mouse stayed put.

"I do. My wife and I have lived here for years. No eggs yet. The weather has been too strange, but once all this passes we'll raise our babies. We do a lot of good, you know. Chickadees eat bugs and larvae."

"Do you live in the barn?" Pewter decided to be social, even if this was a bird.

"No, we have a tidy and tight bird box. Some of the beaglers and basset people put out bird boxes. We used to live in a tree but then we got into an argument with nuthatches who said it was really their home. Wasn't, of course, but as luck would have it, the humans had just put out bird boxes. So the nuthatches can sit in the tree and listen to everyone talk, watch other birds hang upside down from

branches. It's uncivilized, I tell you."

The little fellow, a born gossip, chirped away, and Mrs. Murphy found herself liking him. *"Mr. Chickadee."*

"Bud."

"Nice to meet you, Bud. I'm Mrs. Murphy and this is Pewter. Tell me, have you ever seen the ghost beagle?"

"Ruffy. Yes. He walks about but he's not very talkative. Nice enough."

"He told us he was here because of his friend," Mrs. Murphy replied.

"That's what he's told me, but nothing else. I get the feeling that whatever happened isn't over. Ruffy has a mission."

While the cats and chickadee talked about everything and anything, Harry, Susan, Arlene, Jason, and Mary Reed all struggled with a large tree blocking a narrow trail. This was not visible from the wider walking trails and riding trails, but if the beagles did find a scent, heading in this direction, it would take the humans too much time to find their way around the obstacle, as woods surrounded the trail. The judges would be stymied. Worse, the pack would possibly get so far ahead, the whippers-in couldn't manage them, and the judges wouldn't be able to see the work of the hounds.

Arlene sawed off limbs so Jason, Harry,

and Susan could cut up the trunk. Mary Reed studied the upturned roots, quite large, protruding and taking up a lot of space.

"How can we cut the roots with all the mud?" Mary asked.

"Can't," Harry responded.

"So?" The Master of Bassets peered at the mess.

"We have to cut just above the roots." Jason took charge of the problem. "We can roll away the pieces of trunk we've cut into smaller sections. But to pull away the roots, we'll need a tractor and chains. And then, where do we drag it?"

The women, any of whom could have taken charge, didn't much mind that Jason did. All four ladies operated on the theory, "Keep them working."

After an hour, the large tree had been shorn of all limbs, the thick trunk cut into pieces and rolled to one side in a rough pile.

"Well?" Susan faced the huge root system, then looked upward. "We'll run out of sunlight."

"I have an idea." Mary could be counted on to think things through. "Let Jason go back for the tractor and chains. The four of us can go in each of the cardinal directions to find a suitable place to haul the roots and maybe some of these trunk pieces."

"We should take the trunk pieces back to the Institute. Use a front-end loader and stack them up. Let them dry. This is good hardwood. A chunk of this will burn a long, long time," Harry suggested.

"Good point," Mary agreed.

"We'll walk. Jason, you take the ATV. You know where the tractor is. By the time you get back here, one of us will have found a spot out of the way."

As he motored off, Arlene then said, "Really, it should be dumped out in the open so hounds and people can get around it."

"I'll go west," Harry volunteered.

"East." Arlene picked her direction.

"South." Susan nodded.

"North." Mary checked her watch. "Let's synchronize and be back here in a half hour."

"Mary, will it take Jason that long?" Susan asked.

"Might. The kennel people are using the tractor. With luck, they will have gotten most of their work done, but he'll need to talk them out of it and bring it back if there's a question."

Arlene then questioned Mary. "But what about the equipment in the shed?"

"Not all of that is available to us."

"Right." Harry agreed with Mary, checking her watch. "Four-thirty."

"Four-thirty." Arlene looked at hers.

Susan checked her Fitbit. "Right."

Off they went. Each woman headed for where she remembered an open space. Some were true meadows, others smaller but open areas. The trick was not to clog up an area where rabbits might congregate. This wasn't as easy a task as it appeared to be.

A half hour later all reconvened, discussing what they'd found.

"The bit of a level at the bottom of the ridge, below the high trail, it's more or less out of the way." Arlene pushed for her spot.

Mary, who hunted the Ashland Bassets and knew Aldie well, countered. "It is out of the way, but the creek runs close by. The creek area will hold scent."

Arlene didn't refute this, as she respected Mary's acumen. Mary had hunted hounds longer than Arlene had, so she deferred to what in effect was a senior master.

"If Jason drags this thing down the main path, there's a turnaround, a kind of dead end. No water close by, but the wind whips through there," Harry spoke.

"Possible." Mary looked west. "Susan?"

Mary looked at Susan, whose work boots were caked with heavy mud.

"I found open areas but they're grassy, bush by the edges. Bunnies are edge feeders," Susan wisely noted. "I can't say that I found anything suitable."

"You know where we cross the creek down there? Once across, if you go about one hundred yards, there's scrub. It's not really so flat, but the roots could be dragged there. They're so big, if anyone moved into that area, full of burrs, too, they'd see it," Harry said.

They batted things back and forth, finally deciding that Harry's spot sounded the most promising. Mary, who had walked north, kept encountering a series of low ridges, sort of like terraces, and the creek below would hold scent on the side facing the creek. The scent could literally bounce back. Scent, tricky always, moved with the wind, held on rich soil.

People who hunt, whether on horseback or on foot, enjoy watching hound-work, seeing the beautiful country as they ride or walk through, but they need not learn about scent. The huntsman must. Any huntsman, to which Mary could testify, looks great on a good scenting day. And huntsmen can hold their heads up on a terrible day, say, a drought or high winds.

It's the in-between days that are the true test of a huntsman and his or her pack.

They decided Harry's turnaround would do it. This lively discussion ate up another half hour. Still no Jason.

They sat on the rolled-over big trunk pieces.

More time slipped by.

"Does he have a cellphone?" Susan asked.

"He does. I've seen it in his pocket. He has a leather case." Arlene figured everyone had a cellphone these days. "Does anyone have the number?"

None did.

"Let me call Amy. She's down there at the kennels." Mary dialed Amy, who immediately picked up. Mary asked if she had seen Jason.

"Yeah. He took our tractor about half an hour ago and said he'd be right back. Clare told him he'd better be back. We need that tractor, too. Where the hell is he?"

"That's what we're trying to find out," Mary replied, then clicked off. "Maybe he had tractor trouble."

"Why don't we walk back? We'll probably meet him on the way," Arlene suggested. "If the tractor has acted up, we can all walk back together."

"But we've got to move the roots." Mary was adamant.

"We'll have to do it later," Susan sensibly replied.

"We have to get this done."

"Mary, the light will fade soon enough. It's Sunday and we all need to go home. Come on." Harry sounded firm, then whistled for the dogs, who had been checking out every smell they could.

They dumped their chain saws into a wagon, which Harry pulled. Then Susan took a turn, then Mary, then Arlene. The Institute was a good mile away, probably more, but they didn't want to think about it. They were tired and the mud on their work boots just dragged them down.

Finally, a quarter of a mile from the Institute, sitting on the path, was the old Ford tractor.

Harry climbed up, fired it up. "Nothing wrong with this baby."

"Well, he can't be far." Mary was irritated. He wasn't.

Susan had walked up a small rise by the roadside. "Girls!"

Harry, knowing Susan, ran to her immediately, as did Tucker and Pirate, close on her heels. "Oh no."

Now all four women were running. Tucker

reached Jason first, followed by Pirate.

Flat on his back, eyes upward, Jason lay there, his throat slit ear to ear.

10

April 15, 2018
Sunday, 6:20 P.M.

A lurid red light washed over the corpse. Harry wished the sheriff's department would close Jason's eyes. She, Susan, Arlene, Mary, Tucker, and Pirate waited with the deputy while the ambulance people, a small forensics group, finally loaded Jason onto a gurney. The sun had set at 7:50 P.M., the chill intensified, but the shocking discovery made the air seem cold indeed.

All four women had been questioned but were asked to stay where they were as the other two groups were also questioned, as well as the people at the kennels. Everyone was ordered to stay put.

No reasons were forthcoming, but Harry figured the authorities were aiming to prevent any collusion. No one could warn anyone if the killer was one of a work party. And who would know what Jason's movements would have been, where Jason was? Then again, one never knows of people's secret lives. A slim possibility existed that he had been followed, the perpetrator covered by the topography and some evergreen trees.

She knew if anyone in the other two groups had blood on them, that would sink their ship. But no one did. Then she told herself the killer could have changed clothes. She decided to study whoever she could, once allowed back at the Institute. If someone looked as though he or she wore a complete change of clothing, well, maybe. Then she realized she hadn't truly studied what each person wore. Above all, she felt terrible for Clare.

"Blood has a metallic smell, doesn't it?" Pirate leaned on Tucker.

"Does. Human blood is strong." Tucker nudged next to Harry. She knew Harry was upset.

"Ladies, I'm sorry to keep you here so long, but we can't be too careful in a situation like this," the slim sheriff advised them. "You all have been most cooperative."

Finally released, they slowly walked back toward the large stone building a quarter of a mile ahead. No one spoke until the Institute came into view.

"What do we tell the others?" Mary asked.

Arlene lifted her shoulders, then let them fall. "That we found him."

"Perhaps we might spare them some details," Susan suggested. "Especially Clare. Why didn't the sheriff bring her to the body?"

Harry replied, "Aren't spouses and next of kin the most suspicious people? People are killed by those close to them, not that I think Clare is a killer. Maybe the sight of him would be too dramatic. They wanted to spare her."

"It's hard to get more dramatic than finding a man with his throat slit," Arlene posited.

"Fast?" Mary wondered.

"Not fast enough," Harry told them. "You bleed out but you know you're dying. I expect the shock doesn't totally cover the pain."

"Harry, we don't need to know that." Arlene gently chided her.

"Sorry."

"Our human is practical even about death." Tucker was proud that Harry never lost her head.

The four women gathered in the dining room with everyone else. The kennel group replayed how Jason asked for the tractor.

Amy had made him promise to be quick about it. He was in a good humor. Each person chipped in their impression of Jason in what no one knew would be his last moments. Mary and Amy comforted Clare as best they could, once she was free of questioning. Everyone felt awful for her. She was especially distressed that she had not seen his body. Mary, through her many connections, was allowed to take Clare to see her husband, who would be sent to the medical examiner's office in Richmond early in the morning.

The other work party had nothing to say. They had been far away from the kennels, from Jason on the tractor, and also far from Harry's work party. Naturally, each person expressed dismay and sorrow, but they were one step back from the immediacy of it all.

The dark outside enveloped them. Harry wanted to go to the cabin to let the cats in.

"Given the circumstances, if anyone wished to stay the night, that's okay," Amy told them. "There won't be breakfast tomorrow morning, but you all know you can pick up something once on the road. The bathroom will stay open." She looked to Arlene. "Is there anything we need to do? Clean out the kitchen?"

"No. I'm sure we can round up coffee. I'll

be staying."

"Me, too," Amy said.

"We'll be in the cabin," Harry told them. Most of the group did decide to stay, either in the main building or their cabins. The dark proved intense and everyone had the sense to know they were not at their best. No point driving if your concentration would wander. Although many did volunteer to drive Clare back to Montgomery County, Maryland, tomorrow after she saw Jason. The rest of the family had been called.

Harry and Susan grabbed two sandwiches and had drinks in the cooler back in the cabin. As they stepped outside, the stars loomed overhead so low, it seemed they could touch them.

Mrs. Murphy and Pewter rose to greet them, for they'd been sitting on the cabin porch.

"I'm freezing!" Pewter loudly complained.

The dogs shot inside the second Harry opened the door. Tucker and Pirate told the cats everything while Harry knelt down, poking the embers. A few glowed amidst the ashes. She rolled up newspapers, dropping them into the just placed logs, crossed like a box. The papers caught. She arranged smaller logs over the square, then sat in the rocking chair to warm her feet. Susan had put down food for the animals. She, too, sat down, first handing Harry an iced tea. Neither had thought to bring a plug-in teakettle, but the tea was fine.

"I'm famished." Harry bit into the ham and cheese. "Cold makes me hungry."

"The sight of Jason has dimmed my appetite."

"Susan, it wasn't so bad." Harry remained calm about it.

"Why would anyone kill Jason Holzknect?"

"That's what's shocking, really. The suddenness of it. Now you're here. Now you're not. No signs of struggle. He knew who killed him, I would think."

"They came up behind," Susan reminded her.

"Yes, but he had to climb down from the tractor. He knew who killed him and whoever did it knew how to do it."

"I expect quite a number of people know how to kill." Susan folded her sandwich wrapper.

"Why do you say that?"

"Because of the large number of military and government people, some still active and some retired, in hunting. We're close to Washington. We get all manner of people flying under false colors."

"What do you mean?" Harry leaned forward.

"CIA, FBI, defense department people. Ned has alerted me to that. Not that they're bad. They're not, but Ned says if someone has a business, they make decent money, live in a decent house, but you never see a lot of people in, say, the insurance agency. There's always people in the military service doing double duty. They've all been taught how to handle various weapons. Often, even though retired, they still have one foot in it even if used as a consultant."

"I never thought of that." Harry shook her head.

"We don't have to," Susan simply declared.

"Maybe he made a mistake." Harry wondered.

"For all I know, he stole some money or was sleeping with someone else's wife."

Harry raised an eyebrow. "Jason never gave a hint of, shall we say, such excitements. If anything, he was a bit tedious."

"Now Harry."

"Nice enough. Don't get me wrong. I just don't think excitement was his middle name."

"Well, Harry, he's been murdered. Bam. Under all our noses. He couldn't have been that dull."

The fire warmed the chilled cabin. Harry and Susan removed sweaters and took off their boots.

Tucker rose, walked to the door, scratched.

"Oh, Tucker." Harry reluctantly got up and opened the door. A cold, low air swept by her legs. Tucker halted, then turned back to the fire. Harry closed the door, accustomed to canine changes of mind.

Ruffy had brushed by her, walked to the fire, sat down. The other animals told him about the murder but he knew.

"It's not over," the ghost predicted, then lay down before the fire, something he hadn't done in years.

11

September 13, 1787
Thursday

As the earth neared the autumn equinox, the sunsets arrived earlier and the day's heat cooled off faster. The days, warm, no longer sweltering, presaged a beautiful fall. Better, one needed a blanket at night but not yet a fire.

Bumbee set her loom and rose from her bench, which she preferred to the chair she occasionally needed. The girls spinning yarn or cutting patterns in heavier fabric in preparation for cooler weather had left for the evening.

Moving around the room, Bumbee checked everyone's work. Like any other job, variations in talent revealed themselves, but no one was awful, and a few of the younger women evidenced a flair. Rubbing the thin, light wool between her fingers, she smiled. This would make a blouse or dress draping the female frame and the bit of warmth would be pleasant. On a cool morning Catherine or Rachel could throw over a heavier sweater.

Bumbee checked all the shelves. Sometimes in their haste to leave to go to husbands, children, or boyfriends, the girls would stick the wrong bolt in the wrong place. Bumbee would chide them the next morning, but she remembered those heady days.

She pulled off her shift, the cooler air noticeable. Then she walked over to the large pot over the low fire. She liked to keep warm water going, easy to bring to a boil if someone wanted tea. Mr. Ewing made certain everyone could have a bracing cup of tea. Bumbee mixed her own leaves together. She had her brisk morning tea, an afternoon tea with tiny bits of lemon rind, and then her evening tea with her secret mixture. Put her right to sleep.

She poured out some water into an enamel bowl, grabbed a washrag, and washed herself. After a long day at the loom, this felt so good. A small noise by the back window alerted her. She threw the rag in the bowl and stepped to the window to see Ralston running away.

"That boy will be trouble," she muttered

to herself.

Then she put on a light robe and sat by the hearth. Even though there were no logs burning in the large step-down fireplace, she liked to sit by it. The low flame in the back of the hearth where she'd hung the water pot was flickering out. The aroma of applewood filled the air.

Ewing had planted an apple grove two years ago. The trees, slender, sometimes shed a branch or two and Bumbee made sure to get some. Hardwood stacked by each cabin, a large stack by the weaving room, promised a toasty winter. But a few little branches of apple, pear, peach created a wonderful scent.

She began to doze off. Then a knock on the door snapped her back.

"Who is it?"

"Serena."

"Come on in, girl."

The attractive assistant to Bettina slipped through the door, sat in the old rocking chair across from Bumbee.

"Lord, it's good to get away for a minute."

"Husband?"

"No, he's fine. Tired. Bringing in the last cutting of hay. There was so much of it. By the time I walk back up, he'll be sound asleep. That man can sleep through a thunderstorm. I swear he could have slept through Yorktown if he'd been there."

"Your Joe is a contented man."

Both rocked a bit, then Serena leaned forward. "Bumbee, Ralston is asking questions."

"Well, he tore your bodice."

"Got a big lump on his head, too. I grabbed one of Bettina's tenderizers. She puts a store by beating the meat to bits." She sighed. "She would know. But Bumbee, I can knock that fool upside the head anytime. No, he's asking questions about Marcia."

This made Bumbee sit up straight. "Tell me."

"He knows, everyone knows, that Marcia isn't Rachel and Charles's child. The story about this being the outside child of her distant cousin stuck. All the white people believe it, as well as our people who didn't know."

"Marcia looks white. Selisse blood."

"He asked about the woman who was sick who stayed here. He has figured out she wasn't sick."

"He never laid eyes on her." Bumbee's voice was raised.

"I'm not so sure." Serena folded her hands in her lap.

"I caught him sneaking around just before you came in." Bumbee sharply drew in her breath. "It's possible he was spying. But she had half her face smashed in. If he'd seen Ailee, he would have seen that."

"True. She wore a heavy shawl, drew part of it over her face. But if she went to sit down, he would notice her difficulty. I don't know why he wants to know. I mean, he asks did anyone ever see Miss Rachel's cousin. Stuff like that."

Bumbee ran her hand along her cheek for a moment. "Might be he wants money if he's figuring something out. He never saw her body when we took her out. We buried her in the dead of night and there's no stone. That poor woman." Bumbee shook her head.

"Ralston is a sneak. Money, well, maybe. Buy himself a girlfriend."

"Dear Lord," Bumbee muttered.

"All he thinks about. Or so I hear. And he's fighting with Jeddie."

"That's stupid, bone stupid."

"Barker O keeps his eye on the two of them and Miss Catherine, of course. I worry that Ralston might harm Jeddie, hurt his riding ability. And let's face it, Jeddie is a handsome boy. Girls notice him."

"Yes." A pause. "Yes. Serena, there's not

much we can do unless Ralston opens his big flannel mouth to the wrong person."

"Do you think I should tell Miss Rachel?"

"No. It will only worry her. She loves the child. She believes, as do I, that Marcia will pass. No one will ever know except those of us who cared for Ailee. Even DoRe doesn't know. He thinks the child died when Ailee hung herself. I'm pretty certain he knew she was going to have a baby. I expect he figured it was his son's. I don't know."

"Terrible things happen, don't they, Bumbee?"

"They do. Things have been quiet here. Best to keep it that way."

"But if Ralston gets out of line?"

"Then we go to Barker O. He'll know what to do. They're all in the stables. By the way, is DoRe here?"

Serena nodded. "He slides over two or three times a week now. That will stop when Maureen gets back."

"M-m-m. I'm willing to bet Sheba is in Philadelphia or even Boston. All those years she stuck to Maureen like a tick. Waiting."

"They both smashed Ailee's face. I believe it." Serena's mouth formed a grim line.

"More to it than that, but we'll never know and Ralston must never know. You know, Serena, I believe he will grow to be the kind of man that forces himself on women. Something's not right there. Oh, I understand how they can get. We all do, but usually it stops with pleasing and promising."

"Certainly does when we give in."

They both laughed.

12

April 18, 2018
Wednesday

"What if we get one thousand people?" Mags Nielsen's blonde eyebrows shot upward. "Will cost a fortune."

"If we get one thousand people, we should celebrate that so many want to come home," Harry calmly answered. "And we can start fundraising when the announcement goes out."

Susan jumped in. "Mags, do we need to hire a caterer? We do. But we can still bring dishes. If we're careful, those costs can be controlled."

Janice Childe, another hard worker of the Dorcas Guild, rapped her pencil on the meeting table. "I sincerely doubt one thousand people will journey to St. Luke's from wherever they may be in the world but" — she emphasized "but" — "three hundred, perhaps more, I expect that. First of all, look how many of us still attend St. Luke's. Those of us still in the Mid-Atlantic or even New England may well make the journey. Do we have a great deal to organize? We do, but it is doable."

Mags, not yet convinced, added, "Janice, apart from the food, the chairs, the parking, and the tents, tents' cost. After marrying our oldest daughter, I can tell you about tents. Then there are the games to organize."

Susan held up her hand. "Isn't that why we have the St. Peter's Guild? I think some of this comes under the heading 'Men.' "

This provoked laughter.

"Speaking of men, surely there are those in the congregation who would write a few restorative checks," the much older Pamela Bartlett advised.

"Well said." Harry smiled at Pamela, whom she much respected.

"What about the jewelry that was found with that old body? Why can't the church sell that? I have no idea what it's worth. All the papers said was that there were jewels with the bones, but those jewels belong to us." Janice surprised them with this. "Where are they? Harry, you're in charge of building and grounds. You must know."

"Well," Harry prevaricated. "Almost a year and a half has elapsed. If someone were going to come forward, they would have done so by now. But no one has. Still, we might want to wait longer. Can you imagine the mess if we did something like that and a person shows up, DNA test in hand?"

"Oh, Harry, that's TV stuff." Mags shrugged. "That body was in there for over two hundred years. No one is going to appear claiming to be a relative. Remember when the reverend gave a sermon shortly after the body was discovered? He said, if I remember correctly, that the abandoned, those without a proper service, prayers, or tears still deserve consideration."

"You're probably right, but we live in such litigious times," Susan reminded them all. "Let sleeping dogs lie."

"For now." Pamela's clear voice rang out.

"Have any of you seen the jewels?" Janice's curiosity shot upward with the discussion.

"I did," Harry replied.

"Well?"

"Janice, her necklace was so covered with dirt, I couldn't tell you much about it." This was close to a lie. "Yes, she was wearing a necklace, but maybe the shock of the discovery kept me from closer scrutiny." Another big fib.

"Harry, no one has ever accused you of not paying attention to detail," Janice shot back. "Surely you could tell if the jewelry was genuine."

"I couldn't." This was practically true. "I can only tell you she wore some very dirty pearls."

"We should investigate."

Susan, sharp, interjected. "Janice, the possible uproar doesn't offset the gain."

"Aren't the jewels in the safe downstairs?" Mags asked.

"No. Sheriff Shaw took everything when the corpse was removed. Well, that was hardly a corpse. The bones." Harry sounded calm. "I expect he has them in a secure place. I know that Reverend Jones hasn't asked for them back and I think one of the reasons is that he hopes Sheriff Shaw may be able to piece together something about this discovery. The jewelry might help." She did not reveal that the fabulous jewelry was locked in the big steel safe at Keller and George, an old, established jewelry store.

"This is beyond a cold case." Janice again rapped her pencil on the table.

"Oh, I don't think so." Pamela, highly intelligent, realized this needed to be shut down. "Who knew the body was on top of the Taylors'? Since this had remained undetected since what, 1786 or so, it's doubtful anyone knew other than the person who placed her there. The Taylors died in 1786. Had to be close, I would think, and there were no more burials for a year. Good luck for St. Luke's. But while this may be an old case, it's not necessarily a cold case. It's new to us."

Mags considered this. "True."

Janice then chimed in. "New to us, but someone had to have known. Someone put her there."

"Of course they did." Harry tried to suppress her irritation. "But chances are that person has also been dead for two hundred years."

"Well, what if whoever killed her told someone, or his or her children?" Janice persisted.

"I think we'd know. I would think whoever that might be, subsequent generations would have dug her up." Susan, too, was working to slide away from the jewelry.

"Then why now?" Janice was close to defiant.

"Janice, if we knew that, wouldn't we have solved this?" Harry hit the nail on the head.

As the meeting broke up, the two old friends kept their mouths shut until they were in Susan's station wagon.

"What is wrong with her!" Harry couldn't help it.

"Janice has always been nosey. And I say she became more aggressive when she started frosting her hair."

Harry exploded with laughter. "Oh God, Susan."

"Think about it. Janice hit forty and forty hit back. Granted, it is a good frosting job, but no one frosts their hair until middle age."

They howled as Susan drove out of the parking lot.

Once at Harry's, they sat for a nip of bourbon seasoned in a Madeira cask. Harry rarely drank, but she felt like a special moment and this certainly was that.

"Treats," Pewter demanded.

Harry dutifully got up and tossed out treats, not because she knew what Pewter said but because she knew if she didn't buy off the cat, Pewter would be in her lap. The others would then act up, too.

The back door opened. "Me."

"Come on in. Spirits." Harry instructed her neighbor, Deputy Cynthia Cooper.

The lean woman hung up her heavy jacket and joined them as Harry put down a small, lovely crystal glass with the bourbon gleaming within. "Still cold out there."

"Mid-April. You never know," Susan agreed.

"Heard from the Loudoun Sheriff's Department what happened at Aldie. You all manage to get right in the middle of things, don't you? Well, I'm glad it's up there and not here."

"I am, too," Susan agreed. "We just left our Dorcas Guild meeting. No one knows yet, but it will be in the paper. We would never have gotten anything done regarding homecoming if they knew we'd found Jason. Those girls would have been all over us like white on rice."

"As it was, Mags Nielsen and Janice Childe wanted to know why St. Luke's couldn't sell the jewelry found on the old body. It was ridiculous." Harry sipped her drink.

"What?" Cooper wondered.

"Oh, this all started over money. The homecoming I told you about. The notices haven't even gone out and Mags and Janice are obsessing over money. You know, it's made me tired."

"What did happen at Aldie?" the young officer wanted to know.

The two relayed their experience.

"Not a sound? You would have heard something," Cooper said.

"We were all pretty far away, but what I think is that he stepped down from the tractor, talked to whomever was planning to kill him. No sign of fighting back, and whoever it was sliced him when he turned around. If this had been done face-to-face, blood would have been all over the killer."

"Had to be someone who knows how to kill. You need to clasp the lower jaw, jerk the head back as far as you can, hold it still for a second, and then slice and slice deep enough to cut the jugular."

"Jason was a fairly big man." Susan thought about what Cooper had pictured.

"That he was," Harry agreed. "But again, he knew his killer. He had to, so whoever did it had the advantage of complete surprise."

"They had to be fast," Susan added.

"Which is why I will bet you this is a trained killer," Cooper said.

13

September 25, 1787
Tuesday

A low fire glowed in the elegant fireplace in Ewing's library, which also served as his office. The first blush of fall shone on the trees, and as the sun set, an early chill filled the air. Weymouth, the butler's son, had built a fire for Ewing, who had been glued to his desk since late afternoon.

The large grandfather clock chimed the half hour in the hallway. Seven-thirty. The middle-aged man removed his spectacles, rubbing his eyes. In front of him on his desk rested the Constitution, which had been signed on September 17, 1787, by those delegates still in Philadelphia, a small number, thirty-eight, but the wrangling had gone on since May 25.

A farsighted man, Ewing paid under the table the princely sum of five hundred dollars to Roger Davis, who traveled to Philadelphia with James Madison, acting as the small gentleman's unofficial secretary. As the convention dragged on and on, Ewing made certain Roger received further compensation. After this last spectacular service, he would amend the amount, nearing one thousand dollars to one thousand three hundred. Roger, having recently married, could certainly use this sum.

Many would see this as exceedingly generous, but given that Ewing was one of the few private citizens to be reading the document early, Roger's efforts were worth every penny. Fortunately, the young man's handwriting was clear, for the Constitution, when printed, proved large. This was sent to every state assembly. Virginia used the term "House of Delegates" for the state Senate. But in the main the term "assembly" proved accurate for the proceedings therein.

Ewing had regular fine paper, the normal size, which allowed him to receive this by post, for which he paid thirty dollars. However, the package would arouse little suspicion, the suspicion being: How did this successful businessman receive what state governments had received or were still receiving if further south or north of Virginia?

Once again, Ewing read General Washington's cover letter. "Sir, we have the honor to submit to the consideration of the United States in Congress assembled, that Constitution which has appeared to us the most advisable —"

The appeal continued, as Washington knew full well that this document would create the largest exercise in public debate imaginable. The Constitution had to be ratified by the states to be in force. Knowing the dramatically different economic interests of those former colonies, this would be as much a test of the new nation as had been the war to separate from England.

What pleased Ewing was the phrase in Washington's appeal that this involved "prosperity, felicity, safety, perhaps our national existence. This important consideration . . . each state in the Convention to be less rigid on points of inferior magnitude. . . . And thus the Constitution, which we now present, is the result of a spirit of amity, and of that mutual defense and concession which the peculiarity of our political situation rendered indispensable."

Ewing read and reread Washington's letter and the Constitution three times. He wanted to be certain he understood the contents. Pushing back in his chair, he inhaled the odor of the wood burning, again rubbed his eyes as the candles flickered. While the hour wasn't late, he had been reading, reading for hours. This was far too vital to toss off.

Did he understand it? He thought he did. He feared Massachusetts and, oddly, South Carolina. Would those states, so very far apart in economy, be able to accept this? The representation issue, which vexed everyone, was resolved thanks to the Connecticut Compromise, but there were other issues that were bound to be raised as the memory of an irresponsible and then seemingly vindictive king were stirred up. While the Constitution appeared to be neutral concerning economies, could the difficulties of a New England state enduring rocky soil, really relying on trade by sea, trust a state with soil perfect for rice?

It seemed to Ewing that the New England states, anticipating being overshadowed by the more robust agriculture of the southern states, would naturally be suspicious of the large southern landowners. A banking elite, a concentration of monies, loans, and foreign dealings with other banks loomed large in Ewing's thoughts. If New England could concentrate income through its banks, that would more than offset the influence of the wealthy in the South.

As he was one of those wealthy ones, this deeply concerned him, yet he felt that Hamilton was right. The country needed an economic elite, it needed liquid assets, so to speak, it needed a government, strong and central, to prevent the weaker agricultural states from being held hostage by the richer northerners. But the reverse was just as unsettling. The country needed a securities exchange, which Massachusetts created in 1741, the Land Bank, only to see it destroyed by the British government.

So he put his glasses back on and read again.

Worn out, mind fatigued, he gave up by nine o'clock when Weymouth came in for the second time to refresh the fire.

"Weymouth, thank you. I'm going to retire for the evening." Ewing stood up. "You retire, too. It's been a long day and I hear there was another rumpus at the barn."

Weymouth nodded, not wishing to get caught in the middle. If Ralston learned Weymouth, older and far more powerful than he, had criticized him, the younger man would find a sneaky way to get even.

"It's cooled down even more. Would you like me to start a fire in your bedroom?"

"Ah, yes." He smiled warmly at Weymouth, in his twenties, a good young man but not his father's equal, which troubled both his father and Ewing.

Once in his spacious bedroom on the second floor, the room pleasantly warm, Ewing disrobed, pulling on a light wool navy robe. The windows overlooked the rear garden of Cloverfields, the mountains beyond, the outline just visible in the starlight. The small graveyard reposed below. He always looked out to his wife's beautiful tombstone of a recumbent lamb with a cross between its front legs.

"Isabelle, times are changing, changing so fast. You were always better at seeing these things than myself." He smiled, thinking of her often terse but accurate assessment of events, of people.

Ewing felt intelligent women possessed insights men did not. Isabelle left the business to him, yet she wasn't upset when Catherine took an interest in it. Still, she counseled her older daughter to keep her thoughts to herself, as Catherine also learned from her father.

And as he now sat on the edge of the bed, it was Catherine who filled his thoughts. He would have her read the Constitution tomorrow. Of course, they couldn't discuss it publicly, but they could between themselves. Better for no one to know what he now

146

knew. Once Virginia's governor, Edmund Randolph, and the others came to their conclusion, and he felt sure they would ratify the document after fulsome and tiresome discussion, then he could say he had read the same in a broadsheet distributed after the state's vote.

He was in his late forties, becoming old, although he felt good. When his time came Cloverfields would be held in common by his daughters but not by their husbands. Unconventional as this was, it was a form of dower rights, which could then be again passed on to their children. He needed to talk to their husbands but not yet. He liked John and Charles enormously, saw how happy both sons-in-law made his daughters, but neither man was a businessman. Catherine was. Rachel would follow Catherine's lead.

This new world, this new form of government: He prayed it would hold. He prayed his girls would thrive once he was united with Isabelle. Even if there was another war with a foreign power, he believed Catherine would find a way not just to survive it but to capitalize on it.

As he rested his head on the pillow and pulled up the covers, he prayed for that amity that Washington had written about and he prayed for peace even as he knew France was falling apart and his nation would be urged, seduced even, to help the power that had been so critical to its victory. The country simply could not be drawn into European wars. With that thought and a prayer for his family, he fell asleep.

14

September 26, 1787
Wednesday

Fall coolness filled the air, invigorating horses, cattle, and humans. The birds tended to their nests as those migratory birds took wing. Others had already left Virginia, being able to read the weather and the seasons far better than humans.

Catherine patted Reynaldo as Crown Prince came over for a kiss. Both boys stood in their paddocks, the sun an hour over the horizon. Jeddie had fed them as Barker O had fed the driving horses in the adjoining stable. Little Tulli was grooming two ponies that were now in service for Catherine's two-year-old and Marcia, some months older. Rachel laughed when Catherine put Marcia on the pony, but Catherine's view was that a lady who could ride and ride well was much sought after. So she was giving Marcia a leg up.

"Tulli, how are you this morning?"

"Sweet Potato wouldn't come to me until I rattled the feed bucket." The slight boy grinned at the pony.

Catherine could never remember whether Tulli was seven or eleven. He never seemed to grow, which, given that he labored in the stable, might not be a bad thing. Healthy, she was sure he suffered no wasting disease. He was just little.

She walked outside, pausing for a moment to study the blooded horses. She'd made her reputation on breeding and training those horses. No need to brag. All Catherine had to do was saddle up and ride them. Their quality dazzled people, as did Catherine. She entered the driving stable, with a much larger tack room than in the other stable. It also housed the carriages and took up a large part of the very large building.

Barker O looked up as Catherine softly walked in, a driving bridle in his hands.

"Miss Catherine." He held the bridle for her to see. "English leather."

"Yes." She knew that, of course.

"It's expensive and we are missing two bridles and missing one for the plow horses, too." He didn't mention that the money he kept in his stable coat was also gone.

"What? No one has been in the stables.

No visitors of late. What's going on?"

"Ralston stole them."

"Oh, Barker O, he can't be that stupid."

Barker O blew air out of his nostrils. "Stupid. A liar. I gave him a pretty good beating. He's been sent back to his cabin. His momma can deal with him."

"You did this yesterday? I heard there was a mess at the stables but I couldn't get to you, as I had promised Charles and Rachel to go to St. Luke's. I had no idea it was this serious."

"He's no good. Lies all the time."

"Has he stolen before?"

"Could have lifted something from someone or even carried off tools, but no reports. But this has been going on for a couple of weeks now. He doesn't care."

"Why?"

"Money. He can sell it and make money. Especially the English bridles and the English steel bits. The best in the world. No doubt about that. Jeddie accused him of stealing. That's when the fight started. I heard the noise, came over. Separated them and Ralston turned on me."

"He is stupid, but what does he want with money? He has what he needs, doesn't he?"

Barker O hung up the bridle. "He thinks he's going to be rich as a jockey. I can't watch him. He'll steal again and I'll beat him again but it won't do any good. What if he steals a horse?"

At a race down on the levels outside of Richmond on the James last spring, William, a rider for Yancy Grant, lent to him by Maureen Selisse, rode off with Black Knight, Yancy's good horse. In the process William pulled Jeddie off Reynaldo, who was already a step ahead of Black Knight. Jeddie broke his collarbone and William and Black Knight disappeared. The horse showed up later, skin and bones with his front teeth knocked out. Yancy, having lost money on the race and with Maureen turning on him as well, couldn't help the animal he loved. He asked Catherine to take Black Knight, which she did. He stood out in his paddock sleek and glossy. She had to feed him mash because he couldn't tear up grass effectively without front teeth. He'd had the reputation of being a handful, but at Cloverfields he was sweet, interested in the goings-on.

Catherine knew Barker O was telling her to get rid of Ralston. He could not say that outright.

"Hasn't this come on rather suddenly?" she asked.

"His mind is on women. But that's not —" He thought a moment. "Miss Catherine,

I think William is back somewhere. And I think Ralston knows and the two of them are up to something."

"William! Why in God's name would he come back? We all thought he made his run to freedom."

"He did. But I think he's back for money. Big money. William knows Sheba ran away with jewelry. And Maureen's people hate her. My feeling is William is back to steal from Big Rawly. He must know Maureen is gone for a while. I think Ralston, well, I think they are talking."

This stunned Catherine. "Where could he be? It's not as though people don't know who he is."

"Lot of places to hide at Big Rawly. And there's the caves down by Ivy Creek."

"If I tell Father, he'll sell Ralston. He doesn't like to split up families but no one can afford a thief and troublemaker." Barker O didn't reply and she continued. "But if we turn him out, literally, give him a chit so he can pass, he might lead us to William. William broke Jeddie's collarbone. I don't mind getting even."

A big smile crossed Barker O's face. "I expect Jeddie will take care of that if he can."

"Does DoRe know?" she asked.

DoRe was Barker O's counterpart at Big Rawly. The horsemen at all the estates knew one another, kept in touch, most especially because of breeding. A good breeding outcross could be a step up for the man who suggested and oversaw the match.

"Haven't seen him, but he might have a notion. It's hard to keep these things quiet. You know, Miss Catherine, it's not so much talk as it's a feeling. Someone notices a pretty girl sneaking off at night or someone notices a young man falling asleep on the hay wagon. A feeling."

"Yes. Much as I hate to lose tack, I don't want any harm to come to our horses. I will never forget Black Knight when he arrived. Never. You know, Barker O, I believe I could kill someone over hurting a horse."

"Yes, ma'am." Barker O would be happy to squeeze the life out of someone, but if that someone was white, he'd hang for it even if right. If it were another slave, maybe. He'd seen Ailee when she and Moses were helped by Bettina and Father Gabe, the healer, as they hid during the winter down in the caves. You don't do a woman like that. Seemed like nothing good ever happened at Big Rawly.

"What I will do is talk to my husband and to Charles. They may know how we can trim

Ralston's wings without endangering the horses or losing more tack. I will go to them first and then tell you. Thank you for telling me."

"Anything that has to do with the horses," he simply replied.

Catherine left him, hurrying up to her father's office, for she knew he had materials for her and was anxious for her to read them. She thought it might be another letter from Baron Necker from France. Whatever it was, she also figured she'd be in the office all day. Well, she'd talk to her husband and brother-in-law after that. One way or the other, they'd figure out what to do about Ralston.

But Ralston beat them to the punch. He was already out the gate.

15

Digging into the bag of dog food, securely kept in a trash can with a tight lid, Harry inhaled the pleasant odor. She dipped the scoop in, filled it, then emptied it in two ceramic bowls, names painted on the sides.

"I hate waiting on them," Pewter moaned.

"It's easier to feed them first since the trash can is out on the covered porch. Our food is in the cupboard. Anyway, that's the way she likes it." Mrs. Murphy watched as Harry closed the kitchen door leading out to the porch, a waft of cold air sneaking in with it.

The slender woman hurried over to the cupboard, opened the door, pulled out a delicious-smelling bag of kitty food with a hint of bacon. She put this in two ceramic bowls on the counter, names also on the sides. Then she opened a small can of special moist food, spreading that into each bowl.

Pewter's face was in the bowl before Harry could wash out the can. Then she made herself a strong cup of Yorkshire Gold tea that could wake up the dead.

Fair, called out early as a mare was foaling, had left her a note. Harry could sleep through most anything. She never heard him go.

The TV, new, on the wall, presented the weather. At least no snow was forecast, but neither was it going to be much warmer.

A blip on her cellphone caught her attention. She noted that Susan had just called her. The landlines proved better as Harry was at the base of the Blue Ridge Mountains. Cell service depended on where you were on the farm. For the best reception, she'd need to go outside. She picked up the old wall phone with the long cord, dialed, and sat back down to her tea.

"What?"

Susan's voice, clear, replied, "Amy Burke Walker texted me to go to the Middleburg newspaper. So I did. A long article about the murder."

"Now?"

"Let me finish. It's a weekly paper. Of course, the TV stations from D.C. carried it, but this is interesting because the writer took some time to nose around. It is now four days since Jason was killed. And the writer thinks this is related to his work."

"Jason Holzknect's work? He owned a Toyota dealership allied with Lexus. High and low. What could cars have to do with Jason's murder?"

"Okay, this is conjecture, but the writer relates that questions about contraband came up more than once about Holzknect Motors. Drugs smuggled in the hubcaps. A salesman was charged back in 2009."

"Jason?" Harry was disbelieving.

"He was rich." Susan's voice carried a hint of reproach. "He could have been in on it."

"A lot of people are rich. Doesn't mean they're dealing drugs. He wouldn't have been that stupid. Clare wouldn't have let him be that stupid. I find that hard to believe."

"Would you find other criminal activity hard to believe?" Susan pressed.

"I guess I would. I know, I know, that's how crooks fool us, but I never got a weird feeling from him. He did what he said he would, worked alongside all of us, was good to his hounds. Could he have been some kind of crook? I suppose, but if he was, I sure missed it."

"Somebody didn't."

"I wonder who the reporter interviewed?"

"I guess I do, too," Susan agreed. "You know we'll be questioned again. We're not high on the totem pole, but we are on the totem pole."

"What else could we be asked?" Harry was puzzled. "We were there for hours. Granted, it was pretty awful. It's such a personal way to die."

"What do you mean?" Susan asked.

"Your killer has to be so close to you. Touch you. A gun is impersonal. Sure you can hate that person's guts, but you stand back and pull the trigger. Or even hitting someone with a car. You're not close. This is so close. Like ancient wars, even medieval wars. You were close to your adversary."

"I never thought of that." Susan considered this.

"So it seems to me this is personal. Deeply personal."

"Ew, Harry. Like a betrayed wife or friend kind of personal?"

"Don't know. But I think it could be. The Institute is large. If someone knew the grounds, say, someone who had hunted with Jason, they could slip in and slip out. To the road through the trees. Clare could do that."

Susan thought, then said, "She's strong.

Reach up, pull back his head, and cut through the throat. I don't think Clare did it. It really seemed like a good marriage, a true partnership."

"I don't either, but this is something close."

"Oh, Harry, I hope you're wrong."

"Why?"

"Because the killer would be someone at the Institute. Someone who just blends in."

"Susan, the killer had to be there. Had to know the schedule, the territory, and had to know him. Jason probably liked the person."

"Good God. How do we know this won't happen again?"

"Susan, we aren't close. I swear this was something very personal and close. We're fine. We probably know the killer and have worked with him."

"No way," Susan exclaimed.

"We rub shoulders every day with people who have killed. On TV killers get caught, but in real life not so much." Harry spoke quietly. "If property is destroyed or money stolen, the search is on. But if it's another human being, there's attention, then it fades away. I think this drives law enforcement crazy, the disengagement of the public. People often have information that could be helpful to catching whoever did it. We probably do and don't know it."

"That's hard to believe. I know very little about Jason Holzknect."

"You don't have to know much. We worked with him. He hunted even before he bought the dealership, when he'd come back in the States. He mentioned it to me. Well, most everyone there has hunted for years. Nothing special about that. The killer, I'd bet on this, is a beagler or a basset person. I expect Jason had it coming, at least in their mind. You don't kill without a compelling reason, to you at least."

"Do you think we're in danger?" A ripple of fear ran through Susan.

"No, of course not." Harry paused. "Only if we get in the way. Or get too close ourselves."

16

"Thirty-two dollars and eleven cents." Ralston closed his hand over the money.

"You couldn't get more?" William turned up his nose.

"I didn't have time to get into the big house, the other houses, or the weaving room. I know Bumbee has money in there but I needed to get out. Barker O was getting close. He beat me. He's a smart man. He knew something wasn't right." Ralston looked around the woodshed a mile from the main house at Big Rawly.

Big Rawly comprised twelve hundred acres, nothing like Cloverfields, but the land proved rich, with abundant water, plus Maureen Selisse Holloway made her millions otherwise. She built on what she inherited plus what passed to her when her husband was murdered. Gossip had it that

162

she was the richest woman in Virginia, perhaps in all the colonies.

This shed, tight enough for it was raining, rested on the edge of a hardwood forest. The men would cut timber, split it, and stack it to cure. Once cured, the wood would be moved up to the shed by the house, loaded on wagons, and pulled by two well-cared-for draft horses.

Ralston had followed the creek, hiding if he heard anyone on the bluff above. He had run off from Cloverfields in the night, making it to Big Rawly in the dark. Knowing where to find William, he reached the shed, saw the old tarp left for him on the ground, and fell asleep.

Staying out of sight proved easy for he was far away from cornfields, hayfields, buildings. A hard-running creek provided water. He'd taken bread from his mother's larder but he would have liked something to go with it. William showed up once the sun set. The first thing he wanted to know was did Ralston get any money.

William sat on the tarp leaning up against the stacked wood, which smelled clean, good. "I know where some of the money is, in the stables. Silver in the house. No point taking anything heavy. Selling those bridles taught me that. We need what we can carry but you, well, you should have brought more. Why should I risk myself for thirty dollars?"

"You aren't risking yourself, William. We're both good hands with horses. If this girl takes you to the money, like you say she will, we'll have enough to get clear of here, way clear of here, and hire ourselves out. Then we can make good money."

"Lots of money in Philadelphia. Lots of people wanting to show off their driving horses, racing even."

"Long way away." Ralston shifted his weight, for the ground was hard even with the tarp. "I listened at Cloverfields. Listened to Barker O talk, some of the others. They say there's no slavery in Vermont."

"Well, why go that far? I said the money is in Philadelphia."

"Is, but we have to pass as free men."

"We say we are. There was a reward out for me. No one caught me. We can do it."

Ralston asked. "Why'd you come back?"

"Sulli. I'm taking her with me."

"You didn't tell me that. She'll slow us down." A flash of anger crossed Ralston's face.

"No she won't, and she knows where the money is, where some of the jewelry is. We need her." He took a long moment. "She belongs to me. You touch her, Ralston, and I'll kill you."

"Shit." Ralston shrugged, the picture of noninterest.

This changed when Sulli, shawl over her head, snuck out to the woodshed, whistled low. William whistled back. She hurried into the shed, basket on her arm.

"Sulli, this is Ralston."

She cast her light eyes on him, which shone even in the night light. "Pleased to meet you."

"Yes, ma'am." He put on his best behavior.

"Will, here's food for both of you, two old sweaters. It will be colder tonight. I've got to run back. Elizabetta is cracking the whip because the Missus will be back in a week or more but soon. Elizabetta has sat on her fat ass for months. So now we all got to make up the time. Dust windowsills, wash every pane of glass. Would be easier to keep working, but that is one lazy woman." She paused, a mischievous grin. "She'll be easy to fool. Woman is dumb as a sack of hammers, which is why I think Miss Selisse uses her." She glanced outside. "I'll slip down tomorrow." That said, she melted into the darkness.

William folded back the towel. Ralston wanted to grab whatever was in that basket but he waited.

The two sat side by side and ate.

"The Queen Bitch will be back and we'll be out of here. The best time to ransack the house for money is during church. Sulli will beg off sick. She'll show us where the house money is, in a box, she says. Shouldn't be anyone in the house. We can bust it open and go."

"But what if someone *is* in the house?" Ralston wanted a better plan than that.

"We give them some money and go."

"Never work at Cloverfields."

"This ain't Cloverfields. Everyone on Big Rawly hates that woman. They'll smile to her face, that's for sure, but no one will turn on us unless we drag them into it. I don't want no help other than Sulli."

"Right."

That same night at Cloverfields, Barker O walked to Bettina's cabin, told her about the stolen money from the stable.

"Good riddance to bad rubbish, but I'm sorry it cost you." The powerful woman sat opposite him as the rain pattered on the shake roof.

"He only got what I had rolled up in a saddle pad. Rest is in my cabin. Enough."

"You're a man who gets tips. All deserved."

He smiled. "I try. I'm not telling the Master, not telling Miss Catherine about the money. Find him, bring him back, he'll steal from us again."

"Yes. I mentioned that to Miss Catherine because Mr. Ewing was furious. Wanted to put out signs, a reward. She talked him out of it. Miss Rachel, too. Said, 'Father, let him steal from someone else.' "

"William, now he's clever. Ralston, not exactly dumb as a post but close." Barker O shook his head. "If they get caught, I don't know."

"Won't be killed. Too young."

"Well, Bettina, you're right. They could work but even if separated, neither one is worth squat. I figure they'll be sold to Miss Selisse's birth territory, down there in the waters, and worked to death."

"The Caribbean." Bettina filled in the name he couldn't remember.

"Damn fools."

"They might get away with it." Bettina heard a crack. "Thunder. I'll be."

Barker O looked out the little window. "They're holed up somewhere."

"What makes me fret is our young people. Running might look good to them. Where you run to is another matter, but the idea of being free . . . Oh, as Miss Catherine would say, 'a siren's song.' But if they start slipping away we'll all pay for it. Even Mr. Ewing has limits."

He nodded, face serious. "Well, Bettina, that's the thing, isn't it? When you're young you don't think of anyone else."

Indeed.

17

April 20, 2018
Friday

Sitting in the tack room, Harry checked her email. A missive from Mary Reed appeared announcing that the Hounds F4R Heroes would go on as scheduled: Bassets Friday, April 27; Beagles April 28 and 29. She mentioned that no new information was available concerning the murder of Jason Holzknect. The board decided the cause was too important to postpone, and it appeared that his demise was not related to the Institute.

Harry picked up the old phone and dialed Susan.

"Hey."

"Hey back at you. Did you read Mary Reed's email? I just did."

"Me, too," Harry replied. "She sent it out last night, but I was making up lists of ideas for homecoming and didn't check until this morning."

"Same here. I was at a fundraiser," Susan clarified. "Not for Ned. We've got another year before that, but for the Emily Couric Cancer Center. I didn't invite you because you give to the Women's Center. If I wrote checks to every organization asking for money, I'd be in the poorhouse."

"Wouldn't we all? There are good organizations out there. I pick what's closest to me, like Hounds for Heroes."

"Ditto," Susan agreed. "I'll call Liz Reeser. I'm assuming we can rent the cabin again. I sure hope so."

"If not, let me know. I'll call around. I think the Institute will be pretty full. Maybe that was one of the perks of the job," Harry replied.

A deep breath later, Harry asked, "I Googled Jason. Did you?"

"No."

"More information about his career, how important his work was in Ankara. There was a photo of him, maybe in his early forties, at a conference table. He was standing just behind our ambassador. The other men at the table, all men, represented different countries, and they, too, had a primary assistant behind them."

"He didn't talk much about it," Susan

remarked.

"Probably because the rest of us wouldn't understand it or because we all talked about hunting, as did he. On his Facebook page, still up, he appeared in white tie at a Paris hotel, obviously another big conference, some of the same faces appearing in the background. He certainly ran in rarefied circles." Harry stared into the distance for a moment.

"Switch gears. Homecoming," she stated.

"I put Mags Nielsen and Janice Childe as cochairs of the hospitality committee, hoping that will direct their energy and they won't be, shall we say, so questioning," Susan told her.

"Good idea."

They chatted some more. Then Harry hung up and dialed Cooper, who was driving to work.

"You're the early bird." Her neighbor teased her.

"Both are. But there's more light in the mornings now."

"Is, but I still get up in the dark."

"Will you do me a favor?" Harry's voice rose slightly.

"Depends on the favor. If it involves my work, again depends."

"It does, but let me explain. You know a

man was killed Sunday up at Aldie and Susan and I were there."

"I know what you told me."

"Coop, is there any way you can nose around as one law-enforcement officer to another? We have heard not one thing. Maybe the sheriff's department up there has found something. The reason I ask is Susan and I will return there Friday the twenty-seventh and stay through the thirtieth. We'll be helping with Hounds for Heroes and I, well, I'm not afraid, but I believe whoever killed Jason was working that day with all of us."

Cooper braked for a stoplight, the morning rush hour in full swing. "I'll see what I can do."

The sheriff's department in Loudoun County put Cooper through to the chief investigator for the county on the case. Cooper told the deputy, her counterpart, about her neighbor and asked forthrightly, as she should, was Harry in danger concerning the upcoming Hounds F4R Heroes?

"There's always the possibility of danger," Mark Jackson replied. "But we don't anticipate it during Hounds for Heroes."

"Given what my neighbor Harry Haristeen told me about finding the victim near the tractor, confirmed by her best friend who was there clearing trails also, this seems to be someone who was there or who knows the ground intimately."

"Right. This is in the initial stages, but the one question we return to is his business. Jason Holzknect operated and owned a very successful Maryland Toyota and Lexus car dealership outside the D.C. Line. He was negotiating to buy a Volvo dealership and he had the funds, had the backers."

Cooper mused. "The car business is ruthless, but I don't think it's that ruthless."

"As I said, he had the money. What we're focusing on is potential investors. We think there's a connection. There was the drug-running conviction some years ago concerning a salesman. The money is interesting."

"So often comes down to money, doesn't it?"

"That or someone's fried on drugs or drunk and starts throwing punches."

"Deputy Jackson, thank you. I assume some law-enforcement people will be at Hounds for Heroes?"

"Actually, we would be there anyway and our armed forces recruiters will be there, too. Veterans of Foreign Wars will be there and the American Legion."

"Sounds like everyone will be safe, including the hounds." She joked and he appreciated her humor.

No sooner did she end the call than the dispatcher called her. "Officer Cooper, St. Luke's Lutheran Church."

"Right." Cooper turned on the siren and lights.

"Attempted break-in just discovered when the pastor unlocked the door, which was 7:50 A.M."

18

September 30, 1787
Sunday

The faint sound of beautiful singing intermittently drifted up to Sulli through the open window at Big Rawly. Given that the night had turned cold, the window, allowing just a gap of daylight, let in the sound with a slight breeze.

In general, Maureen Selisse Holloway, driven and ruthless as she was, thought her slaves singing and praying on Sundays quite a good thing. The Old Testament, that paean to monotheism, justified dictatorships, one-man rule. Justified slavery, too. Her late husband ran the place with her help, but she was in charge and everyone knew it. Her father, who used the same methods, equally impressed her. Being a widow would have been a form of freedom, but when Jeffrey looked at her with that handsome face, those sensitive eyes, well, a

lady must live. So he was her screen. Everyone knew, of course, but fictions must be
preserved.

In Sulli's hand were topaz earrings, a
lovely but modest necklace, no large stones.

"Where's she keep her jewelry?" William
wanted to get out before the service ended.

"Elizabetta has the key."

"Where's the stuff?" he demanded.

Rather than argue with him, Sulli glided
through the main room, Ralston in tow,
moved into the hall and down to the small
pantry. She turned left, stood at the top of a
solid wooden stairway leading down to a
root cellar. Halfway down the stairs a metal
door, large, filled part of the wall.

"It's in here."

"Even if we had a crowbar, we couldn't
open that." Ralston's jaw dropped.

"Dammit!" William turned, nearly knocking over his beloved, and charged upstairs.
"There's got to be something we can turn
into money."

"Tack?" Ralston thought.

"Too much to carry. The pieces you
brought me were hard to sell. We need
jewelry and cash." He turned to Sulli.
"Everyone has a box of money to pay little
things."

Sulli wordlessly walked to the kitchen and

opened a drawer. "Household stuff."

He pulled the drawer all the way out. Some scrip and coins rested in the bottom. He scooped them up.

"William, we need to get." Ralston knew that while services were long, more time not to work, they weren't that long.

"We need two heavy coats," William ordered Sulli.

"Wait here." She left, returning with two woolen jackets, dark gray, plus a beige one for herself and a scarf.

William sighed, taking a jacket from her. Ralston also lifted a jacket off her arm. If Ralston had thought about this, he would have realized William didn't have much of a plan. Sulli tried to come up with useful items, but what could she do? Big Rawly, well run, treasures locked away or hidden, would yield little.

"Do you know where the key is to the wall safe?"

Sulli stared at William. "Around Elizabetta's neck."

"Why can't we wait until she comes back? We can tear that key off her neck." William rubbed his hands together.

"She'd scream," Ralston sensibly noted.

"Put your hand over her mouth and I'll hit her upside the head."

"William, don't be stupid. Everyone on this place would turn against you." Sulli may have loved him and believed he loved her, but she was beginning to doubt his intelligence.

"She serves Maureen. Who would care?"

"She's not like Sheba." Sulli had known Sheba since she was a child and Sheba was hateful to everyone, including children. "She does the Mistress's bidding, but if she can help without that witch knowing, she does."

"What's that to me? We need things to sell." William nearly spat.

"We can steal along the way." Ralston wanted to get moving.

"He's right." Sulli smiled at Ralston.

"Goddammit." William stalked off, looking over his shoulder. "Well, come on."

Walking behind hedges and trees, fall now obvious, they headed down to Ivy Creek. The idea was to go east-northeast, to get through Virginia and Maryland. Once in Pennsylvania they could decide whether to keep moving north or find work with rich horsemen. Pennsylvania boasted fine carriages, and people needed good hands with horses.

Running to freedom. Three young people, Ralston sixteen, Sulli eighteen, and William twenty-two. They weren't just running to freedom; they would find money, maybe even fame. Silk breeches awaited them and patent leather shoes with gold buckles. Low-cut dresses with sheer lace bodices and exquisite bonnets, such fine things to adorn young heads. The world beckoned.

19

April 20, 2018
Friday, 8:50 A.M.

Harry, Cooper, Reverend Jones, his animals, and Harry's shone a bright light on the door to the back of the church itself, which sat in the middle of the arcades.

"Pretty primitive." Cooper knelt down.

"Whoever did this splintered the wood." Reverend Jones knelt down beside her.

"Amateur. If someone knew what they were doing, a true break-and-enter robber, this would have been easily popped if carrying the right tools."

"I'll buy a new lock and install it today," Harry offered.

"Actually, Harry, let a locksmith do this, and while he's at it, let him check all the exterior locks. These doors, locks included, have to be forty years old."

"Cooper, the doors are from 1787. The

locks, yes, they've been updated," Harry replied.

"Update them again." Cooper stood up, as did Reverend Jones. "You have crosses, candelabra, expensive embroidered vestments. The chalice alone is worth a fair amount of money. Am I right?"

"Yes."

"Have the locks changed on your house, too," Cooper suggested, a bit forcefully. "You don't think about it, but everything in this church, even the baptismal font, is from right after the Revolutionary War." She smiled. "And your office, Reverend Jones, well, Victoriana."

He smiled back. "It is. I will call today."

"Do you have any idea what they wanted?"

He shook his head no.

"Harry?"

"I do have an idea. I wonder, are we stirring the pot? I wonder if this isn't about that body, or more likely the jewelry. It's not here, but whoever is trying to get in doesn't know that."

"Possibly." Cooper raised her eyebrows.

"I believe the jewelry belongs to the church. We should sell it and put the funds into our small endowment," Harry said.

"Set aside some for treats. We work hard,"

Elocution, one of the Lutheran cats, meowed.

Herb picked her up, rubbed her ears. "Well, I hope not. Keller and George has been extremely helpful keeping the jewels, but maybe we should move them or give them to the Virginia Museum of Fine Arts."

"Rev, why?" Harry was aghast.

"The exquisite workmanship. The museum has that incredible Fabergé collection, Mellon's equine art, and even those Degas figures that Degas worked with, so wouldn't something like this be special? Maybe the sight of this ought to be available to all. Sometimes the museum sets up clothing exhibits."

"You are too kind, Rev. I say it belongs to us and we should use it for our endowment and even take a few thousand for work here. The church itself could use a new heating and cooling system, one that is more efficient and cheaper to run."

He furrowed his brow. "Actually, this is a puzzle for the board."

"What do we really know about the victim? A female, thirties at the most, and probably African American. Isn't that what the medical examiner told you?" Harry looked at Cooper.

"That's what she told the sheriff. She also

said that one can be about ninety percent sure on race. Also, with what they could tell from bones alone, she was probably healthy." Cooper shone her light beam above. "Have the locksmith check the roof, too."

Harry bristled a little, thinking about the work she had put in, but thought better of saying anything.

"Thank you for responding so promptly. I'd best be getting back to work. Need to write Sunday's sermon," Reverend Jones said.

"You could just say, 'Thank you, Jesus.' " Harry teased him.

He laughed at his longtime parishioner. "That's at the bottom of all my sermons, but I think I'd better expand." With that, he walked back to his office at the end of the western arcade.

Harry, Mrs. Murphy, Pewter, Tucker, and Pirate escorted Cooper back to the squad car.

"I Googled Jason Holzknect," Harry told Cooper outside. "Funny, when you hunt with people you don't really care what their business life is or was. His career was a lot bigger than I thought. Then I switched to Facebook and found photos of him from his career."

"We did, too. Then I set about, with help from our forensics folks, identifying the other people in those photos. Lots of translators, policy wonks. Some faces recurred regularly. Usually translators from Russia or Greece. Not one Kurd, by the way."

"If you sit down at the table to talk to a political group, then you have recognized that group politically. The Kurds don't really have a state, so they aren't invited to the table," Harry added thoughtfully. "How can thousands of people be denied basic rights?"

Cooper leaned against the squad car door. "How terrible is it to give them a bit of land to call their own? It's a big, wide world."

"Not if it's your land. What are wars fought over? Land, money. This business about wars being fought over ideas or ideology or improving someone's lot is pure bull." Harry wasn't the historian Susan was, but she had studied a bit.

"The point is to always look like the good guy. I guess you're right — it's always smash and grab. Which keeps bringing me back to those damned pearls. Why not grab them?"

"I want to know who she was. And I also want to know why Jason had his throat slit ear to ear," Harry commented.

Cooper crossed her arms over her chest.

"We have a much better chance of finding Jason's killer than the woman found buried here. When is Hounds for Heroes, by the way? I'm sure you told me but it's slipped my mind."

"Next weekend, but I think Susan and I will go up earlier. There's still some cleanup to finish. When you think about it, there's been so much death at Aldie. Well, that's not exactly murder, the war, I mean. It's an impressive place and yet I feel a kind of sorrow. Especially when I walk along the path by the slightly raised mound, I feel a little cold air at my ankles and sometimes I feel that elsewhere."

Cooper said, "Little wind currents?"

Tucker raised her head. *"Ruffy."*

Harry glanced down at her corgi and the others. "Well, let me haul this crew back to the farm and put them to work."

"I'm not working without more tuna," Pewter declared as she leapt into the back of the Volvo station wagon.

"Then you'll fall asleep," Tucker teased.

Mrs. Murphy, right behind Pewter, said, *"Given recent events, we'd better stay wide awake."*

20

April 21, 2018
Saturday

"You did it." Cooper teased Harry as they studied her garden's neatly plowed rows.

"Yes, I did." Harry, hands on hips, looked for even one little shoot in the kitchen garden, then focused on the garden. "You know the weather has been too crazy. Eventually the corn will come up and the tomatoes, but we are late this year. So, what did they decide happened at the church?"

"Nothing. Someone had simply tried to pry the lock on the front door. Pretty stupid. They would have had even more trouble if they had known the pearls were at Keller and George. All these businesses have security systems, some better than others. Jewelry stores have good ones. The unearthed pearls are safe."

"Yeah, but if someone understands electronics, I bet any of these expensive security systems can be disarmed."

"Maybe," Cooper responded. "A thief would need to be tremendously well trained plus have the means to disarm a system. Some of these systems cost hundreds of thousands of dollars. Granted, the actual size of the store reflects some of that cost. Can you imagine the security system for Tiffany's, what is it, five floors?"

"Something like that. It's been years since I passed through those doors on Fifth Avenue." Harry knelt down to brush the moist soil with her gloved hand. "Still holding moisture. Then again, we got enough of it."

"No more snow," Cooper pronounced with finality.

"I doubt it. Then again, we aren't living in Wyoming or Montana. Can snow there in May. Well, upstate New York, too. But we'll get rain. Actually, the year has been wet and I think it will get wetter."

"Good for the water table." Cooper, not a country girl, was learning.

"That it is. We'll be grateful come August and September. I love the changing seasons."

"Me, too." Cooper glanced up at the sky. "Not a cloud."

Harry looked up. "Sometimes the blue is

almost turquoise; other times, robin's egg blue; and other times, a pale blue. Never fails to fascinate me. Now back to your garden. You really have to put up chicken wire or something because the second — and I mean the second — those first shoots finally make their appearance, so will the deer and the rabbits."

"You never have any problems," Cooper said.

"I have two dogs and two cats. I also have doors so they can come and go. The deer can't pull their tricks up at the house in the night. I don't care if they eat some of what I have as a crop, but not my little garden. One thing we have in our favor is there's lots to eat for wildlife."

"Harry, when you go to some of the places I do, you understand there's lots to eat for people." Cooper laughed.

"What is it, something like eighteen percent of Americans have diabetes?" Harry queried.

"Can't be that many." Cooper shook her head. "Least I hope not but" — she shrugged — "too much sugar and not enough physical labor, I guess."

"Back to the failed break-in. Are there a lot of break-ins at businesses in the city and county?"

"Actually, we're below average in the county. Keller and George is the province of the city. But even in the shopping centers there's not much planned theft. It's impulsive. Someone gets caught shoplifting. And as we all know, impulses usually land you in hot water. Add drink or drugs and it's a given."

"Ah. So the big crimes, big brains?"

"Pretty much. Cyber theft has taken over for armed robbery. That used to attract the bright and the bold. Now the crooks sit their fat asses behind a computer. I assume their asses are fat. Anyway, the crook could be in Bermuda, in Mumbai, in St. Petersburg."

"M-m-m, St. Petersburg. Wouldn't that be a political crook?"

"Harry, there are young people hired by older people all over the world who want to crack into credit card systems, bank systems, medical records. You name it. They are already here."

"What about the records of the sheriff's department?"

Cooper thought a moment. "I don't know if they find us that important. A large city police department maybe, but those of us in law enforcement have to combat these cyber crooks, too. Our small department has two computer whizzes."

"Gregory Dwayne and who else?"

"Sheriff just hired a young woman from UVA, Regan Moore. Both she and Dwayne will be out and about, but if anything is odd or we confiscate a computer, it's their task to unlock it."

"I'm hardly in their class, but I did research Jason Holzknect. Good career in foreign service. Specialized in communications, especially electronic communications."

"He was on the wave of the future," Cooper stated.

"He was. He was good with people and I assume good with money. He always seemed sensible to me. I mean, neither he nor Clare threw money around."

Cooper smiled. "Thinking about crime, murder usually is an easy crime to solve because most murders are impulsive, like shoplifting is impulsive. The impulse isn't gain, it's rage, uncontrolled rage. Again factor in drugs or drink and there's not an ounce of thought to it. Half the time the perp isn't far from the corpse. Easy." She paused. "A planned murder, like planned theft, isn't easy. If you think about it, Harry, most everyone has someone who doesn't like them. Maybe that tips over into murder if there's an old wound, an old theft even.

You get even."

"You can kill for material gain," Harry posited.

"You can, but there's usually a trail. The motive is clear. Add political power to wealth and it's doubly clear."

"You think the late Andrew Mellon had people who wanted to kill him?" Harry named a former secretary of the Treasury back in 1921–1932. He died on August 26, 1937, of cancer.

"M-m-m, political enemies, yes, but I doubt most people knew what he was doing. As it turns out, he was right for his times. He cared about our country. Now even fewer people know what a secretary of the Treasury does, but they'll want to kill him anyway. Crazy times."

"Crazy people." Harry turned to head for Cooper's house.

Once inside, Mrs. Murphy, Pewter, Tucker, and Pirate woke up, all asleep on the kitchen floor near the hearth, a fire burning, for it was still cold enough. Cooper gave them so many treats, they chose to stay inside thanks to bowls of food, eating themselves insensate.

The two women sat down, Cooper having made hot chocolate.

"Bums." Harry chided her pets.

"It was too good." Tucker lifted her head, then rested it again on Pirate's flank.

"You go back up to Aldie next weekend?"

"Unless we're needed earlier." Harry smiled. "Such a good idea, Hounds for Heroes, and anyone can bring hounds and hunt. You don't need to be a member of a recognized pack."

"What's the goal? How much?"

"Last year they raised twenty thousand dollars. That's just Virginia."

"Wow." Cooper's eyebrows raised up.

"Apart from the murder, I still see him flat on his back, but apart from that, every now and then I feel a little touch of cool air on my lower leg up there. Comes and goes. Odd. Then again, topography creates wind currents. A good huntsman knows how to use them."

"I expect."

"Thinking about what you said about murder, whoever killed the woman in the Taylors' grave got away with it."

Cooper nodded. "I don't know if it was easier then or not. Killing in the dark would be easy. Other than that, I don't know. If there are people willing to help or to keep their mouth's shut, it's still easy."

"And yet someone knew."

"What do you mean?"

193

"Why would the grave have been disturbed if someone didn't know?"

Cooper, cup in hand, thought about this. "I guess some stabbing in the soil is a form of disturbance; knocking over the tombstone, too. I wouldn't bet on that one being figured out. Someone would have to make a terrible slip or reveal hidden information, hidden for over two hundred years, but I'd say the chances of finding Jason's killer are pretty good as opposed to the killer from the eighteenth century."

"Why, because the murder's not over two hundred years old?" Harry reached for a chocolate chip cookie.

Cooper, who had put the plate on the table, reached for one, too. "No, because it has to be someone who was there."

"You don't think someone could have snuck onto the grounds, killed him, then left?"

Cooper shook her head. "No."

Harry waited a minute or two. "I know."

21

April 22, 2018
Sunday

A light rain failed to dampen efforts to brighten up the Institute in preparation for the Hounds F4R Heroes. The women had been asked to come up early. Harry, along with her pets, swept out the stables. Susan, Mary Reed, and Arlene focused on the Institute building itself while Amy, her husband, Jeff, Dr. Rachel Cain, up from near the North Carolina line, and Beth Opitz, Virginia, crawled over the kennels. The fixed rooftops held tight in the rain, which threatened to grow stronger. The kennel group checked for dropped nails, any nail sticking out from the kennel itself. Looked clean.

Inside, floors swept testified to the good wood. The walls, having recently been painted, to Susan's eye a pale mint, were welcoming and all the furniture was vacuumed. The porch outside, some white chairs tucked back up to keep out of the rain, gleamed white.

Harry rarely minded working without other humans. Mrs. Murphy, Pewter, Tucker, and Pirate were with her. She washed out every water bucket and hung it back up inside the stall. She thought about filling each bucket, then decided against it because the water would sit until Friday. She stacked good square bales of hay on a raised pallet. Again, no need to put hay in a stall's corner. People preferred to feed their own animals. Some horses wanted three flakes, others two. Some needed a bit of grain, which the two judges would bring if they wished. Too much grain proved as bad as too little, so best left to the owner. The mule who would be in the barn was reported to have a healthy appetite.

"Tidy," she announced.

"Because we killed all the mice." Pewter lounged on a sturdy wooden bench between two stalls. This stood there for odds and ends each rider might put down, but Pewter commandeered one by stretching out.

Off to the side was a sturdy yellow cart.

Mrs. Murphy, like Harry checking each stall, puffed up her friend. *"We did kill a lot."*

"Bud the chickadee will tell everyone. Bet

mice don't dare come back in here for months," Pewter predicted.

A wheelbarrow at the end of the open aisle, rain blowing in a bit, filled with sweet-smelling shavings, next attracted Harry. She lifted up the handles, going to the first stall. A wide shovel allowed her to pitch in the contents. She returned to the shavings shed outside, moving quickly, filled the wheelbarrow, and returned to repeat the procedure. Once both stalls contained shavings, she took a rake, carefully spreading the shavings evenly. She wasn't sure if one animal was coming or two, so she set up two stalls.

Most all barns have nails so one can hang up shovels, rakes, brooms, even lunge whips. Keeping equipment up off the ground guaranteed a longer life for same.

Finishing, she leaned on the rake, admiring her handiwork. "Ought to do it."

"Who will pick out the stalls?" Tucker asked.

"Arlene, she's in charge," Mrs. Murphy answered.

"If she doesn't, Mom will." Tucker watched as Harry made certain everything was just so, including tack hooks, which she brought and hung up.

"She's so orderly." Pirate was learning to love Harry.

"A greatly overrated virtue," expressed Pewter, who was not.

The rain, steady now, drummed on the barn roof. Harry walked to the end of the aisle, looked out. Checking her watch, she walked back and sat next to Pewter.

"Let's give it a little time before we make a run for it."

"It's not going to stop." Pewter put her front paws on Harry's thigh.

"Sky's gray. Coming down in sheets now," Tucker observed.

"We should have left when it started," Pewter complained. *"Now I'll get wet paws, which I hate. Takes so much time to dry between your toes."*

The five creatures listened. A tiny mouse peeked out from its hole in one stall. No one saw her at all because of the shavings. She ducked back in. No need to set off the cats, and her living quarters were dry, filled with rag bits, lots of rag bits.

"Jeez." Harry listened.

"I'm telling you. It's not going to get any better. Make a run for it," Tucker advised.

"She can carry me." Pewter rolled over to reveal an overlarge tummy.

"You can run, Fatty," Tucker undiplomatically barked.

Pewter sat up. *"I'll scratch your eyes out."*

No time for scratching as Harry stood up, walked to the end of the aisle, took a deep breath, and sprinted for the cabin. It was far enough from the barn that she was soaked by the time she reached it, threw open the door, and everyone piled in, dogs and cats shaking themselves dry. Not being able to shake, Harry stripped off her wet clothes. She'd started a fire when she and Susan first arrived, for the lowering clouds kept the mercury in the high forties, low fifties. The threat of rain, the dampness, added to the coolness. The slight chill cut right through her. She draped her clothing over the one rocking chair in front of the fire, wrapped herself in a heavy towel, which she'd brought, and sat down to dry herself.

"Susan will get wet," Pirate said.

"She's in the Institute. She can find an umbrella if she decides to come back here before the dinner," Tucker told him. *"Susan can run between raindrops."*

"She can?" Pirate questioned.

"She's pulling your leg." Mrs. Murphy smiled.

Feet propped up on a heavy log turned on its end, Harry dozed off. Her animals did, too, as the rain beat down. The aroma from the fire filled the room.

A half hour passed. The door flew open.

Susan, umbrella overhead, turned around, shook the umbrella outside the open cabin door, then shut it. Harry, awakened, knocked over her makeshift footstool.

"Get the work done?"

Susan, wearing a Barbour raincoat, slipped out of it, hanging the dripping garment up on a peg. "We did. Glad I brought my raincoat." Noticing the drying garments, she said, "You didn't."

"I did." Harry pointed to her Filson tin jacket. "I didn't wear it. When we left the cabin, I really didn't think it would rain. Wrong again."

Susan dropped into the rocking chair next to Harry after carefully removing the drying clothing, folding them over the coat pegs. "I'm bushed."

"Me, too. Fell asleep, obviously. I hardly ever do that."

"Get the barn ready?"

"Oh, sure. Takes time, but it's all easy enough. I don't know who they buy their shavings from, but they're good shavings. Personally I prefer peanut hulls, but they are so expensive. So I use shavings like everyone else."

"M-m-m." Susan inhaled the fragrance. "It's not cold, cold but it's raw. Know what I mean?"

"What time do we need to be back at the Institute?"

"Hour. Dinner. The Ogdens are coming." Susan named a couple who had served for decades in the foreign service, and Geoff had also been president of Middleburg Hunt Club.

"Good. I don't know them well, but the times I've been in their company have been interesting." Harry smiled. "By the way, this bath towel is warm. I usually don't wrap myself in a bath towel. Always have my robe, which I forgot. Actually, I forgot a lot of stuff."

Susan turned to her, the light flickering on her face. "You're too young for a senior moment. Is it sheer stupidity?"

"Aren't you hateful?" Harry pointed a finger at her.

"No. Actually, I'm tired, too. It's been a week, you know. Ned was in Richmond the entire week and he's there now. Then there's the planning for the homecoming. Great idea, don't get me wrong. Now I'm stuck with Mags Nielsen and Pamela Bartlett. Everything is an issue."

"There are just people like that and my feeling is there are more and more or maybe I'm just noticing."

"No, Harry, I think it's true. Everything is

a potential problem, a potential lawsuit or, given the homecoming and food, how about ptomaine poisoning? You would not believe the bullshit."

"Actually, I would. Not so much for me since I farm, although I receive pages and pages of questions annually from the U.S. Agricultural Department as well as Virginia's. Given that no one in the cabinet or in Congress farms, the questionnaires are really about their careers, not my farming." She smiled. "I'm a cynic."

"We all are now. I imagine Fair handles his share of paperwork, sidesteps lawyers, has to account for controlled substances."

"Fortunately, horses don't have lawyers but their owners do. He fills out insurance forms, no kidding, and they get longer and longer. And now there is health insurance for horses. I'm not kidding."

"I suppose if you have a horse worth two million dollars, that's not such a far stretch," Susan reasoned.

"No, but a foxhunter? A pleasure horse? Not one of my horses is insured."

"Of course not. You're married to the vet." Susan let out peals of laughter and Harry joined her.

An hour later, dry, a bit of makeup, squeezing under Susan's umbrella, they sloshed to the Institute. The work party, comprised of ten hard workers, sat at the table, glad to be finished, hopeful for the upcoming event. Some drank wine, others beer, and, for the purists, bourbon and scotch. Even Mary, hardly a drinker, would not have downed vodka. Bourbon still reigned in the South.

Geoff and Jan, sitting in the middle of the table, surrounded by old hunting friends, pepped up the conversation, as always. Geoff's career in the State Department hit many high notes from being counsel general in Istanbul to specialized work on economics to personnel to being director of maritime affairs. Jan also covered many bases, truly enjoying it when she and Geoff were posted to the same countries. It seemed they knew everybody; they had known Jason well and later Clare.

Harry, fascinated, listened to Geoff having five Turkish bodyguards as he was the PLO's number one target in Turkey. Like many people, she took our State Department for granted, not considering how lives could be at risk. Given the murder of Ambassador John Christopher Stevens in Benghazi, Libya, during Obama's presidency, the dangers were apparent. What wasn't apparent and what she was listening to was what happens when the secretary of state and then the president do not correctly evaluate information from abroad. The first step was that U.S. diplomatic efforts were weakened or undermined by enemies. The worst outcome was death.

Fortunately, few people in the foreign service are killed, but one receives postings and must go. A posting to Russia proves quite different from one to France. Both are vital.

Harry realized how naive she was.

Jan, wonderful to look at, was telling the group how the public and private sectors can cooperate. The leadership starts with the president.

"For instance, and I bet no one knows this except for Geoff and me, it was President Nixon who brought together the private and public sectors. He considered it important and part of our education. I wasn't in service then, obviously, but I stepped into it as a young woman. A person like the president of Westinghouse might be sitting next to a senator from Utah. I always thought of it as cross-fertilization. Nixon would have meetings and he used state dinners to good effect. The big prize was a private lunch with him."

"Good things." Mary Reed smiled. "Don't

you think plenty of good things are still happening? The media focuses on the bad?"

"Fundamentally this is a Puritan society." Susan, the history major, threw this out. "Bad news sells. Cromwell proved that." Everyone started talking at once.

Harry leaned toward Arlene, an old friend of the Ogdens. "Arlene, how did you meet the Ogdens?"

"They were back in Washington when I was at the Agency. The secretary of state's office is on the seventh floor of the Harry S. Truman Building and I'd see Geoff in the elevators because sometimes I was called out there. We got to talking after many trips and I found out he foxhunted; he found out I beagled. Then he, Jan, and I hunted together. I'd follow the foxhounds by car. They'd join in on the beagling and basseting, and that's how we all met Mary Reed. A former Vietnam combat helicopter pilot, Al Toews, was Master and huntsman of Ashland Bassets then, a big, tall — and I mean tall — fellow. What fun we had."

"Sounds like it."

"Al died of a heart attack on December twenty-first. I remember because it's the winter solstice. Unexpected. Everyone came through, as you would expect. The hunting world is tight. Mary then took over. The club supported her, but what a shock."

"I can imagine. It's odd, isn't it, how big and strong men are, but they go first. For the most part they do."

Arlene nodded. "My mother used to say God gave women something extra."

Harry laughed. Hours passed before anyone noticed.

Finally, Rachel couldn't help herself as she asked Mary, "Nothing about Jason?"

"It is disturbing."

"Murder is." Geoff Ogden flatly spoke. "As the senior officer here," he said with a smile, "I'd advise you all to have security." He tapped the table with his forefinger. "You never really know, and both covered some sensitive areas."

"Will you be here for the Hounds for Heroes?" Mary inquired.

"We'll certainly try," Geoff replied.

Harry sidestepped the Jason issue to ask Geoff, "Did you ever lose anyone in service?"

A silence followed this. "I'm not sure."

All eyes turned to Jan and him.

Jeff Walker, Amy's husband, a man who had spent time in Nepal, had a grasp of, if not foreign service, at least what can happen when one is immersed in another culture and another language. "That's enigmatic."

Geoff Ogden paused, his distinctive voice low but clear. "When I was in Istanbul I had an M.C., a minister counselor, Paula Devlin. A career officer, obviously. She'd spent four years in Helsinki, two in Cape Town, said it was beautiful, and another two in Vienna before being posted to Istanbul. Her specialty was economic development and the Turks needed that. She spoke good Turkish and worked well with her Turkish counterpart."

"What happened?" Rachel wondered.

"That's just it. I don't know." He looked to Mary.

"She hunted with Ashland Bassets after she retired. She and Al were great pals."

"And?" Everyone looked at Mary.

Mary thought a moment, then spoke. "Al swore she was CIA. As a combat officer he had a nose for things. Like he could tell even before he was told if another person had seen combat. I don't know, it was a sixth sense. And he seemed to have it about the CIA. Paula disappeared. Vanished. Not a trace."

Jan added, "Apart from being a good Master and huntsman, Al did possess a sixth sense."

"What did you think?" Arlene asked Geoff, adding, "I knew her from hunting. We discovered we both worked for the government. We didn't usually discuss work. She asked me once about being wounded but we clicked. She was a lovely friend. We also talked with Clare about her shipboard days in the Gulf of Finland. She was a Russian expert and would listen to Russian chatter. For three women, and it was tougher then, we had good careers."

"In any embassy or consulate there are CIA people. There have to be. And there are some telltale signs. They have money. Never run out. Maybe not lots of money, depending on their job, but money. If they are operating inside our borders, they usually have a business front. There are times when they can be opaque. If you're smart, you don't ask too much, women or men. For one thing, most government employees can't tell you the truth." Geoff looked outside the window into the darkness. "Still raining. Well, the ground should be good for the fundraiser."

"Hope so." Amy stood up as the others followed.

Rachel then asked, "No one ever found Paula?"

Jan said, "She didn't come home. Her

neighbors in Hume noticed. No sign of her. Just poof."

Geoff added, "Her little dog didn't come home either." He held the chair for his wife. "Everyone got their umbrella?"

Back at the cabin, Harry and Susan took off their clothing. Harry snuggled into her comforter, Susan into her sleeping bag.

"Make room for me," Pewter demanded.

Harry patted a place for Pewter and one for Mrs. Murphy. The dogs stretched out in front of the fire, which Harry had fed.

Ruffy slept with them.

22

October 1, 1787
Monday

Summer's last kiss brushed Catherine's and Bettina's cheeks as they sat outside in the late afternoon, the garden and Isabelle's tomb drenched in gold.

Charles West designed and had a bench built so his wife and sister-in-law and whomever could quietly view the mountains and Isabelle's lovely monument. Apart from Charles's excellent education, the Baron had sent his sons on a Continental tour, considered vital for a young man of means. And so it was for Charles, who absorbed everything, most particularly loving Italy. Dutifully, he went into the Army, but he was an artist. No wonder he loved this new nation, for he could be what he was born to be.

Feet outstretched, eyes half closed, the two women felt the warmth. A clip-clop popped their eyes open. Tulli, with John-John in front of him, rode Sweet Potato up to the women.

"Momma, Momma, I can ride."

Catherine, trying not to resent her repose being disturbed, smiled. "And so you do." She then smiled at Tulli. "I think we need another matching pony so the two of you can be a team."

"Yes, Miss Catherine." Tulli bobbed his head in agreement, knowing JohnJohn wouldn't be riding on his own for maybe another year.

Catherine's son, two, was big like his father. He was well coordinated like his mother, so age three, riding on his own with Tulli next to him, might be possible. At any rate, it fed the child's ambition.

Bettina, hands folded over her ample bosom, shook her head. "You two are growing too fast. Why, Tulli, I think you've grown an inch since yesterday."

As Tulli, age eleven, was slight, or what horsemen called "weedy," a thin, small fellow, this sounded wonderful. "I have. I can feel it." He sat up straighter and Sweet Potato turned his head to look.

Ah, yes, humans, but then Sweet Potato had long ago learned to humor them.

"I want you to turn around and trot

halfway to the barn. And I'm watching. You do it correctly, Tulli."

"Yes, Miss Catherine." He carefully turned Sweet Potato toward the barn, visible in the distance, a lure for the pony.

A little cluck and squeeze and off the two boys went, JohnJohn screaming with delight.

Catherine looked at Bettina. "I will never be the woman my mother was. Both you and Mother loved mothering. Strict. But still."

Bettina reached for Catherine's hand, squeezing it. "There will never be anyone like your mother. I loved her. We all loved her. She understood life."

"She did. But Bettina, you liked being a mother."

"Most times. I never thought to outlive my children. Well, the little one, so frail. We all lose the little ones. My momma used to say, 'If I can get you to seven, I can get you to seventy.' "

"Mother said that. Heard it from you." Catherine watched clouds slowly slide overhead, long stratus clouds in an achingly blue sky. "I don't really remember your mother."

"You were tiny when she died. Just dropped. Boom." Bettina inhaled. "The older I get, the more I want to go like my mother."

"Bettina, don't say that. You need to live forever."

"When Rosalinda died, oh how my girl suffered. She wasn't even twenty."

"I remember." Catherine nodded. "The coughing. Weakened her so and then she could barely breathe. Oh, why are we talking about dying!"

"It's the light on your mother's marker, the lamb with the cross. Gives me peace. But you're right. You were talking about motherhood."

"I am not cut out to be a mother. I love my son, I do, but I force myself to listen to his prattle, to his hundreds of little requests and questions. I swear, if someone isn't watching over him, he'd probably walk off to Mr. Jefferson's and ask him questions." She laughed.

"Give him two more years. By four the worst of that is over. Tell you what, not enough babies at Cloverfields."

"Does seem to be a lull," Catherine remarked.

"Goes in cycles. I hope." Bettina rose and pulled over a low bench, placing it in front of them.

Sitting back down, she rested her feet on the bench, as did Catherine.

"Hurt?"

"M-m-m."

"You're standing all day."

"And I'm fat."

"You're not fat. You're upholstered." Catherine teased her. "Men like what you have."

"As long as DoRe does." She sighed. "Things settled at the stable?"

"Better. Ralston was creating one problem after another. It seemed to me to happen suddenly."

"M-m-m."

"Bettina, what do you know that I don't?" Catherine asked the cook, the head woman slave.

"Oh, a little of this, a little of that." Bettina patted her own arm. "That boy broke bad when his parts started working. Well, and his people are no-count."

"I think he's been stealing from us for a while. I'd leave a few coins in my little leather box in the tack room, or a bracelet would fall off and I'd drop it in. Then last month, I noticed those things would be gone. I'd ask Jeddie. He knew nothing. I'm not so sure he didn't know."

"If he did, what could he do? Ralston hated him."

"Meaning he'd get even?" Catherine took

214

a deep breath. "And how would it look if Jeddie ran to the Missus. I love Jeddie, but" — she took another deep breath — "it's complicated, isn't it?"

A long, long silence followed this, then Bettina finally said, "You have to follow your heart. Thieving isn't like hurting someone. If Ralston would have lifted a hand to you, Jeddie would have tried to kill him."

"I understand." And she did.

"I thank you for talking your father out of trying to get Ralston back. Offering rewards. No good would come of it."

"Rachel and I both talked to him. Rachel is better at it than I am because she's so much like Mother. I'm too logical. Father was incensed that Ralston ran away. He didn't know about Ralston pulling down Serena's dress, or the fighting with Jeddie or the stealing. That made him angrier, but we told him he has so many large issues on his mind, these were things we thought we could take care of, give him some peace. And we made the point that Ralston's disaffection might spread. The thieving wouldn't stop. Once a thief, always a thief."

"Ain't that the truth." Bettina nodded her head, the slanting golden rays illuminating her head rag, bright green today.

"Barker O is happy. Things are quiet. And

Tulli has taken on some of Ralston's chores. That child is one of the sweetest children I have ever known. Sweet."

"He is. Goes down to Ruth's cabin to play with the babies. I know we might need some more young ones, but Ruth has four down there all wailing and needing to be held. Tulli holds them, rocks them, sings to them when he's finished his horse chores."

"You think people are born that way?"

Bettina turned to her. "I think we come out of our mommas exactly who we are."

"I expect." Catherine agreed and they sat in quiet harmony for a good fifteen minutes.

"Sugar Baby." Bettina called her by her childhood name.

Catherine knew this was important. "Yes."

"DoRe has asked me to marry him. I said yes."

Picking up Bettina's hand, Catherine kissed it. "He's a smart man."

A low, rolling laugh followed this. "I don't know about that, but I think he loves me. I do. And I love him. Never thought it would find me again."

"Happy. Happy forever." Catherine kissed Bettina's hand again. "You tell Rachel. She should hear it from you."

"I will. But you and Little Sister need to tell Mr. Ewing."

"We will. He'll be happy for you. I know he will."

Bettina smiled. "He's a feeling man." She then said, "It's Maureen Selisse will not be feeling happiness."

"Oh, God." In her excitement, Catherine had forgotten, just for a moment, that Maureen owned DoRe.

Not that the now named Mrs. Holloway would refuse the marriage. Not at all. But she'd make it hard for DoRe to leave Big Rawly.

"Your father said he didn't want a big supper. I'll go in and start a nice light soup for him."

As Bettina left, Catherine got up, walked to her mother's tomb, the recumbent lamb promising Christ would shepherd them all to a better way. Little crosses marked the back of the base. Bettina once told Catherine that when someone is loved, people will ask her for help and make a little cross. If they want to call down harm, they scratch a square. But no squares were on Isabelle's base, for no one could imagine her heaping harm on anyone.

Francisco Selisse's monument was at Big Rawly, an awful thing really, the angel with the flaming sword guarding the East of Eden, covered with squares. Even in death

Francisco called down wrath. Big Rawly never seemed to be at peace.

Catherine touched the cross between the lamb's front legs. "Mother, I need your help. Bettina has found love. Maureen Selisse owns him. Help me find the way to free DoRe of Big Rawly." A pause followed this. "I miss you, Momma. I'm not as good or as wise a woman as you were. I try."

23

Yancy Grant accompanied the barrels of oats being hauled to Cloverfields. Ewing's purchase enabled him to pay some bills as well as buy much-needed spring seed. Yancy's finances were declining. Maureen Selisse Holloway had sued him after the duel with Jeffrey. When she'd drawn enough blood, she dropped it, knowing full well he couldn't afford the legal costs.

The overcast day, a slight chill in the air, enlivened the horses. Yancy, finally able to visit his Black Knight, smiled at how healthy his boy looked. Ewing was with him.

"Splendid, splendid," was all he could say as Barker O and Jeddie slightly inclined their heads.

Catherine, too, had come down to manage this first visit. When Black Knight originally arrived at Cloverfields after being stolen at the races, Yancy couldn't bear to see him or say goodbye. He loved Black Knight, who had not forgotten him.

The animal let out a nicker, galloping to the fencing to nuzzle his old master. Tears rolled down Yancy's cheeks. He couldn't help it.

"Would you like me to bring him in the stable, Mr. Grant?" Jeddie respectfully asked.

"No, thank you. He's happy out here, still a lot of grass, and he's with friends." He turned to Catherine. "Bless you."

"Yancy, you bred a fine animal." She smiled at him.

"You flatter me."

He did breed a fine horse, and Catherine and her stable boys, as she thought of them, having brought Black Knight to a shiny coat, taut muscles, and a bright eye, would use him in the breeding shed. She now owned two extraordinary stallions, Reynaldo, hot as a pistol, and Black Knight, now sweet.

"Well, shall we old men repair to the house? A light repast is not out of order." Ewing touched his friend on his back and the two started walking toward the house.

Jeddie, Barker O, and Catherine headed to the large, tight storage shed where the oats were being loaded and placed. The barrels proved heavy enough that it took three men to move them about: one to lift the barrel off the wagon, one to guide it down, and one to roll it and, with difficulty, tip it upright.

"Let's have a sniff." Catherine looked to Barker O, who took out his penknife, running it under the barrel lid, which he then lifted off.

She lingered over the barrel, filling her hands with the oats.

Handing them to Barker O, she lifted her eyebrows. He, too, sniffed. Then Jeddie did the same.

"Good," Barker O pronounced.

"We'll be glad to have them, even though Father resisted. He said we had glorious hay, three cuttings, a miracle, but oats help those hard keepers." She used the term for a horse who had difficulty putting on weight.

Usually this betrayed a high metabolism, in animals or people, but sometimes difficulty putting on or holding weight pointed to a hidden illness. Catherine watched Tulli, nose at the top of the barrel, wanting to be part of the group. She wondered if his growth wasn't in some way stunted. He stayed thin, too, yet seemed full of energy as well as ideas, lots of ideas.

Rousing herself from this, she turned to watch her father and Yancy pace up to the house.

"Old friends are the best friends. Mother used to say that, and I begin to believe it."

Barker O's deep voice was comforting. "Miss Catherine, you will never get old."

"Ha." She laughed, then tossed a handful of oats up in the air.

Before Ewing could reach for the elegant curved brass doorknob, the door swung open. Roger bowed to Yancy, beamed at Ewing.

"Ah, Roger, you anticipate everything."

"Mr. Ewing, Bettina has set out oh, tender veal. The aroma alone, well, Bettina has put out food for you two gentlemen to enjoy. She said she hasn't seen Mr. Grant in so long, she wishes to spoil him."

"Ah!" Yancy clapped his hands together.

Seated in an alcove, they chatted, discussed the weather as only farmers can, wondered when Maureen would finally be back at Big Rawly, wondering, too, what she would bring back from England.

"What hear you from your friend Baron Necker?"

Ewing leaned forward, a tiny, perfect carrot speared on his fork. "No hope of solving the financial crisis and the Notables have been dismissed."

"I thought, now this is some time back, reading a paper from Philadelphia, that the Court had devised new financial measures, new taxes."

"The Court did, but the Parliament refused to endorse same. If they sat regularly like England, perhaps, but the Baron fumes, fumes, truly, that no nobles will surrender or even share special privileges. For instance, if you had the fishing rights, say, for Marseilles, you would neither surrender nor utilize same to relieve the kingdom of its financial distress. Every single noble cared only for preserving his rights."

"The Baron?"

"Actually, no. A few of the highborn realize the time has come to put the welfare of the state first. But who is to say? It takes so long for word to reach me here, perhaps this has been resolved. France is too important to be set adrift."

"I would think we might have created an example." Yancy leaned back in his chair for a moment.

"We are or were Englishmen, Yancy. The French are, well, the French."

"Quite so." Yancy half laughed, then changed the subject. "My man, my indentured servant, Sean, said he thought he saw your Ralston down by Scottsville. A fleeting glimpse with another young buck and a comely girl. His words."

"Ralston did run away."

Yancy's eyebrows shot upward. "There's a young fool."

"I agree, I agree, but Catherine and Rachel told me he had been pressing himself on the girls, even ripped Serena's bodice. Not able to control himself."

"A fast way to die young." Yancy patted his lips with the linen napkin. "Men have killed for less."

"Had anyone touched my Isabelle, I would have killed him. My angel."

"Of course, we all feel that way about our wives, daughters, sisters, but Ewing, there are men who prey on women. Rich, poor, free, slave, young, old. Some illicit thrill, I suppose. Will you bring him back if you can?"

"No. My girls are adamantly opposed to it. I said I must make an example of him, but they said it would be worse to bring him back. Catherine even used the word 'rape.' "

A sharp intake of Yancy's breath testified to that powerful word. "Good Lord."

"And she said, 'Why harbor a thief?' She

has a point, but I think a wrongdoer should be punished."

Yancy nodded. "Perhaps the solution is for someone else to punish the wrongdoer." He beamed when two of the young kitchen girls being trained removed their plates, and Serena, balancing a tray, carried in cherry cobbler. Following her was another youngster with a hot pot of tea. "Heaven. This is heaven." He smiled up at Serena, who smiled back.

Ewing liked seeing his friend awash in pleasures. The last year had not been kind to Yancy. His kneecap, shattered, pieced back together by a new young surgeon, held, but he walked with difficulty, needing a cane. Maureen's blaming him for the loss of William, her stable boy, and the subsequent miseries with the law also dragged him down. Finally she relented, but he was exhausted and demoralized and broke. Yancy, slowly reviving, truly glowed in his old friend's presence. The excellent food helped.

"The horses and Charles's dog, Piglet, are already growing winter coats. Might be a harsh one."

"My woodpile is full. What else can one do?"

"True. How is this Sean fellow working out?"

"He puts in a good day's work, and if a larger chore needs doing, he seeks out day laborers. This saves me a great deal of money, though I can't tend to as many acres."

"Your oats certainly are fine. Perhaps when finances improve, you can buy more hands."

Cup of tea in hand, Yancy sipped it, then set the fine china cup in its saucer. "No more slaves. The more I think about feeding, housing, clothing, medical things, I believe the slave system to be highly uneconomical. Harmful, really."

"Slavery is the way of the world," Ewing simply stated.

"Yes it is, but that doesn't mean it's efficient."

"You're not turning into a Quaker, are you?" Ewing smiled at him.

"Ah, well, in my trials I have thought much about their teachings. No, I am not a Quaker but" — he leaned forward, his voice low — "I much admire them."

24

April 24, 2018
Tuesday

" 'I am the resurrection and the life, saith the Lord: he that believeth in me, though he were dead, yet shall he live: and whosoever liveth and believeth in me shall never die.' " Reverend Jones took a deep breath, read the next paragraph of the Order for the Burial of the Dead, then concluded with, " 'We brought nothing into this world, and it is certain we can carry nothing out. The Lord gave, and the Lord hath taken away; blessed be the name of the Lord.' "

The Dorcas Guild, the St. Peter's Guild, and a few parishioners feeling they should attend watched as the unknown bones, in a simple casket built by Fair Haristeen and Ned Tucker, was lowered into the open grave.

The site, under the red oak as Reverend Jones had suggested, seemed perfect this first day that felt like spring. Tree buds swelled finally, promising to open soon.

Arlene Billeaud, next to Harry, observed the burial with interest. Harry had told her about the circumstances of unearthing the bones. Arlene, at Harry's invitation, had come to stay with Harry for three days, then Harry, Susan, and Arlene would drive up to Aldie for the Hounds F4R Heroes.

"If you have to be buried, a wonderful day." Janice Childe walked up to Harry, Arlene, and Susan after the service.

"You're right," Harry agreed, as Mags also joined them.

"The casket glowed. Fair and Ned must have rubbed it with oil for hours." Mags praised the men.

"They wanted it to be of her time." Susan spoke for her husband. "I think we all feel a little uneasy that she was tossed on top of the Taylors."

"And you say she wore a fortune in roped pearls and pearl and diamond earrings?" Arlene was intrigued.

"Isn't it something?" Janice waited for the reverend to shake her hand, as was proper.

They all did.

Reverend Jones then said, "Let's hope she's with the Lord. Everyone deserves a proper Christian burial."

The cats, reposing in the office window, which was a series of paned-glass windows to allow as much light as possible, observed the ceremony.

"Poppy takes this so seriously." Lucy Fur loved her human.

"Well, you can't just let human bones lay about," Elocution added.

"The dogs could chew them. They wouldn't last long." Cazenovia flicked her long-haired calico tail.

"That's the point," Elocution replied.

After the burial, the three women drove over to Big Rawly. Arlene enjoyed historic homes. Big Rawly qualified. As they drove down the narrow road off of Garth Road, they turned left onto Big Rawly land, passing the imposing graveyard with the large tomb of Francisco Selisse guarded by the angel with the flaming sword.

"East of Eden." Susan filled Arlene in. "When Adam and Eve were driven out of Eden, the Lord placed an angel with a flaming sword to keep people out and guard the tree of life."

"A little like closing the barn door after the horses have fled," Arlene wryly commented. "Shall I assume that Francisco Selisse was rich and powerful?"

"He was. He was murdered, so they say,

by one of his slaves who escaped. As it turns out, he wasn't much loved, including by his widow, who quickly remarried Jeffrey Holloway, my ancestor," Susan replied. "Before I married Ned, I was a Holloway."

"You're still a Holloway," Harry affirmed.

"There's no end of drama around here. We bury an unknown woman, not a Lutheran, right?"

"Right. If she were, we would know who she was, but she was found as we told you, on top of two Lutherans who helped found St. Luke's. Old crimes. And now we face a new one. Killing is a part of being human, I fear." Susan stopped at the rear of the French-designed home.

As Susan walked Arlene around the gardens, pointing out garden features as well as the elegant home, Arlene said, "I suppose the mystery of an unclaimed body, bones, an old crime has a kind of pull. When we were all at Aldie, Geoff Ogden recalled Paula Devlin. Another unsolved crime, the body never found. I miss her. Once, shopping, we walked into an expensive woman's clothing store in Washington. We walked right out," Arlene mused.

"Let's hope it doesn't take over two hundred years to find her," Harry blurted out.

"It's the killer I worry about, just like the killer of Jason Holzknect." Susan opened the graceful wrought-iron gate leading to the back door.

"I'm not too worried about Jason's killer," Arlene said.

"Why not?" Harry inquired.

Arlene didn't answer as Susan's mother and grandmother greeted them at the door, inviting the ladies inside, where Susan's mother gave Arlene another tour.

Tea followed and both older women told stories about Big Rawly, starting with the questions unanswered about all that Caribbean money Maureen's father made, much of it sent on to Big Rawly by his daughter. But Big Rawly, well served throughout the centuries, stood firm and remained beautiful despite all.

Back in the car, Harry returned to the question about why Arlene wasn't worried about Jason's killer at Aldie.

"I think the murder was specific to him," she answered calmly.

"Like his money or something?" Susan wondered.

"I've been asked by the sheriff about his finances, did I know anything, but I just don't think this is broader-based. I hunted with Jason twice a year at Aldie over the years. Also visited Chesapeake Beagles to hunt on his territory. He was a good huntsman. He never lacked for anything. I can't say I felt close to him or Clare. They were good members of the National Beagle Club. Very helpful. It does seem dramatic that such a seemingly bland fellow would be killed, but this has nothing to do with us."

Susan asked, "You think we're safe?"

"I do. You aren't going to get your throat slit."

25

October 17, 1787
Wednesday

Her back laid open in long strips, Elizabetta fainted. Her dress, ripped down the back, streaked with blood, evidenced her beating as she was tied to a vertical pole. Fincastle, Maureen's overseer, performed the service. While not a harsh man, he did his employer's bidding, for he had five children to feed, no education, and an ailing wife.

Given his faithfulness, he stayed on the good side of Maureen, if she had a good side. The slaves at Big Rawly, called together to witness the punishment, hung their heads. Who would be next, for the Missus seethed in a fury?

Maureen, herself, wouldn't be seen during any beatings. Not that she was squeamish — she wasn't.

Better to let her people wonder where she was, was she viewing, and, even better, wonder what she was thinking.

What she was thinking was she would beat the truth out of all of them. She had come back from Europe with stops at Guadeloupe, a tiny Spanish colony, and Santiago, on Santo Domingo, which held some of her father's fortune.

Satisfied that the funds were growing, she handsomely rewarded some of her father's old employees, now hers, and sailed back to the United States, disembarking at Charleston, where she also lingered to attend to banking matters. Jeffrey languidly strolled the streets, soaking up the perfect architecture, listening to the women sing in Gullah outside the churches as they sold baskets, brightly woven scarves, all manner of delights. The sun would set, Maureen would be freed from her meetings, the black folks would sail back to the islands off the tip of Charleston.

Finally home, she allowed herself a day or two of rest. Jeffrey made a beeline for his coachworks, far happier to be working than to be the adopted brother of a baron, the Baron West.

Needing pin money, Maureen went to the drawer, pulled it out — no money, no inexpensive but pretty topaz earrings. Furious, she checked all her little hiding places.

Gone. Not a penny. Granted, it wasn't much, but the Mistress of Big Rawly couldn't abide a thief. Then Elizabetta told her that Sulli had escaped.

Naturally, Maureen had to blame someone, and her lady's maid, ostensibly in charge of the house in her absence, fit the bill — hence the lashing.

Fincastle picked up the full wooden bucket, sloshed the water on the poor woman's flayed back. That brought her back to consciousness. He then reached up, cutting her down, where she slumped in a sodden pile.

No one would touch her. Jeffrey, unaware of the punishment, hurried up to the site once one of the men in the huge workshop informed him. It was he who knelt down, picking up the swooning, in-shock woman.

"For the love of God, someone help me."

DoRe stepped forward. He picked up Elizabetta's feet while Jeffrey held his hands under her arms, careful not to touch her around to her back.

"Can you carry her to the last cabin, Master?" DoRe asked.

"Yes."

The two men carried the woman, not terribly heavy, to the herb cabin wherein a young woman had been grinding herbs in a bowl. She managed to avoid the beating spectacle. Looking up, she stopped.

"Kintzie, help." DoRe moved toward the pallet in the corner.

"Lay her on her side." Kintzie walked over, kneeling down. "He cut through to the ribs here." She pointed. "DoRe, fetch me one of the clean rags by the lavender." He hesitated, so she pointed up. "Under the hanging lavender."

"What can I do?" Jeffrey asked, but Kintzie feared giving the Master an order. "I think, sir, given your wife's temper, you had best leave us."

His face reddened. "Of course." Then he looked at DoRe. "I'll do what I can."

DoRe simply tilted his head in response as he also carried a bucket of clean water. As Kintzie dabbed the deep wounds, Elizabetta refused to scream — she held one hand over her mouth.

Tears saturated Elizabetta's cheeks. Kintzie reached out with her left hand, picked up another rag, handed it to the suffering woman.

"Hold my hand." DoRe knelt before her, taking her hand. "The pain will be fierce. You'll live."

Elizabetta, tears running, nodded.

Kintzie wrung out a rag, dipping it again.

"Near as I can tell, no bones broken. Sugar, I need to get you as clean as I can. This will hurt. I will rub some salve on you. It's a lot of beeswax but it will help you heal. I'll wrap a bit of gauze over your back. Can't have anything sticking on these wounds. DoRe is right, you'll live and you'll heal. You're strong. You'll heal." She asked DoRe, "What did she do?"

"Nothing. It's what she didn't do."

"I never knew." Elizabetta choked that out.

DoRe said, "Missus found money missing, what she calls her pin money, then she found some earrings missing. She came down to the stable, asking me had I seen anyone? Well, I hadn't, but by her questions I knew jewelry again. She's got the big stuff locked up but if she owns it, it matters. She'll never get over Sheba stealing those pearls. I didn't think too much of it, figured we were all safe at the stables."

"Yes." Kintzie placed a soft, dry cloth over Elizabetta's back.

"It was Sulli," the wounded woman gasped. "She ran off. I never knew."

"DoRe, did you see her?"

"No, Kintzie, but I felt William was back. Saw someone moving toward the woods. Moved like him. I doubled the watch at the stable. Figured he'd steal a horse, but why would he be so damned stupid as to come back?"

"Sulli." Kintzie supplied the answer. "I caught sight of her carrying a basket in the dark, tiptoeing down to the firewood sheds. Never thought it would be William. Maybe they had taken up with each other before he ran but he or someone was here and she was feeding him."

"Ralston ran off from Cloverfields," DoRe told her.

"H-m-m." Kintzie fanned the thin cloth with another cloth to cool down Elizabetta's back.

"Stupid little bitch. I never watched her. I trusted her," Elizabetta said.

"You've paid for it." A long, long pause followed this. "We'll all pay for Sulli, the slut." Kintzie couldn't help herself. "And wherever she is, she'll have a swollen belly before Easter."

"How long before I heal?"

"Months. You'll be walking about in days but you won't be able to sit and lean back. And you will be scarred for life," the kind young woman told her.

"At least she didn't tear half your face off like she did to Ailee." DoRe's voice fell. "Blinded one eye. Smashed half her face."

"We didn't know. We never saw Ailee

again." Elizabetta, working at the house at the time, did not see any of this.

Ailee and Moses ran. But DoRe had seen them and both Kintzie and Elizabetta were prudent enough not to ask.

"I'd better go back to the horses." DoRe released Elizabetta's hand.

"Thank you." She meant it. "And I will thank the Master someday."

"He knows." DoRe smiled, then left.

As DoRe reached the stables, the odor of cleaned leather, sweet hay, and oats filled his nostrils. Out of force of habit, he walked into the large, well-organized tack room. Counting bridles and saddles and running his fingers over the steel bits to search for little pits calmed him.

Seeing the beating, Elizabetta's wounds, infuriated him. The night Francisco was killed came back and he heard Maureen's screams enhanced by Sheba's wails. He had run to the house as he could just make out two figures in the distance running for all they were worth. One moved like Moses, his son. Later he found out Moses and Ailee had fled, Moses being accused of killing Francisco.

Even in the midst of the blood, blood on both Maureen and Sheba as they tried to stanch Francisco's wounds, even then he knew they were the murderers. Maureen's revenge for years of infidelity must have been sweet. As for Sheba, she would do anything to intensify her power over Maureen.

DoRe never knew if Sheba had killed Francisco and Maureen had then smashed in Ailee's face or the reverse. No matter, they were both guilty as sin. Moses and Ailee's disappearance was considered proof of their guilt. It was enough proof that if they hadn't run, Maureen would see them hanged. What chance did two slaves have against one of the richest women in Virginia, if not the new nation?

The burden of those memories weighed on DoRe. He sat heavily on a tack-room chair. Back then, when the opportunity had presented itself last October, he had snapped Sheba's neck. She'd paraded around Big Rawly in Maureen's celebrated pearls. The Mistress was off the estate. Darkness shrouded DoRe as he tossed Sheba in a cart, covered the body, and drove to St. Luke's, where the Taylors had just been buried.

Every spade of dirt he had thrown on her face once he'd opened the grave made him thank God he'd lived to kill the evil bitch. She was with the Devil by now.

His heavy breathing subsided. DoRe folded his hands together. Someday he needed to tell Bettina, but not now, not now. He wanted no secrets between himself and the woman he loved.

As for God's punishment, DoRe felt none would occur. If anything, the Lord would rejoice as he rejoiced over Old Testament warriors' victories over unbelievers. Sheba was an unbeliever. He had done his duty.

In the meanwhile, Jeffrey had stormed up to the house, where his wife, low-cut bodice prominent, sat at her card table. He swept the cards off the table, yanked her to her feet, and slapped her hard across the face.

"Don't you ever do anything like that again." He towered over her as she sank to her knees.

"I didn't do anything." She was stunned.

"You had Elizabetta cut to ribbons. What's the matter with you?"

Flaring, she spat out, "You can't let those animals get away with anything. Beat them, beat them into submission. She was in charge of the house and money is missing, jewelry is missing, and Sulli has run off."

He slapped her hard again. "Don't you ever do anything like that again! As for Sulli leaving, well, she was a petty thief. Elizabetta couldn't have known. Do you think she'd be stupid enough to be here knowing or being a part of this? Never. Never. Never. Never. Do you hear me?" He gripped her wrists until they hurt.

"Yes."

He kept holding her wrists. "I am your husband. I am the Master of Big Rawly. You will obey me. Do you hear? You will never beat anyone again."

She nodded. Whether she agreed or not was another issue.

The bosoms were not lost on her husband. He pulled her up, ripped her bodice right off her bosoms. The material hung at her waist. Then he kissed her hard, holding her so tightly she could barely breathe.

"Do you hear?" he whispered.

"Yes, husband."

Having never seen Jeffrey like this, Maureen was equal parts frightened and thrilled. The fear subsided. The thrill remained.

26

October 19, 1787
Friday

"Your brother wished for you to have this." Jeffrey handed Charles a lovely wooden box, the inlaid wood shining.

The two men sat together in Charles's parlor, having enjoyed a light midafternoon meal prepared by Rachel with Bettina's help. Rachel left to help Catherine write out some of their father's correspondence and to allow the two men time alone.

Charles carefully unhooked the brass latch, opening the box to find a mate to the beautiful Nicolas-Noël Boutet pistol his father had given him.

"Oh," Charles exclaimed as he lifted the work of art from its housing.

"The Baron knew you had forfeited your pistol to John Schuyler when he captured you. He thought this would please you."

Charles grinned. "Wait until John sees

this." Then he rubbed his forefinger on the rich wood of the flintlock. It was accurate. When one pays that much for a weapon, it had better be, and his late father had paid plenty.

Jeffrey, happy to have made Charles happy, said, "I never understood how you and the major could become so close, but now after my duel with Yancy Grant, I somewhat understand."

"John originally thought we were lucky to be living. You can imagine. But he knew the Articles of War, and he treated my men and me with respect, even on the march from Saratoga to here, now the prisoner of war camp." Charles shook his head. "I have never been so cold in my life."

"I saw it once. Delivered a chest for the wife of the commandant. All those cabins, wooden chimneys, and the rooftops, evergreens. I suppose the needles were to keep out the snow."

"Well, Piglet and I snuggled up each night." Charles reached down to pet his devoted, aging corgi. "But I give my captors credit. When I approached the guard with the suggestion of thatching the roofs — that we could do it because no one here really knew how — he took me to the commandant, who seemed relieved, actually, that there might be a way for more protection from the elements. He had no money. The Continental Congress had none, nor did the colony of Virginia."

"I certainly saw many thatched roofs in England. I liked them, actually."

"Well, my men and I found reeds, mostly in lowlands near the camp, and we thatched our roof. Then the other fellows did it, those who could. Kept the rain out and the snow. The next thing was cutting firewood. I remember a Hessian from another cabin sneaking over to steal some of our firewood. We caught him and thrashed him worse than we would have thrashed a colonial." Charles laughed.

"Having seen where you were raised, I would imagine we do appear barbaric," Jeffrey remarked.

Charles quickly replied, "I do not feel that. Are there castles and kings, are there the great piazzas such as exist in Italy or estates of twenty and thirty thousand acres owned by dukes, no. But the homes in Philadelphia are graceful. I hear Charleston is beautiful, and even Richmond, a bit less refined perhaps, contains touches of elegance."

Jeffrey brightened. "Technically you and I are brothers now."

Charles tapped his forefinger on Jeffrey's

hand. "A good addition to the family. I am grateful that you and your wife have rescued my brother. That's the only word I can use. 'Rescued.' Our father, a man of immense charm and sociability, left us in tatters, as you know. Well, insolvent, as he did inherit the title."

Jeffrey leaned back in the comfortable chair. "My wife sets such a store by such things. Lord Holloway. If anyone would call me that, I would be embarrassed."

"I doubt any Virginian will, but when you leave our country, you will be so addressed."

"Maureen insists I have your family's coat of arms painted on our carriage, on everything, engraved on the silver. My God." Jeffrey couldn't help himself.

"Ah well, she was raised where such things still matter."

"I saw where she was raised. More splendor, which she has reproduced at Big Rawly. She was educated in France."

"Yes." Charles smiled, for Maureen spoke impeccable French, as did he. "You didn't cross the Channel?"

"We didn't visit France. Maureen, who keeps up with foreign developments, judged it not a good time to see her old friends there. She says the dismissal of the Assembly of Notables in May was unwise. Your

246

brother, when this was discussed, called them the Assembly of Not Ables."

Charles laughed. "He would, but they didn't do anything anyway. I can't see a dismissal as much to worry about, but, then, I am here and very grateful to be here."

"You don't miss it?"

"Oh, I miss the shires sometimes. I miss Oxford. I don't really miss London at all. Every time I would visit, which my father insisted upon for our social education, if you will, I found the city had grown even more. People everywhere. I'm not meant to sit in soirees."

"Yes, well, I now understand." Jeffrey smiled. "Italy proved a revelation. I tried to remember my school Latin, but the light, the color of the homes, the furniture" — he paused, blushing slightly — "I will ever be a cabinetmaker. I was enchanted."

"Business is good?"

"My wife has had that large shop built for me, encouraged me to hire specialized labor. The orders pour in." He paused. "And you?"

"The work at St. Luke's has brought me attention. I've received a commission to design a home along the James outside of Scottsville. I will take you to St. Luke's. I would like for you to see it."

"I would like to see it. I can't speak for Maureen. She is a dedicated Catholic, which means she likes the ritual. What she believes, I couldn't say."

"Ah well, perhaps none of us can really understand any church. I read my catechism — oh yes, Church of England has catechism. I still don't know what it's about, although I can recite the Nicene Creed by heart."

They both laughed.

The clock struck five o'clock. The late-afternoon light streaked across the land like butter.

"I have taken up too much of your time. I'd better find DoRe and we can drive home before twilight. I assume he is visiting your cook." Jeffrey smiled.

"Or she him. When DoRe and Barker O are together, they can talk." Charles again opened the box to admire the pistol. "Thank you for this."

"I am merely the messenger. Your brother wished to restore the mate to the one John has as the spoils of war. He knew how you valued it."

"My father gave me an excellent education, a Continental tour, clothing, but he wasn't much for gifts to his sons. He didn't want us to become, in his words, effeminate.

I don't think either Hugh or I was in danger, but he gave me the pistol when I left for the Army. I wasn't close to my father, but I liked him. Does that sound strange to you, having worked with your father?"

"One sees the distance with many sons. Then again, fathers are often absent. I call upon my father often for help in my work. He is astonishingly good, you know, and I don't say that because he is my father, but he can put his hands on a piece of wood and feel it."

Charles smiled. "A gift. You possess it, too." He rose and Jeffrey rose with him.

As they walked to the door, Jeffrey confided in him. "There was an unfortunate incident at Big Rawly yesterday."

"Elizabetta."

"How do you know?"

"Word travels fast."

Jeffrey nodded. "I believe the slaves have ways to reach one another of which we know nothing. Bad as it was, it is settled and that will never happen again." Then he paused again, cleared his throat. "You have been married a few years now."

"To the best woman on earth." Charles lit up.

"Certainly a woman of great beauty and

uncommon sweetness. Her mother must have been a beauty."

"I never met Isabelle, but Yancy Grant declared she was a breathtaking beauty, which her daughters reflect, but he also said she possessed an intense allure. His very word, 'intense.' "

Jeffrey smiled. "Charles, yours is a good marriage."

"It is."

"Do you understand women?"

A burst of laughter followed this question. "No. Does any man? I love my wife. I worship my wife. Do I understand her, no, but" — he took a deep breath — "I believe she understands me and sometimes better than I understand myself."

A look of relief crossed Jeffrey's face. "I see."

Charles slapped him on the back as he still laughed. "Brother, don't even try."

They talked about Florence, about how restorative it is to finally come to one's own home. They walked to the stables where DoRe sat with Barker O, a basket of food in front of him, for Bettina had also been visiting before returning to the house. Charles and Jeffrey shook their heads about both of their wives swooning over fabrics.

When Jeffrey climbed up next to DoRe on

the light, lovely, one-horse carriage, he looked down at Charles, smiled, and tipped his hat. "Thank you, brother."

Charles touched his forehead with his finger. "The pleasure was mine, brother."

27

April 25, 2018
Wednesday

Walking toward Jefferson's house, Harry stopped to admire the work, the restored slave quarters, the food plots. Then she ducked into the underbelly of Monticello, alleyways and, of course, the kitchen. Arlene, never having seen Monticello, even though she now lived in Virginia, gave Harry the excuse to visit again. Harry never tired of Jefferson's estate, nor the restoration over the years. Dan Jordan, the former director, and his wife had the vision to take Monticello back to the time in which it was lived in as opposed to latter-day "improvements." Well, perhaps they were improvements, but Jefferson never enjoyed them, nor did the other people living and working on the incredible estate, a view worth a trip across the Atlantic, at least in Jefferson's mind. The current director, Leslie Greene Bowman, was bringing the world to Monticello and vice versa.

A bit of breeze swept through the alleyways, which was how Harry thought of the ground floor of Monticello. Must have been a hive of activity, people moving to and fro, ladies attending the cooking fire, people poking their heads in storage rooms for this or that.

"Being here, being anywhere where a powerful man lived, I am always reminded of how many people it takes to free one to do major business," Arlene commented as they walked along a corridor.

"Still does," Harry rejoined.

"You know, you're right. Technology can perform some of these services, but it still takes people, highly trained people. I learned that when the Agency sent me places. If I had a long land time, I would rent a car and, if a friend was, say, in Amsterdam, off I'd go. Once Paula Devlin was in Paris when I was in London. We'd hunted together a few times when I was home on leave, so I called her, crossed the Channel, and she drove me everywhere. That's when I got to know her. Versailles, of course. Impressive. Beautiful. The reflection of the Sun King, yes, but it was too much. Here at Monticello, more, u-m-m, what am

I trying to say, in proportion."

"I know what you mean."

"You've been to Versailles?"

Harry nodded that she had. "I was an art history major at Smith and one summer Susan, who was at William and Mary, and I traveled to Europe, the hostel route." She smiled. "We'd worked that year at our respective schools, saved everything, and off we went. I wore out three pairs of sneakers."

"Ha." Arlene enjoyed the detail.

They took the tour through the house, walked on the raised walkways to the small buildings at the ends, then walked along the path by the food plots, where some of the sturdy slave cabins once stood. They reached the graveyard, Jefferson's monument simple, unadorned. Other family members slept behind the wrought-iron fence.

"Isn't it odd that both Jefferson and Adams died on July Fourth, 1826?" Harry remarked.

"And the stuff they argued about we're still battling over." Arlene shrugged. "Maybe that's good. Right now it seems like a bad time, but we've been through worse, and this going back and forth between a strong centralized government, which we do have, and states' rights, growing again, it's good. My time in Washington taught me that if we harden, we lose."

"You know more than I do. You and Ned Tucker should talk. I'm not much of a political person." Harry swept her eyes over the tombstones. "Did you know that Monroe also died on the Fourth of July? Eighteen thirty-one."

"We will never see public servants like our Founding Fathers." Arlene thought a moment. "And mothers. In so many ways they were ahead and, in other ways, creatures of their times. I think that can be said of all of us."

They walked down the path through the woods to the parking lot and the visitors center.

"These last few weeks, it's sure been a focus on the dead, hasn't it? We go to Aldie, all those cavalrymen somewhere. Then Jason. And then you come to Crozet and we put that murdered woman in the ground, a proper Christian burial."

"Have you ever noticed that on a woman's tombstone it never reads, 'She was a good housekeeper'?" Arlene laughed.

"So true. You've just given me an excuse to put off doing the laundry. I hate doing laundry."

Arlene smiled. "I hate folding it."

"The worst."

They reached the parking lot. "Do you want to go into the store? It's got some beautiful things."

"No, thank you. I'm trying to save my money for a new coffee table. I saw one when I was last in New York and the sides were like a ship's rigging. Sounds weird, but it really is elegant and my old coffee table is, well, old. I looked at a new office chair. One of those that you can adjust a thousand ways." Harry unlocked the doors. "One thousand six hundred dollars. I nearly passed out."

"It is crazy, but if you sit at a computer all day, that's not so outrageous. I kind of think we've reached a point where we can't afford ourselves."

"Boy, is that the truth." Harry cranked the engine and they drove out.

She chose to go up the mountain, drive along Carter's Ridge, pass Highland, Monroe's place, and cruise through the beginnings of spring.

"If the weather holds, a lot of entries for the fundraiser. I'm looking forward to it." Arlene looked down the long drive to Highland.

Coming down to Carter's Bridge, Harry

turned left, heading south on Route 20. She thought she'd drive Arlene through Scottsville, the county seat during Jefferson's time, then follow the James back toward Crozet. It would take a good hour, but the drive was pleasant and they could visit.

As they neared Crozet, Harry said, "Arlene, let me stop at St. Luke's for one minute. I want to check my mailbox to see if any of the ladies from the Dorcas Guild left me brochures for caterers for our homecoming idea."

"It is a good idea." Arlene had heard about it from Harry and Susan.

"We all can reach one another via our computers, but I like to go over a brochure or a catalog and I like to lay them out on my desk to pages where I can compare services or prices. Drives me nuts flipping back and forth on the computer screen."

"Bad for the eyes." Arlene waited while Harry parked and dashed in.

She returned with her hand full of shiny catalogs, one *Southern Living* magazine that had pages marked, and a few envelopes. She tossed them in the divider.

When they reached the farm, the cats and dogs rushed out to greet them. Once inside, Harry put the materials on the kitchen table. The animals were petted and loved,

257

and a few treats were handed out. She turned on the teapot.

"Something stronger?"

"No, this will be restorative. Do you need to bring in the horses? I can help."

"It's my husband's turn to do it. But I never mind. They make me happy, my horses." She ran her hand over the mail, moving it about. "You know, thank you for putting Susan at ease over our being at Aldie. I'm not worried."

"Me neither."

"People are so strange, it might even pump up the numbers of visitors or even competitors."

Arlene smiled. "Well, then, we can all say Jason didn't die in vain. He helped raise money for Hounds for Heroes."

Harry slit open a heavy, good-paper envelope with her one long fingernail, about to break. She could never keep them long. Hard to do when you're pitching hay, cleaning out hoofs, rolling a wheelbarrow.

"What the hell?" Harry handed Arlene a piece of paper, expensive paper, too.

"Maybe we'd be safer at Aldie." Arlene studied a perfectly round blackball in the middle of the paper.

28

October 20, 1787
Saturday
"He said Royal Oak. Seven miles from the river." Ralston repeated what the carter had told them.

"We've gone seven miles," William complained.

"Maybe not. The land rises above the Potomac and getting over that takes longer. It's rolling here. This road looks well used," Ralston, doing his best to think ahead, said.

"That river runs fast," Sulli, tired but keeping up, observed. "You all were smart getting us a ride on the ferry." She looked adoringly at William when she said this, which made Ralston want to throw up.

Not wishing to call undue attention to themselves, the three had waited on the Virginia side of the Potomac. While they had enough for their fare, they still waited. If they could align themselves with a white man, they might pass not unnoticed but unquestioned. Hours later, the air brisk, the day bright, a carter moved toward them and, as luck would have it, his cart stopped. He didn't know why so he whipped the horse.

Ralston called to him. "Stop, sir. The problem isn't your horse."

Ralston remembered what Catherine had told him: "Never spur a willing horse."

He and William walked to the cart as Sulli watched. William held the bridle as Ralston crawled under the empty cart.

Pulling himself half out on his back, he told William, "Get me a thick stick. Well, Sulli can find one." Then he said to the carter, "A stone is wedged in the wheel well. I think I can pry it out. Your axle is fine."

"Good" was all the fellow grunted.

Sulli, casting about, picked up two sticks of differing lengths but thick widths, handing them to Ralston, who pulled himself back under the cart, working on the wheel from the underside.

They heard one stick crack, a groan, then, "Got it."

Ralston pulled himself out, looked at William. "Take a few steps."

William did and the cart freely moved.

The man reached in his pocket to pay Ralston, but the slender young man instead asked, "If we could stand with you, sir, and you might pay our fare, that would be a fair trade, I think."

As the fare was only sixpence for all three of them, not outrageous, the portly fellow nodded his agreement.

The three stayed with him as though he was their master, and on the Maryland side, Ralston asked if the gentleman knew of any breeding farms, preferably blooded horses. He named Royal Oak, owned by an Irishman, Cinian Finney. And he also mentioned that given the man's temper, he always needed new help.

The sun hung low, the air cooled, and on they trudged. A mile down the road, southeastern direction, a zigzag fence appeared. Seemed to stretch on for miles. They walked along, seeing horses in the fields, divided.

"Royal Oak." Ralston breathed the name hopefully.

"Whatever it is, money. Money and good horses." William paused to look over the pastures, all well kept, as were the horses.

"Must be the broodmare field," Ralston observed.

"No one has babies by their side." Sulli liked the setting sun glistening on their coats.

"Not yet," Ralston simply replied. "There's a road up ahead, turns into the farm. I say we go on down. Got to be someone around. Time to bring in the horses anyway."

They did, and that trek seemed like miles as they were tired. A wiry man, close-cropped ginger hair and a neat mustache, a horse on each side of him, nodded as he walked toward stables in the distance.

They followed.

"Can I help you, sir?" Ralston called over the horse's neck. "I'm a dab hand with a horse."

"Are you now? Cheeky, I'd say." The fellow had an Irish accent. "Here."

Ralston took the lead rope from the fellow's hand, walking in rhythm with him and the horse, a dark bay mare, mane pulled, tail tidied up, hoofs trimmed. This was a first-rate operation.

They walked into the stable, brick floor, painted wooden stalls. The man put the first horse into a stall, then took the second one from Ralston and did the same. Hay was already in a hay crib and buckets of water hung in the corner. The back of the stall remained open and the horses were tied to their cribs with enough room to move around and even lie down if they so chose.

But they couldn't walk out of the stall.

"Sir, Ralston Moore."

"Ard Elgin."

William stepped forward. "William" — he paused for a moment — "Fields. And this is my wife, Sulli Fields."

"If there's work, put us to it." Ralston smiled.

"Runaways are you?" Ard noted William's pause and he figured, correctly, that the fellow was thinking of a last name.

"No," William replied too loudly.

Ralston had learned a lot in his brief run for freedom. Well, it didn't seem brief: He'd lost weight, his feet hurt, and he wanted to sleep on a pallet. No more sleeping on the earth, where the dampness crept into his bones.

"I see." Ard smiled. "What can you do?"

"We're both good with horses and my wife can cook or help in the house." William puffed out his chest.

"Can always use hands." Ard, tired of the turnover, wanted to keep his own job, so if he found some good workers who stayed, and he figured runaway slaves would stay, he'd receive a reward from the Boss.

"Day's over but you can stay in the cabin there." He pointed to a high-roofed cabin. "We can sort this out tomorrow. Pump out behind the cabin. If you head up this path you'll come to the bunkhouse. Food's in an hour. Miss Frances don't like dirty people, so wash up. Any clothes?"

"No, sir."

"I'll tell her, otherwise she'll get her nose out of joint. If I can get you hired, you give me your first week's pay. Then we'll be even. I'm taking a chance on three people I don't know. Hear?"

"Yes, sir. You won't be sorry." Ralston extended his hand.

Ard shook it. "You got a wife, boy?"

Ralston shook his head. "Not yet."

Ard laughed. "Clean up. Do the best you can and don't mind Miss Frances. She has a tart tongue." He focused on Sulli. "I expect she'll put you to work. Keep your mouth shut and do what she says."

"Yes, sir."

They left him, hurrying for the cabin. No one wanted to be late for food.

Sulli opened the door. "A fireplace."

William stood in the opened door, looked at the bunk beds, and said to Ralston, "You take the top." Ralston looked around for blankets. Six were neatly folded on a shelf. He walked outside with a bucket, filled it with water, took off his shirt, washed himself as best he could while William brought in firewood stacked at the side of the house. The sun had set. Ralston shivered but it felt good to be a little clean, even if he had to put his old shirt back on.

Sulli inspected every nook and cranny. An old pot sat on the shelf underneath the blanket shelf. It was a start.

Miss Frances lived up to her billing, but she handed the three of them patched shirts and two pair of pants. She told Sulli if Mr. Finney hired her, she'd find a decent dress. In her own way Miss Frances had a kind heart but no backtalk, no laziness.

As the three walked back in the darkness, Ard walking halfway with them, Ralston asked, "How many slaves here?"

"Royal Oak doesn't have slaves. Mr. Finney says they're worthless. Cost too much. He'll give you a wage, a place to live. If you want to eat with us, Miss Frances is a fine cook, you pay three dollars a month for food and Miss Frances doesn't stint on food. You have to make your own breakfast. Mr. Finney is a demanding man. Do what he tells you. Even if he cusses you like a dog, do what he tells you. For that matter, do what I tell you."

"Yes, Mr. Elgin." They all three replied nearly in unison.

"Dawn. Be at the stables. Sulli, Miss

Frances will be coming to the bunkhouse kitchen. Best you meet her there."

"Yes, sir."

Back at the cabin, warm now, for there would be a frost tonight, William and Sulli went outside in the cold to wash each other. Ralston climbed up in the bunk, a straw pallet on top. Felt good. He took off his clothes, pulled the blanket up, happy for his small comforts. He knew not to trust William, who had proven to be a liar, out for himself. As for Sulli, well, she wasn't his worry. He liked her. Thought she deserved better. He would work hard. He would make good. He was a free man and he would stay a free man.

The fates played games with people. Sometimes they were cruel, sometimes kind. But no matter what they did, how they rolled the dice, Ralston was free.

April 26, 2018
Thursday

Warmth still proved elusive since the temperature, at 50°F, would drop even more when the sun set in about an hour, at a little after 7:30 P.M. Harry, Susan, and Arlene drove in two vehicles up to Aldie. The basset trials would begin tomorrow and the ladies wanted to help the attendees get settled the night before, rise early to do whatever the organizers wished. The weather, not comfortable, wasn't bitterly cold, but spectators and participants would need layers. Also, a light rain was forecast for tomorrow. Harry decided not to focus on it. She'd wake up and deal with whatever fell from the sky.

The problem wasn't what fell from the sky but what had sneaked into the car. The two cats burrowed under the comforter, as did Tucker. Pirate, larger, remained in the farmhouse where he would be with Fair. But the others were sneaky and neither Harry nor Susan knew they carried stowaways until they reached the outskirts of Culpeper. Given that the two talked nonstop even if Tucker snored or Pewter coughed, they might have missed it. Also, Susan's Audi station wagon was big.

Once they discovered their passengers, the two decided to keep going. Turning back would cost them about an hour each way, so the plan was to secure the very bad children in the cabin. Once at the cabin, the two cats and the dog were literally bundled inside, the door rapidly shut behind them. Given the chill, Harry set to building a fire while Susan unpacked, hanging up their raincoats — as well as short, flannel-lined front-zip jackets for use if it didn't rain — on the pegs by the door. Each had brought silk underwear, three sweaters apiece, four pair of silk socks, and four pair of thin wool socks to wear over the silk. Both hated for their feet to get cold, which happened often. One would think Harry, a true country girl, would have figured out the secret to warm feet, but even with Thinsulate-lined hiking boots, her feet grew cold. Gloves were easier, plus she could stick her hands in her pockets. The temperature for tomorrow, the first day, was predicted to nudge up to 53°F. If it didn't rain, that would be refreshing, especially if one was running.

"There." Harry stepped back as the flames touched the logs.

"Given that these cabins, the first three built in 1917, have no insulation, the fire is a godsend. As it is, even in this small space it takes about an hour to really warm up." Susan found the history of the Institute and its buildings fascinating.

"Our ancestors were tough. Even the rich were tough." Harry had brought water in plastic gallon jugs.

She poured water, which she'd brought for tea, into a large water bowl for the animals.

A knock on the door sent Harry to open it a crack to keep her pets in. She opened it farther and Arlene slipped in.

"Didn't read your text until I parked." She stared at Mrs. Murphy, Pewter, and Tucker. "You're going to really need to keep them in."

"I know. If it gets impossible, I guess I'll borrow Susan's car and drive them back home."

"Thought I'd check around. We have about an hour of sunlight."

"Good idea." Susan reached for her short coat.

Harry did likewise and they stepped outside, Harry carefully closing the door behind her.

First they walked over to the kennels. Almost everyone drove in early to get their hounds settled.

Ron Ausman and his wife, Lei Ruckle, waved to them.

"Are you ready?" Susan called out.

"You bet," Lei called back.

They waved, heading back toward the Institute, when Arlene saw Clare.

"Clare," Arlene said, then turned to Harry and Susan. "I didn't expect to see you."

"Jason always hunted the hounds for the contests. I brought two couples of beagles, which I'll hunt tomorrow. I think he would want Chesapeake Beagles to participate. He loved this fundraiser." Clare, although grieving, was determined to show off Jason's pack.

"I'm sure you're right," Arlene agreed.

Harry encouraged her. "Just seeing other beagles work, that's exciting. And tomorrow we can all watch the bassets."

"I love their voices." Susan flipped up the collar of her jacket. "Getting close to sunset."

"Well, it is a little damp. I guess there's a front coming in." Clare smiled, then turned to Arlene. "Let's go to where Jason was found."

"Twenty-minute walk, thirty if you poke," Harry offered as they started down the path, first climbing the low rise, then walking along.

The buds seemed larger and they were. Some daffodil shoots poked up their heads, late, but it had been a hard winter and a very late spring.

They chatted about hunting, about looking forward to meeting veterans tomorrow.

Reaching the flat stretch where the tractor had been parked, Susan stopped. "We're close. The rains since then have washed the tracks, but we're pretty close."

Harry walked off the road, over a mound, then dipped down again. "Here."

As she sounded sure, the others joined her. Harry, with her fine-tuned sense of direction, was almost on the spot.

Clare peered down, saying nothing.

Arlene, consoling, said, "It was quick."

"I hope so," Clare, heartfelt, uttered, then turned to get back up on the farm road, the wide path. "I just wanted to see it, you know. Give me energy for the hunt. I'm doing it for him."

As they all walked back, the sun set. The twilight lingered, as it does near the change of the seasons, on either side of the equinoxes.

Clare spoke again. "I can't imagine why someone would kill him. I regret every time when we'd have an infrequent fight and I'd say, 'I could kill you.' "

Harry fell in beside her. "Every wife says that. A husband can pluck your last nerve."

They walked quietly, then Clare, obviously somewhat overcome, said, "The damned police. Crazy questions. Did he have a mistress! They sure asked a lot of questions about money, which I also resented. I told them we didn't steal anything, we invested our own money, and we built a very successful car dealership that survived through hard times as well as flush."

Arlene, more familiar with Jason's history than Harry or Susan, changed the subject. "Did you bring any whippers-in?"

Clare's face registered more discomfort. "No. I mean, Jason had registered for the Hounds for Heroes and I decided at the last minute to come over. I called our whippers-in but everyone was committed. So what? I was coming."

"We can whip-in to you. Plus a brace is easy," Harry volunteered.

Arlene smiled. "There, you have two whippers-in if you wish. I am the director and will be on the wagon, but Harry and Susan can run."

"Thank you," Clare replied with feeling. She looked up. "Low clouds."

"I think the bassets will be hunting in the rain, but then again, unless it's a downpour, it will intensify scent."

"They have spectacular noses," Clare mentioned.

"They do. My grandfather always said bloodhounds first, bassets second, and beagles third. Foxhounds fourth. Of course, when he and his friends would get together, this order would change according to who was hunting what. Those old guys loved their hounds," Harry said.

"We all do." Arlene grinned as they reached the row of cabins, bidding one another good night.

Harry opened the door enough to peek. She felt a bit of cold air at her ankles as Ruffy trotted in. The three animals slept by the fire. Susan hurried inside as Harry shut the door, which awakened her animals. They hung up their coats. Harry tossed more logs on. The cabin felt wonderful.

Ruffy sat next to Tucker. *"I'd hoped you'd be here."*

"We're not supposed to be here. We sneaked into the car." Tucker stretched.

"We're in the doghouse." Pewter laughed.

"Well, I'll go in and out and keep you posted," Ruffy promised.

"Nothing on finding the killer, I guess." Tucker figured Ruffy was in the middle of things.

"No. The killer is here, though."

"What?" The tiger cat was surprised.

"Do you want us to help you catch him?" Tucker felt certain she could be of service.

"No. I want to make sure the killer doesn't get caught."

30

October 22, 1787
Monday

Virginia creeper winding up a pin oak outside Ewing's library window pulsated deep flaming red. Fall arrived in fine raiment. However, Ewing slapped his desk with his right hand while Catherine pulled out the accounting books, opening them on her side of the desk.

"It galls me."

"Yes, Father."

"We are reorganizing as a nation; you read the Constitution as well as I have, and yet there is nothing in there about postal service. How can we be an organized nation without good service? I am tired of paying these high prices for mail. The Romans could do it. Why can't we?"

"I don't know, Father."

"And furthermore, I reread the papers sent me from Philadelphia. What is to prevent Congress from instituting a state religion down the road? The French still have no toleration for Protestants. And that is in writing, the intolerance, I mean. And I guarantee you one other thing." He picked up the handwritten copy of the Constitution sent to him by Roger Davis. "Nothing in here about postage costs for members of Congress. I tell you they will get all this for free and we will pay for it. I know it."

"Father." Her voice was soothing and cool. "If our new representatives enumerate their privileges, they may not be representatives for long. Better to keep their powers general" — she pointed to the papers — "than to list them."

He stopped smacking the desk. "Quite so."

She closed the account book to begin sorting the mail. Ewing, still irritated, had paid little attention to the mail other than the cost, paid by the recipient, which also irritated him. If someone wanted to cost you money, all they had to do was send heavy mail, heavy items.

"Father, here." She stood up and walked behind the desk, handing him a quite fat letter, the handwriting serviceable but not beautiful.

He slit the letter open with a long, narrow, silver letter opener.

"Well." He read the first heavy letter.

"Well what?"

"From Gabriel LeSeur. He writes that one-quarter of what he owes me for the tobacco has been sent to England. I can draw on it there as it is in my account in London." He pulled out the second paper. "A rather detailed account of sales. Now why would he send me that?" Ewing handed the accounting to Catherine.

She read the odd letter, citing half a hog's head to DeJarnette Tobacco Shop on the right bank of the river, near the former Philip Augustus's wall. "This is odd and the paper feels a bit odd." She held it up to the light. "Father, hand me your letter opener."

He did so and she carefully slit the paper lengthwise, exposing a parchment, tissue-paper thin.

Seeing this, Ewing now stood up to walk over to his daughter. "What is this?"

"It is for you." She carefully handed him the delicate paper.

He gave it back. "Your French is better than mine."

Catherine slowly read the letter then read it aloud. The lines were small, jammed together, the handwriting cramped.

"My Dear Monsieur Ewing, I trust you are

278

in good health. We have done business for close to two decades. It pains me to inform you I do not know if I will be able to pay for the rest of the tobacco. I also ask your forgiveness for I write plainly, not being a man as educated as yourself. Things are uncertain here. The Crown will not pay its bills. The Crown has no money, truthfully. This has given rise to unscrupulous people who order goods without a desire to pay. If one presses, they run to an advocate. My only comfort is I doubt the lawyers will be paid either, although in my darker moments I believe the lawyers are forcing the banks, the church, and the Crown into the abyss. Calonne has fled to England, accused of hiding the state of the nation's finances from the King. We now endure Brienne hovering over the Treasury like a vulture. The Queen has gotten her way. My Dear Ewing, there is no money. My wife declares she has never seen events at such a pass, but I tell her we French excel at argument. The ship will right itself. She begs me to leave Paris. She is a good woman but given to women's foolish fears. Again, forgive me."

"It's worse than Baron Necker has written." Ewing exhaled.

"Written by a man outside of government, Monsieur LeSeur clarifies the difficulties in a manner easier to understand. At least for me."

He grunted. "For me as well." He ran his hand across his forehead for a moment. "He will not be the only merchant to fail us, but I believe he is the only one who will give us warning."

"He is an honest man. Perhaps he should listen to his wife." Catherine reread the letter. "What will happen if the Crown does not solve this problem? What will happen when men like LeSeur cannot pay their bills inside of France? And what happens if the bakers must pay more for flour and then the people must pay more for bread? Look what happened to us when the Articles of Confederation failed. The states were at one another's throats. Granted, we don't have a king or a hereditary nobility, but people must be able to make a living."

He listened to his oldest daughter, then spoke. "You have an old head on young shoulders."

"You flatter me, Father. My head is filled with the history drummed into it by those costly teachers you and Mother provided. Whether it was ancient Athens, Rome, or now Paris, whoever is in power must tend to the people."

"Do you think the states will ratify the Constitution? Since I paid for those history lessons, what do you think?" He teased her a bit.

"After endless talk, yes." She smiled at him. "It's better than what we had before. Who knows, Father, it might work."

His gaze again fell upon the accounting. "I don't know how to address this loss or the ones sure to follow."

"We can cut and plane more timber. People will build. Times are better. Of course, this will not address all of our losses, but it will be a start."

"Perhaps." He sighed, then changed the subject. "I heard another slave ran away at Big Rawly and Maureen's lady's maid was severely punished."

Catherine thought to herself Roger must have told him. News flies. She reminded herself to be constantly vigilant about Marcia. Ewing believed the story about Marcia's illegitimate birth. He did not know Ailee was buried on Cloverfields. Better this secret be buried with her.

"Yes," Catherine simply replied.

"I can understand Maureen's anger. I'm angry at Ralston. But she is unusually harsh." He breathed in. "Her Caribbean upbringing, I'm certain of it."

"The thing is, I don't think her beating anyone does any good. It just makes everyone else watchful, ready to run if the opportunity presents itself."

"Do you think any more of our people will run?"

"Ralston, well, I think he was a special case. He broke bad. He was always jealous of Jeddie, but the thieving, the exaggerated interest in women. The only thing I can think of is he broke bad."

"Maybe he should have married young." Ewing found this reasonable.

"Getting married and staying married are two different things." She shrugged.

Marriage didn't enter Ralston's mind. Nor did it enter William's, despite his lie that Sulli was his wife.

Mr. Finney hired them. Ard kept William and Sulli in the cabin, shifting Ralston to a bunkhouse with the other single men.

Ralston was glad to be away from the two of them. He groomed the horses, fed them, was watched by Ard, who was not yet ready to let him or William mount up.

Walking a gelding back into the stable, Ralston heard wheels on the drive. He put the fellow in his stall, walked outside, coolish, to behold a large cart painted a bright yellow now pulling up at the stable entrance.

Two men sat up top. One was Moses and, before Ralston could hide, Moses spied him.

"Ralston."

Ralston turned. "Yes, sir."

"What are you doing here?"

"Mr. Finney has hired me."

"That doesn't answer my question."

"I ran away."

Moses then asked, "Have you seen my father?"

"Before the leaves fell but the color was changing. He looked well."

Moses grinned. "Good. Good."

"What are you doing here?" Ralston asked the question back to Moses.

"Sam and I, we work together, are delivering a cart Mr. Finney bought from Mr. Studebaker. I work for Captain Graves but he lets me work with Mr. Studebaker if he doesn't have anything for me. Man builds a solid cart and his axles rarely break."

"Does he paint them all yellow?"

Moses laughed. "No. That was Mr. Finney's special request. Makes it harder to steal, I would think."

Ard was walking toward them, Sam with him.

"I better get back to work." Ralston

thought for a moment. "Did you know Sheba ran off with a fortune in pearls?"

"No." Moses's eyes widened. "She had a low cunning."

"I only saw her once or twice, but people would talk about her. Said she knew all the Mistress's secrets." Ralston left to fetch another gelding.

Ralston didn't know that Moses and Ailee had hidden at Cloverfields. Because of working with the horses, he had seen Moses at Big Rawly working with his father, DoRe. But without knowing what, Ralston suspected something was under wraps when Father Gabe and Bettina kept disappearing at night, Bettina carrying baskets of food.

Moses and Sam had been followed by another cart, one with a canvas top stretched over four supports. This had canvas sides, too, so the three men could sleep inside, Moses, Sam, and the other driver. It was of ingenious construction.

Ard carefully studied this. He would draw it later, presenting it to Mr. Finney as his own idea. Ralston watched Ard watching. He realized if he worked with this fellow, helped him along, he, too, might benefit.

Moses, swaying in the makeshift carriage, would have two days to wonder why Ralston ran away from Cloverfields and how he wound up at Royal Oak. He was happy to hear about his father. It had never occurred to him that his path would cross Ralston's now or in the future.

31

April 27, 2018
Friday

"I feel like I should sing like a canary." Harry, reins in her hands, swayed as the cart pulled along, one wonderful mule doing the honors.

Arlene, as the director, watched every competitor. She would get closer than the spectators. She didn't want engine noise to disturb the bassets. Also, the smell of gasoline, depending on the weather, offended her and them.

The weather was a light rain, cool, perfect for hunting.

The first draw at 7:30 A.M. was Rachel Cain with her Reedy Creek Bassets. Using three whippers-in, one on each side of her and one behind, she cast into the wind.

A huntsman prefers casting into the wind, for the game's scent will blow into their nostrils. Casting with the wind at their tails does the opposite. However, this being Virginia, the wind could and did change. A huntsman needed to be alert and calm. No point shifting every time the wind did. One needed to watch and make a judgment. Often one's hounds made the judgment for you.

Rachel's four girls hunted like stars. Noses down, fierce concentration, plus they got a good draw, they opened within five minutes of being cast. Arlene, letting Harry hold the reins so she could concentrate, used binoculars. Being the director, in case of a dispute or confusion between judges, she made the decision. Decisions came naturally to her. The Army taught her to lead and she did.

The spectators, veterans, some mobile, others more compromised, wore light raincoats; some pulled rain caps low on their heads. As many of these people had hunted before service, most of them knew what was going on. A few, new to the game, had interpreters, and a few of those interpreters were handsome or pretty, working with a serviceman or -woman. Happy people.

The deep, resonant voices of Rachel's two couples ricocheted off the woods. They slowly worked their way west of the Institute building, then hooked north, picking up speed as they trotted.

Clare and Susan, also in the canary-colored cart, occasionally wiped down Arlene's binoculars. They kept the coolers between their feet. No telling what would happen out there, so a bottle of water or cola might be necessary.

"Tallyho," Arlene quietly called out, pointing in the direction where the rabbit broke out.

The three other women watched as the rabbit, fast and evasive, quickly disappeared into dense underbrush.

Rachel, running now, reached the underbrush. Those basset tails moved like windshield wipers as their huntsman and best friend encouraged them.

"Oops." Clare giggled, pointing beyond the underbrush.

"That devil." Susan smiled, for the rabbit burst from cover, high-tailed it to what had to be his or her den, because before you could say "Jack Rabbit," all that could be viewed was a white tail popping down into a little den.

The bassets patiently worked, moving all around the underbrush. They hunted well together and with drive. They were sisters and when one opened, the other put her nose down to open, too. Reaching the place where the rabbit had disappeared, they

marked the den but couldn't flush out the rabbit.

Harry's watch beeped. She wore one of those watches that gives the wearer's steps, their heartbeat, stairs, the time, even worked as a stopwatch.

Hearing the beep, Arlene put her grandfather's big cow horn to her lips, blowing deep, mournful notes that they probably heard all the way to Middleburg.

Rachel called her bassets to her, the whippers-in quickly on either side and the third whipper-in bringing up the rear.

"That was a damn good run," Clare said low.

"Well, we'll have a long day, but I would be surprised if the judges didn't give Reedy Creek Bassets a high score. Rachel has a nice touch." Arlene sat down on the hard seat. "This wasn't built for comfort."

"We should have brought pillows," Clare remarked.

"At least we don't carry around a lot of padding back there." Susan laughed as Harry turned the mule, Madam, back toward the Institute, where they would go out with the second team, this one from North Carolina.

The two American Kennel Club judges walked together, discussing the run. They'd be pooped by the end of the day. This wasn't a job for sissies.

"Clare, Jason gave me a long story about this yellow cart. Said the original was built in 1790 by Studebaker and it is indestructible," Harry said. "This is a replica. The original is in the Studebaker Museum."

"True. You know how he was about automotive history. It was built in York County, Pennsylvania, but I guess the son or grandson of the Studebaker who built this moved to Ohio, then the western territory, to build carts and, in good time, the cars."

"Isn't the history of this nation something?" Susan enthused. "Even pottery has a story."

"Here they come." Arlene focused on four dark-colored bassets.

Harry waited for the team to pass her. The huntsman, a young man, which was always a good sign for the future, carried the horn. He was perfectly turned out, too.

"Is that Milton Riddle's son?" Clare wondered.

"Is. He's got a good draw, too, and I'm sure he heard how well Rachel's girls hunted. His blood will be up."

So was that of his hounds, who hit right off the mark flying, truly flying up the hill toward the east as the rain intensified a bit.

As the wind, slight from the east, blew right into those sensitive basset noses, Nattie Riddle ran like the devil to keep up. One of his whippers-in could match him, a young woman, Caitlin, but on his right side an older man fell behind.

This age disparity played out in all forms of hunting with hounds. Hunting on foot, one needed to be strong. The older fellow was, but he'd lost his speed. Why use an older person? Because of what they knew. They'd seen it all and a word from a wise old hunter could save a huntsman many miseries.

The older man, Jake Deloria, kept behind the pair. He couldn't move up to the side, for they picked up more speed, stopped, lost scent, cast themselves before Nattie reached them.

Clare muttered, "I'm not sure he has control of that pack."

Her words, prophetic, made Arlene, Harry, and Susan sit bolt upright. Sure enough, the hounds took off, flat out took off, and no amount of blowing or cracking a whip could bring them back.

"Shall I try to follow?" Harry asked the director.

"Yes. It's rather hard to be discreet in this yellow cart," Arlene wryly replied.

Harry clucked to Madam.

Hounds crested the hill, running straight as an arrow. Up ahead two rabbits ran together. Not all that common but not unusual either. No one saw them break cover so the hounds weren't rioting, but they were not listening to their huntsman and this would cost points.

"Madam, good girl." Harry praised the mule, who watched with excitement and trotted with vigor.

This continued for five minutes, which doesn't seem like a long time, but when one's fillings are being rattled by potholes, it is. And it promised to go on longer.

"Harry, can you get closer? We have to stay on the road," Arlene asked.

"Sure." Harry clucked and Madam showed some surprising speed herself.

They reached a spot where the two rabbits had disappeared and the hounds ran in circles. Harry held up Madam while Arlene climbed down. Susan climbed down, knowing not to say anything about Arlene's artificial leg. Arlene didn't want help and she really didn't need it.

Being a huntsman herself, Arlene quietly walked toward the confused hounds. "Good hounds. Good hounds."

Susan knelt down, a posture most dogs

find reassuring.

Harry stayed in the cart, as she held the reins.

"Maybe I should help." Clare hopped out. "Do you have a leash?"

"Under my sweater, around my waist," Clare called over her shoulder.

Approaching the two bassets, wondering whether to go to Susan or not, Clare also knelt down.

"Good hounds," Arlene soothingly said. "Come along."

The larger hound hesitated, then walked to Arlene, who bent down to pet her, sliding a finger under her collar.

Clare quietly came up and snapped the leash on the collar. "I think, Arlene, if we walk back, the other one will follow."

"Let's give him a minute. You're probably right, but it's better if he comes to us."

Susan, on all fours now, was almost at eye level with the basset, who decided this was okay and bounded up to her. She grabbed his collar.

Hoisting him up, for she didn't have a leash, she grunted. "My God, these hounds are heavy."

"Hold on a minute." Arlene unbuckled her belt, handing it to Susan, who slipped it under the hound's collar.

"Good."

The three women slowly walked the hounds to the wagon just as Nattie, Jake, and Caitlin came into view.

"I'm sorry to have put you out." Nattie apologized to Arlene.

"We've all been in this situation. Don't worry about it."

The two whippers-in, leashes around their waists, put those on the bassets, handing back the belt and leash to Arlene and Clare. They walked, crestfallen, back toward the Institute.

The rain, steady, made dampness seep into bones.

"Give me a minute to see if Madam would like a drink when we get back," Harry said.

They passed spectators, umbrellas up now. Everyone wore mud boots, so that was a plus. No wet feet.

However, every now and then a raindrop would slide down the back of Harry's boot or down her collar. Being a country girl, she ignored it.

The day, rain notwithstanding, proved exciting. At the end, Mary Reed's Ashland Bassets won, with Rachel coming in a close second. A hairsbreadth separated them, but the reason Ashland won is that there wasn't one check, not one.

The dinner couldn't have been better. Harry talked to everyone, being especially fascinated by the women wounded veterans. But the men, military service being part of manhood for centuries, truly were impressive. What touched her was that no one complained. No one.

Once back at the cabin, fire going, Mrs. Murphy, Pewter, and Tucker having had a potty break and now in front of the fire with Ruffy, whom the humans couldn't see, the two women replayed the day.

"Supposed to rain tomorrow for the beagles, too." Susan put her feet on a little stool, hoping to warm them.

"As long as it isn't heavy, it helps scent and really, this place is full of rabbits. I think they'll have a booming day."

"Hope so." Susan leaned her head on the chair's back, looking up. "I forgot that Arlene has one of those space-age legs."

"She can run better than we can." Harry nodded.

"Yes, she can, but I think about that moment when the device blew up. I can't imagine that, and here she is. Thank God for our medical corps."

"And technology. I can't imagine it either, Susan. All these people here, each of them with a story of service. We're pretty spoiled, you and I."

"That we are," Susan agreed.

"We'll be in the canary cart again. I would think Madam would be embarrassed."

"If she isn't, I am." Susan laughed.

Harry inhaled the lovely odor of the hardwood fire, thinking again that Jason's killer had an intimate sense of the territory, which could be difficult.

"I'm beginning to think Jason was a good actor. You don't just get killed for being a nice guy."

"She's got that right," Ruffy said, ears sharp.

"Let's not dwell on it," Susan advised.

"I won't. Let's remember to find pillows for tomorrow." Harry smiled, closing her eyes, bone weary but happy to be useful.

32

April 29, 2018
Sunday
Saturday's runs pitted husband against wife as Mandy Bobbitt and Billy Bobbitt wound up with two fabulous hunts. Also right up there was Sherry Buttrick with four Farmington Beagles descended from her glorious Peanut. Overcast but no rain, the day delighted everyone. Arlene, being director, wanted to hunt her two hounds but turned the horn over to her first whipper-in, a young man, Lonnie Parrish, stationed at Quantico Marine Base, who fell in love with the sport at the base.

Now Sunday was day two for the beaglers, as there were so many of them, and they were undeterred even though the light rain had returned. Clare drew a ten o'clock slot. Harry and Susan whipped-in to her. Arlene, binoculars at the ready, really needed to watch over everything, so Nattie Riddle drove Madam, Jake Deloria aboard. Although basset people, a hound man is a hound man, and both wanted to observe hound work. Sitting in the canary wagon gave an excellent vantage point.

Clare walked her four Chesapeake Beagles up over the hill, for the day's territory had to be different from the last two days'. Rabbits shouldn't be overhunted and since the Institute covered 512 acres, the game could be fairly protected. One would be hunting fresh rabbit.

Well, Clare certainly hit a fresh rabbit, and the bugger shot straight uphill, a fairly steep rise above a small but swift creek. Harry, on the right, had the presence of mind to vault the creek to begin the climb. Susan hung back slightly should the game turn, because if the rabbit did pull a one-eighty — and they had a bag of tricks — she'd be able to turn with it, keep up with the pack. But this rabbit harbored Mount Everest dreams, going ever upward. Harry, cool though it was, sweated. Susan knew she couldn't catch up to be on the hounds' left shoulders, so she sensibly climbed but conserved her energy.

The rabbit hit the crest, the four beagles perhaps five or six minutes behind. They poured over, followed by Harry, determined to keep up. No human can keep up with canines at full tilt. She hung in there as she heard Clare reach the crest, whooping encouragement to hounds who needed none of it. A beagle possessed is in his or her own world.

The high ground, wet, slowed Harry down, but not the light animals. She kept them in sight, only realizing as she reached the middle of the high meadow that it was where the cavalrymen had thundered on, to their regret. The rabbit did not stop to say a brief grace but zoomed over that meadow, the cottontail bobbling, eyes determined. Farmwork makes one strong but doesn't necessarily give one great wind, and Harry's lungs burned. Still, she kept up, as did Susan, closing slightly. Both women, in shape, decent runners, realized this run was very, very good. The rabbit hit the tree line of a northeastern woods, cut into it, and then swerved west. Hounds roared in, full cry, then silence.

Harry could drop it down to a trot, for she saw the Chesapeake hounds casting about. They tried everything, but to no avail. Clare blew her horn, calling them back. She then walked along the wood's edge, pushing them into the woods. She might have done better sticking to the edge, for rabbits are edge feeders. Then again, one never knew. After fifteen minutes she turned to recross the meadow and hunt downhill, but the timer watch on Nattie's wrist went off and Arlene blew the horn.

Madam flicked her ears. She wasn't a big horn fan.

Clare told her hounds how good they were and began walking back to the kennels at the Institute. Harry and Susan walked on either side of the proud beagles, tails upright.

Arlene had Nattie drive her back to the top of the hill for the next hunt, which was Waldingfield Beagles.

"I should have kept on the edge." Clare kicked herself.

"They put in a super run. And who knows where scent might be? You did a good job." Harry praised her.

"Clare, you've been hunting these hounds less than a month." Susan put things in perspective.

She brightened. "I think Jason would be proud."

"No doubt. I personally would like to have a word with that bunny. Nearly straight up. Hateful climb."

"Was." Both Susan and Clare agreed.

Reaching the kennels, Clare checked the hounds' paws and refreshed their buckets of water, putting them in their tidy kennel. She also mixed up a kibble mash into which she threw what she swore were secret ingredients.

Each small kennel sat separate from others, a good plan, and the fencing gave enough room for stretching legs, too. Everything at Aldie had been thought out for generations, literally, for the good of the hounds.

Meanwhile, Dr. Arie Rijke, Amy Burke Walker, and her brother Alan Webb, survived one of the most incredible runs ever. Einstein and Yeovil, led by Empress and Voicemail, nosed about for ten minutes. Nothing. Dr. Rijke, carrying the horn, pushed them along.

"Find your rabbit," the huntsman said.

Amy began to wonder because, of course, they'd all heard about Chesapeake Beagles' run.

Dr. Rijke, not one to fret, kept pushing his beagles. His wife, Suzanne Bishoff, Joe Giglia, and Bob Johnson, all able to attend the weekend, remained with the spectators. Often someone who knows the pack, and these three did, can be helpful as spectators, seeing what the huntsman and whippers-in can't. Amy and Alan had an intuitive understanding of what the other sibling would do.

Empress snuffled, tail starting to feather. Voicemail came alongside her and within five seconds both opened at once. Yeovil and Einstein came alongside. They ran for one solid hour. Damn near killed the humans, but the work was so exciting. Somehow those Waldingfield people kept the hounds in sight. The spectators, the young ones, kept up. The older ones fell back. The veterans in Gators and the other ATVs also kept up.

The rabbit shot out of the territory, literally passed the monument erected by the First Massachusetts Cavalry and crossed the road. Dr. Rijke had to blow back his beagles. Amy and Alan had to break them off the line. Voicemail gave up before Empress, who was a hound possessed. Einstein, the youngest, and Yeovil hurried to the horn. For Empress the party was unfortunately over.

Arlene, Nattie, and Jake, who had convinced Madam to go off the dirt road, a bit muddy now, and onto the pasture, waited at the top of the slight rise.

"Best run I ever saw," Jake declared.

"It's been a terrific weekend," Arlene said. "But Jake, I'd have to agree, best run I ever saw. We all dream of a run like that."

Nattie, jaw dropped, simply held the reins lightly in his hands.

Three tired people gathered the four hounds, turning for the long walk back.

"Let's let them get ahead. If anyone poops out, we'll pick them up," Arlene suggested.

Those spectators in Gators and ATVs cheered when the happy beagles passed them. Dr. Rijke lifted his proper soft black hunt cap. Amy was too tired to do anything but smile, and Alan was dying for a cigarette. Of course, he wouldn't smoke one, but right about then the hit of nicotine would have been heavenly.

By the time the Waldingfield people had reached the kennels, everyone there had heard about the run. Harry and Susan wished they had seen it but their run was plenty good and rule one was to take care of the animals first.

Clare, hands on hips, beamed as Amy, Alan, and, lastly, Dr. Rijke walked by. "Think you beat me."

"Everyone wins at Hounds for Heroes." Alan tapped his black baseball cap with his crop.

"We made thirty thousand, ten thousand more than last year." Amy grinned. "Everyone did win, but I have to admit, best run I've ever whipped-in to, the best."

"Are your legs jelly, because mine about are." Harry, who knew the Waldingfield people well, laughed.

Jeff Walker, Amy's husband, who had been helping both Bobbitts, hound Masters, ran up to her, put his arm around her shoulders, and kissed her on the cheek. Her legs felt a little better.

Harry, seeing Madam and the humans, left them all to go to the barn. She wanted to freshen the shavings for Madam and wipe her down, as the girl had been in the light rain all day. Arlene started to help her unhitch the placid mule.

"I'll do it. You're the director. Go on over to the kennels."

Nattie stepped up. "I'll help."

Turned out he was a good man with driving gear, more to handle than riding tack.

Jake walked with Arlene as they replayed the day.

"Where'd you learn about driving?" Harry asked Nattie.

"Lexington, Kentucky. My mom has fine harness horses."

"Ah." Harry nodded, for that meant his mom knew a great deal.

Madam, wiped down, put her face in her food bucket, which had two scoops of delicious, sweet feed.

After seeing to the mule and the canary cart placed in its parking spot under roof, Harry, too tired to sprint, walked back to the cabin, where she put Tucker on a leash and walked her away from everyone.

"I could go with you," Mrs. Murphy offered.

"Stay inside. It's raining," Tucker prudently advised.

Pewter, one eye now open, muttered, *"You spoil that dog."*

"She's a good egg." Mrs. Murphy watched embers glow in the fireplace.

Fifteen minutes later, Harry and Tucker returned. Harry wiped the dog's feet and brushed her corgi's fur, for the rain fell a bit harder now. She then fed the dog and cats juicy scraps she'd taken from the Institute kitchen.

She really did spoil them all. A human would have enjoyed the scraps.

As they ate, she freshened the water, put four logs in the fire as an open square, and put twigs in the middle with old papers she'd brought from home. As the embers pulsated, she didn't need to use a match. The twigs caught, so Harry then placed logs over the square she'd built. This would warm things up nicely and she'd put more logs on after the dinner.

No one had time to clean up for the dinner as the hunting ran overtime. Also, awards needed to be given. A few speeches were made but were kept mercifully short.

One couldn't have asked for a better dinner or awards ceremony.

Arlene handed out awards. Clare received a third place, which pleased her. By the time all was finished, including bottles of bourbon, scotch, wine, and vodka, people were ready for bed or to leave if clear-eyed and if the drive home wasn't too long.

"I've got a headache. Just wore myself out," Clare said to Arlene, next to her.

"Wait a minute." Arlene fished in her purse, handing her two pills. "Knock it right out."

Clare thanked her and checked her watch as she slipped out the back door. Most everyone's cars were parked in the front, so they left that way. Some with cabins at the end of the cabin line left by the back, hoping the run through the rain would be shorter. It wasn't.

"Susan, I'm going to throw a light rug over Madam. She has to be dry by now. Will you put more logs on the fire?"

"Of course."

Harry opened the door, the rain falling hard enough that she was glad she had a good raincoat. People scurried about for their cars, their cabins. What a happy group.

No one would suffer from insomnia this Sunday night.

Monday morning, those with hounds in the kennels cleaned them and cleaned the kennels. Some put their hounds in their trucks or cars, as each competitor only brought four. A few pulled a little hound wagon, but most hounds sat in someone's lap.

Harry and Susan walked over to say goodbye to Arlene, who had to oversee it all.

Clare's beagles were unattended.

"I'll see where she is." Arlene made sure the hounds had food and water.

"I'll come along." Harry fell in with Arlene as Susan stayed back to talk to Dr. Rijke, Amy, Alan, and Jeff.

Arlene knocked on Clare's cabin door. There was no answer, so she slightly opened it.

"Looks like she isn't packed yet," Harry noticed.

"That's not like Clare. I didn't think she tied one on," Arlene said.

They called in the Institute hall. They checked back at the kennels. No one had seen her.

"Ah, here's Madam's transportation.

Arlene, let me help load the mule."

"I'll help. Maybe Clare's in the barn."

"Who knows? She's around somewhere," Harry replied.

Once in the barn, Harry put Madam's halter on, walking her out for Geoff Ogden, who owned her. Not really a mule man, he had fallen in love with the sweet girl years ago and, like all love stories, or most love stories, they wound up together.

Madam happily walked into the aisle, and as Geoff, leading her, passed the space for the canary cart, he glanced over, then half laughed. "Someone had too much to drink, I fear."

As Madam's hoofs reverberated on the aluminum walk-up ramp to the trailer, Harry looked at the cart.

"Arlene."

Arlene came over. She poked Clare. "She's dead."

Harry checked her pulse. Her wrist was cold. "Good God. What's going on here?"

Clare was emphatically dead.

33

April 30, 2018
Monday, 6:00 P.M.

Harry, Susan, and Arlene remained at Aldie until the ambulance removed Clare's body. Death appeared to be from natural causes. However, the Loudoun County Sheriff's Department wanted to ask a few questions. Deputy Mark Jackson returned to perform this duty since he was on the Jason murder case. Two deaths at Aldie close to each other was unusual. As Clare was relatively young, an autopsy would be performed.

After he left, the three women repaired to the cabin, where Harry let out the two cats and the dog for a quick run through the rain. Tucker and Mrs. Murphy flew to the barn, having heard everything. Pewter chose not to get her paws wet.

"Would you like a drink? We've got water, cola, and iced tea. I can also make hot tea over the fire. Brought my teapot and hanging rod," Harry offered.

"No, thanks. I'd like to sit for a moment." Arlene dropped into a chair.

Harry pulled one up for Susan, then sat on the cooler. No one said anything for a few minutes.

"She appeared in good health. After all, she ran with her beagles," Susan offered.

"She did," Harry concurred.

"A heart attack or a stroke can hit you at any time. She was what, late forties?" Arlene wondered.

"Fifties," Susan said with finality. "She had a good face-lift. I can always tell."

Harry glanced at her friend. "You can. I can't."

"I never thought of Clare as vain." Arlene raised her eyebrows.

"I don't think she was. Face-lifts are a lot more routine these days. I mean people say, 'It's not the real me, it's the best me,'" Susan replied. "No one really wants to look old."

"I guess." Harry sighed.

"Well?" Susan held her palms upward. "Whatever took her away, I doubt it was a result of a face-lift."

"That's the truth. She looked like she was sleeping," Arlene murmured.

"But here's the thing. What was she doing

in the cart?" Harry asked.

Arlene gave her a sharp look. "Maybe she wanted to visit Madam."

"Why would she crawl into the cart?" Harry's mind ever worked. Logic, there had to be logic.

"Maybe she thought she'd left something in the barn or cart and when the party was over, the dinner and all, she went back to look. The deputy searched her room. Suitcase not packed. The other deputy said her purse was in her truck. So?" Susan was at a loss.

"So," Harry started explaining her point of view, "there are ways to kill people to make it look natural if you know what you're doing. Any doctor or nurse can kill pretty much with impunity. We have doctors and nurses hunting hounds."

"Oh, Harry, Dr. Rijke didn't kill Clare," Arlene responded.

"Of course he didn't, but I'm simply saying we don't know that it was a natural death because, if you think about it, the circumstances aren't natural. She leaves the Institute. Nothing unusual there. Doesn't return to her cabin, or if she did, she didn't pack. No goodbyes or anything, which to me means she's coming back. So why was she going to the barn?"

"She rather liked the mule. Really," Arlene posited.

"Well, it's too bad Madam can't talk." Susan was frustrated. Madam wasn't there to talk, but Mrs. Murphy, Tucker, and Ruffy were.

Mrs. Murphy jumped into the cart, sniffing everywhere.

"Anything?" Tucker and Ruffy wondered.

"A lingering perfume." Mrs. Murphy again sniffed everything. *"And some mud from her boots."*

"It doesn't matter," Ruffy said.

"Why?" Mrs. Murphy leapt down.

"Dead is dead." Ruffy rubbed against Mrs. Murphy and she felt a cold little shiver.

"Yeah, but it will upset the humans." Tucker knew this would set off Harry.

"Don't humans have a saying? From their Bible? 'An eye for an eye, a tooth for a tooth,'" Ruffy questioned.

"They do," the cat replied.

"Clare's death is an eye for an eye." Ruffy wagged his tail.

"Oh, dear." Tucker sat down. *"This means this will go on until everything is cleared up."* The corgi looked at the ghost beagle. *"Our human won't rest until it is. She has a sense of justice."*

"I see." Ruffy did, too. *"My human lies in*

314

an unquiet grave. If your human figures this out, perhaps she will at least be at peace, and we can go for walks, happy walks."

The cat swept her whiskers forward. *"It's important to humans to say prayers for the dead. Not necessarily the evil dead, but they do that, too. Everyone is entitled to, what can I call it, a send-off? So if our human can figure out what happened, she can say prayers for your human."* Mrs. Murphy then asked, *"Will that bring peace? Justice and peace?"*

"The justice is done. But I think perhaps prayers would bring her peace." Ruffy hoped this would be the case.

"We will do what we can," Tucker promised.

"Then I will see you all again. I would like that." Ruffy lifted his floppy ears.

The three returned to the cabin, Tucker scratching at the door.

When Harry let them in, Pewter pronounced with relish, *"Mom has them all upset. She says it's murder."*

The three looked at one another.

Tucker murmured, *"Maybe this will be easier than we thought."*

"What's her reasoning?" Mrs. Murphy got down to brass tacks.

"She says there's no way Jason and his wife and vice president at the dealership would die

so close together. There has to be a connection." Pewter loved having the news. *"Arlene said maybe the stress did Clare in. She and Jason were close. Maybe it really was a stroke or a heart attack. Mom says, no way. Susan is now fretting. She says it looks like a natural death."*

"Mom won't give up." Mrs. Murphy knew her human.

And the humans were at it.

"Harry, why do you do this? You drive me crazy. I say the woman had a heart attack. Maybe it was stress. Maybe she had a weak heart anyway," Susan vented.

"It's too convenient. Okay, a doctor could shoot her full of potassium. Granted, the needle mark would show. If it were cyanide, someone could snap it under her nose. Death would be pretty fast."

"Harry," Arlene gently said, "it would be pretty fast for the person snapping the cyanide."

"Well, yeah. But then again, what if they wore a gas mask?"

"Harry!" Susan threw up her hands.

"Listen to me. I know I am nosey and maybe too suspicious, but this is suspicious. And what if she knew and trusted her killer? Jason did. So maybe whoever gave her a pill, she was tired, she had a headache, she was a little tipsy, say. It is possible."

"Well, if that's the case, it will show up in toxicology." Arlene thought it through. "Then what we do, I don't know."

"Here are the facts. Two people who owned a company together are dead. One murdered. One, we don't know. But here's what I come back to and I thank Geoff and Jan Ogden for this. Jason was in the foreign service. He was posted to Ankara. Okay, Geoff was general counsel of Istanbul. Jason was moving up the ladder. Turkey is a very important ally. So what was Clare doing at this time? She was in the Navy, right?" Harry asked.

"Right," Arlene answered.

"And she was in the Gulf of Finland. That's a critical area."

"And potentially dangerous. She knew Russian. I don't know really what her duties were, but I expect because of her language skills, she had important ones and, then again, she made captain," Arlene remarked.

"Jason spoke fluent Turkish," Susan remembered from an old conversation. "Of course, they all spoke French. In the old days everyone in the foreign service who wished to rise or was in diplomacy spoke French."

"Whatever for?" Harry asked.

"For centuries it was the language of diplomacy," Susan, good with languages, replied. "I wish it still was, as we need two or three languages that can span the world."

"Well, English sure does." Harry felt quite smug about her own language.

"It's not the same," Susan fumed. "French can be marvelously subtle. English, well, you can be subtle but you have to work at it. We need French. We also need Chinese. If those two languages could be taught and taught early, it would help those who go into government and it would help business."

"Russian," Arlene said. "Maybe not as important, but Russian and Chinese. And I would have to say today, Arabic."

"So if someone knows at least one of those, they'll have a good career?" Harry wondered.

"They will if they keep their nose clean." Arlene exhaled. "So Harry, what you are saying is that this goes back. Somehow this isn't really about a car dealership or the onetime employee who smuggled drugs inside hubcaps."

"Well, drugs can always be a motivator. So much profit." Harry lowered her voice. "But I think this goes back to their thirties. I am missing something, but I believe Clare was murdered and I believe it is connected to Jason getting his throat slit."

Arlene exhaled loudly again. "Remind me never to underestimate your brainpower. You could be right."

"Don't tell her that!" Susan nearly shouted. "I have to live with her."

"Lucky you." Harry half giggled despite all.

Susan pleadingly looked at Arlene. "We were placed in the same cradle together by our mothers. I can't get away from her, and let me tell you, she has always gotten me into trouble and she can be bossy, too."

"I am not. I am clear thinking most times."

"I need a drink, a real drink," Susan complained.

"I'll drive. There's bourbon in the cooler," Harry volunteered.

"No." Susan shook her head. "What truly pisses me off is now you've made me think there is a connection. I just want to go home and forget it."

"We can't forget it," Harry replied.

"Perhaps for a night. I need to drive home and so do you. I'll take Clare's beagles with me and call Chesapeake Beagles tomorrow. Little things probably want to know why everyone has left the kennels but them," Arlene told them.

"We'll help you load them up," Harry offered.

"Harry, you go help Arlene. I'll load up our stuff. It's about a two-hour drive and now it's dark. I mean, we could stay the night, but it feels creepy."

"Does," Arlene agreed as she and Harry left the cabin to drive Arlene's truck to the kennels.

The four sweet beagles wiggled because they were going to ride in a truck like house dogs. Big deal.

As Harry returned, Susan had everything organized, including pouring water on the fireplace coals and swooshing them about.

Ruffy sat by the station wagon as Tucker was lifted in. The two cats jumped in, making a beeline for the comforter.

"We'll be back. I don't think it will be too long," Tucker called down.

"I hope not," Ruffy replied, and as Susan pulled out the beagle felt hope for the first time since he had been killed with his human.

34

October 25, 1787
Thursday
A light frost silvered the earth. Fall truly arrived, and with it the lavish colors beloved of Virginians living by the Blue Ridge Mountains.

Ewing would be finished with his breakfast, filled with Bettina's wonders and rich, fortifying coffee. The two sisters slowly walked to the big house. They'd put this off as long as they could.

"Father," Catherine called as she opened the back door.

"Me, too." Rachel's light, liquid voice followed her sister's. Already in his library, Ewing nearly sang with delight. "My angels. Both of you."

Catherine stuck her head in the kitchen. Bettina had been using the winter kitchen since the beginning of October, as the nights proved cold. "Wish us luck."

Bettina came to the sisters, held each one's hands for a moment, her kind face bright. "Bless you. No matter what, I bless you."

"Oh, Bettina." Rachel impulsively kissed her on the cheeks, cheeks she had kissed since infancy.

Catherine, less demonstrative, squeezed the good woman's hand. "We really will do our best, but Bettina, this might take Father some time."

Bettina nodded, letting go of Catherine's hand.

The two sisters, nearly equal in height, took each other's hands to walk down the hall. As unalike as they were in their abilities, they shared their mother's kindness and their father's hopefulness and the deep reverence for life that Bettina had taught them as children.

Just before they reached the open door of the library, Rachel turned to her stunning sister. "Catherine, I pray Mother is with us."

Catherine, searching her equally beautiful sister, but beautiful in a classically feminine fashion, nodded. "She will be."

As they walked into the library, Ewing stood up, strode to his daughters, kissing them. "Both of you at the same time. What a wonderful way to greet this frosty morning. Come, come, sit by the fire. You both wouldn't be here if this were not important."

He was hoping one would tell him she was with child. Ewing had turned into a predictably besotted grandfather.

"Coffee? Tea? Anything?"

"No, Father. I have actually learned a bit of cooking and made a breakfast today that even my husband gobbled." Rachel laughed.

"Rachel, you're a good cook." Catherine meant it.

"Well, before you tell me whatever it is, I can tell you, Catherine, I received an inquiry yesterday — you were at the stables all day — from a London firm inquiring about tobacco. Now, if we can reach an accord, it will somewhat offset our French losses."

Rachel, at the edges of European doings, mostly listening to her husband, said, "No one likes to lose money. And imagine what Maureen is thinking? No more fabrics from Paris."

"Oh, I think Maureen will compensate. She has a cleverness." Ewing stretched out his legs.

Apart from being a bit portly, he was in good health, but his knees ached a bit, as did his finger joints.

Catherine took a deep breath. Best to get

on with it. "Father, we are here to ask a boon."

"Yes." He really did expect a notice of a forthcoming child.

"DoRe has asked Bettina for her hand. She has accepted," Catherine calmly reported.

Rachel jumped in. "They're very much in love."

Ewing's eyes widened. "Does Maureen know?"

"I don't know, but surely you must have suspected the friendship was deepening." Rachel leaned toward her father.

"I knew he was calling on her but well —"

"We are here because we hope you will convince Maureen to let him go."

This provoked a grunt. "Let him go? She'll sell him for twenty thousand dollars. Once she knows the situation, she will be merciless. She is a Midas in her own way."

Catherine and Rachel looked at each other. They knew their father was right, but what to do?

Catherine spoke first. "She will make it as difficult as possible because she knows how much we value — adore really — Bettina. Here are a few things Rachel and I have considered. If Maureen could get her hands on Bettina, she would finally have the best cook in the state. Naturally, never, never, never."

Rachel added, "Never."

"I quite agree."

"She can't forbid a marriage. As a Christian, at least in name, and she certainly makes a show of her faith, she must agree," Catherine continued.

"True. We will throw a sumptuous wedding here at Cloverfields." He paused, voice dropping. "The only thing I can think of is giving Bettina time to visit at Big Rawly and we can only hope Maureen will do the same for DoRe."

"That's just it. She'll seem to agree but I believe she will find impediments each time DoRe is to come here." Rachel folded her hands together to keep from shaking. She desperately wanted Bettina to be happy.

Ewing rubbed his chin, then his cheek. "Ah, my dear, you are right. Of course I agree to the marriage. We are all Christians here. The wedded state is the best state and he has properly courted her. I can't think of any way to get DoRe from Maureen unless I were to agree to what will be an exorbitant price."

A silence fell over the room. He was right. It wasn't that Ewing wouldn't pay for

DoRe, but to be held up — and by Maureen no less, even though he didn't know what she had done to Moses or Ailee. Had he known, this would be even more painful.

"We could free Bettina," Rachel quietly suggested.

"She wouldn't go live with him. Bettina will not go to Big Rawly." Catherine was right, too.

"If we freed her and she left, perhaps DoRe could run away," Rachel blurted out.

"Daughter, think what you are saying. Apart from the fact that I don't believe in slaves running away, this would be a death sentence for DoRe and he would be easy to identify. The limp, his size, and his age. She'd kill him for pleasure when he was returned." Ewing shook his head.

Catherine, mind whirring, said carefully, "There might be another way. What if — and this will cost us but force Maureen to work closely with us — what if you plant a huge apple orchard for her. We pay for everything. All she has to do is prepare the ground, and we can help there, too." Catherine held up her hand. "And as a nod to her power, we pay a reasonable sum for DoRe."

This struck Ewing forcibly. "Why?"

"Well, Father, she is uncommonly shrewd.

326

If we both have orchards, then she will work hard to see that those apples bring a high price on the market. And I would not be surprised if she sought markets in England touting the wonders of apples grown by the Blue Ridge Mountains. Knowing Maureen, she'll concoct a story about learning the secrets of longevity from the Monacans who used these very apples, and they lived forever." Catherine couldn't help but laugh.

Her father did, too.

Rachel, smiling, added, "In a sense, Father, we will be in business together, at least by growing apples. Vile as she can be, Maureen never does anything halfway."

Folding his hands over his chest, he played with the chain of his heavy gold pocket watch, which his daughters had given him for his birthday. "Girls, you may have hit upon something."

"If you agree, the next step is we must call upon Maureen, and we'd better make sure Jeffrey is there." Rachel liked Jeffrey and knew he could sway his wife.

"Yes, yes." Ewing exhaled from his nostrils. "Roger."

Within seconds Roger was at the door, so of course he had heard everything. Roger was born to be a politician, whether elected or unelected. White or black, he could gather information and closely observe, then gently guide, others.

"Yes, Mr. Ewing."

"Will you prepare my pipe and bring it to me? I need an infusion of my own tobacco." He smiled broadly.

"Of course." Roger disappeared.

"Whatever price she sets upon DoRe's head will not be the price she accepts. We have to take the first blast in good grace." Ewing was already on board.

Rachel, realizing they had won, nodded. "No one can negotiate better than you."

He waved his hand. "I wouldn't go that far."

Roger reappeared with the pipe, took a taper, held it in the fireplace, then touched it to the pipe bowl while Ewing took a deep draw. "God bless the Monacan."

"Did they grow tobacco?" Rachel wondered.

"I expect they did." Catherine steered them back as Roger bowed out. "Shall we leave it to you to discuss this with Bettina?"

"No, no. You girls are closer to her and it is women's desires that count in these matters. Your mother taught me that."

Rachel, out of the blue, hearing about her mother, said, "I think Mother would wish us to free Bettina and DoRe after we procure him from Maureen."

Catherine looked at her sister as though Rachel had lost her mind.

"What?" Ewing sat bolt upright.

"Mother would want this. Bettina sat by Mother's bed, she washed her, sang to her, she prayed over her. And she with Mother raised us. Set her free, Father."

To his daughters' surprise he burst into tears. "Oh, my dear, Bettina keeps your Mother close. How can I part with her? I —"

"She would be free. That doesn't mean she would leave. She and DoRe might stay. This is her home. She was born and raised here. But Rachel" — Catherine paused, shocked at the lump now in her throat — "Rachel is right. This is what Mother would want now that Bettina has found love."

Tears cascaded down Ewing's cheeks. The three of them cried. Rachel, on her feet, now knelt before her father, kissing his hands. Catherine stood next to him, her hand on his shoulder.

Finally able to speak, he rasped, "I will see to it."

When the sisters left, they briefly stopped to tell Bettina that they would do their best to get DoRe to Cloverfields. They promised to talk more in detail later, as both were overwrought and unexpectedly tired. Ewing, pipe in hand, put on his jacket, took a deep puff, and went outside to his wife's tomb. He dropped the pipe into his pocket absentmindedly as he placed both hands on the recumbent lamb with the cross. He sobbed. He sobbed as hard as he had sobbed when he had buried this glorious woman.

"I am about to do something highly unusual, Isabelle, but I believe as our daughters have pressed me that this is your wish." He continued to sob. Then he smelled his pocket burning.

Looking down, he saw that his pocket had caught fire, and little tendrils of smoke billowed out of his right pocket.

He slapped at his pocket, pulling out the pipe, dumping out the tobacco from the bowl where he stomped on the lit tobacco. His pocket was ruined. His coat was a mess. He stood there for a moment, then threw back his head and laughed. He laughed until the tears flowed again, for he knew Isabelle had sent him a sign. She had a wicked sense of humor.

35

May 3, 2018
Thursday

Curiosity bit Harry like a mosquito. One bite, a scratch, then another. She couldn't get Aldie out of her mind. Doing her chores, she ran through possibilities. The weather, perfect early May days, should have diverted her attention but no, she couldn't get the two deaths out of her mind.

Sitting in her tack room, low sixties, a lovely light breeze, the door finally open, she could hear the horses outside playing. Spring fever didn't just affect humans.

Mrs. Murphy sat next to Harry's computer. Pewter, colossally bored since this wasn't about her, snored, splayed out on the sheepskin saddle pads. Tucker sat by Harry's chair.

"What's she doing now?" Tucker inquired.

Mrs. Murphy peered over the top of the computer.

"Murphy, what are you doing?"

"She's looking at pictures of a car dealership," the cat answered her canine friend.

Lawsuits were public record. The very first thing Harry had done on Tuesday was to see if Montgomery County in Maryland had lawsuits on record. There was the one about drugs, and the dealership was dismissed from the case. The guilty party was still serving time. One case in 2009 proved a bit interesting in that a buyer sued for the entire replacement of the computer brains for a Mercedes that had been traded using a Lexus. Now there was a jump in taste. Harry read this with interest. The entire Mercedes had died, fritzed right out, for the rain had somehow driven up under the windshield wipers, seeping down into the brains of the car. Clearly human brains were becoming less and less necessary, according to carmakers. Anyway, the cost was well over seven thousand dollars, and that did not include the labor. The buyer's insurance found a way to wiggle out. Understandably furious, one Mr. Samuel Bonfoy sued the dealership. This dragged on. Holzknect had inspected the car before the sale. Low miles, new tires, it seemed good, and it was until that unusual driving rainstorm. Harry, a motorhead, devoured the voluminous proceedings. Mercedes knew this was a design flaw but very few of their cars died in this fashion, sort of an automotive brain hemorrhage. They did not publicize the flaw. Holzknecht again was exonerated. Fascinated, Harry checked on Mr. Bonfoy's subsequent suit against Mercedes-Benz USA. Naturally, they initially refused to pay. Ultimately, they replaced his vehicle because Mr. Bonfoy hired the best law firm in the state of Maryland — and there were plenty — but these guys had fangs. Mercedes saw the wisdom of simply giving the plaintiff a brand-new car.

"Wow." She continued to scroll.

It became clear that Jason and Clare were responsible people, took good care of their customers, plus they had the advantage of selling two of the most reliable brands in the country, if not the world.

"*She's still scrolling. You'd think she'd go blind,*" Mrs. Murphy remarked.

"*Computer screens ruin your eyes,*" Tucker declared.

"*How do you know that? You don't have one.*" The tiger cat teased her friend.

"*Fair read it out of the paper. He likes to read aloud and I remember everything he reads. You know now he turns to the obituaries first.*" Tucker was mystified.

"He turned forty and that is important to them. He's what, forty-three? I forget, but I think he's one or two years older than Mother."

"Sets them right off, doesn't it?" Tucker laughed.

"Sure seems to, but this death thing, I mean I understand the obituaries, sort of. She likes to send sympathy cards and go to services. She's respectful that way, but unexplained death, she gets obsessed."

"Jason getting his throat cut, well" — the corgi tilted her head upward — "pretty awful and now this thing with Clare. She doesn't believe that it was natural. You smelled everything."

"If Clare was murdered, it had to be without scent and clever, something we don't know about. But Tucker, humans do keel over."

Mrs. Murphy stuck her head over the computer again. "She's trying to find Clare's service record. Shouldn't take long. Can't be that many Lazos in the Navy. No matter when."

"Why?" Tucker wondered.

Harry whispered to herself and the cat called down. "Clare's discharge. It was honorable and now she's seeing all the awards Clare won. Do they call them awards in the service?"

Tucker thought. "They get to wear ribbons

on the left sides of their chests. But I don't know if that's called an award. It's pretty, though all the colors and certain of those little ribbons mean wars. Then there's the stripes on their sleeves. Humans put a big store by this stuff."

"So Clare did well?"

"As did the dealership. Everything seems to be in order." Tucker knew Harry still wouldn't let this go.

Then Harry returned to the Google information on Jason, returned again to Facebook. She peered intently at the photographs, noting that the same Russian translator appeared, as did his Turkish counterpart. Given the centuries of tension between Russia and Turkey, this seemed in order. Jason's linguistic abilities had to have been critical in assuring U.S. interest in both nations remained stable. Even with her limited understanding of foreign relations, Harry began to see Jason's usefulness to the country's political interests as well as economic ones.

The bribery, the threats, the military forays over the centuries added to the needs and dreams of the nations surrounding Turkey. For a mad moment Harry thought about Catherine the Great bribing Turks, Greeks, anyone to open that wedge to what was then called Constantinople, now Istanbul.

How much money was squandered the world over to buy friends, information, to open the back door?

She was suddenly glad she didn't know but so much.

Harry got up out of her chair, walked into the center aisle of the barn to pace. Up and down, up and down.

"Don't watch her. You'll get a crick in your neck," Mrs. Murphy advised.

Hands behind her back, Harry stopped in front of the open tack-room door, took a big breath, strode in, sat down, and picked up the old phone.

"Jan. It's Harry Haristeen."

"How odd. Geoff and I were just talking about you. You have the unenviable distinction of seeing two corpses at Aldie. Geoff saw one. That was enough."

"He thought she was asleep, passed out."

"Here, you talk to him."

A deep voice came on at the other end of the line. "Harry."

"Mr. Ogden."

"You have, of course, spoken to the sheriff, as have I."

"Yes. Let me get to the point. I don't believe Clare's death was natural and I believe it was connected to Jason's. I have no idea why these two people were murdered, but may I ask you some questions about the foreign service, about our State Department? I don't think I'm using the correct terminology."

"Doesn't matter. Go on."

"When you were general counsel in Istanbul, Jason Holzknect worked in Ankara, the capitol, right?"

"Yes. This was a good assignment for a young man, only his second assignment. His fluency in Turkish made him valuable."

"So I assume he was low down on the totem pole?"

"Well" — a pause followed this — "yes, but to be assigned to the capitol of an ally is a plum posting."

"What would his duties entail?"

"He would speak directly to his counterparts in the Turkish government. He could call and chat with probably another young person, and the two could set up meetings for their bosses. He would also be expected to read the newspapers, any official bulletins from the Turkish government. He could speak to any other ambassador's assistant fluent in Turkish."

"But he had no real power?"

"No, but over time if his assessments of

government proclamations, of economic development, officials in the Turkish government, proved correct, he would rise, and he did."

"What about the Kurds? Would he have contact with them?"

"No, but he would keep us apprised of the government's position on them as well as their relations with bordering states because people in those governments would be dealing with Turkey and someone in each office would be fluent in Turkish."

"Most of the bordering states would speak Arabic?"

"No. Southeast of Turkey sits Iraq and Iran. Iranians speak Persian. Due south it's Syria, a complete and terrible mess. Due west, Greece and Bulgaria. North sits Russia, the traditional enemy. Across the Black Sea is Sevastopol, ever famous because of the Crimean War. Georgia and Russia as well as Greece have a long, long history with Turkey. No one forgets the Ottoman Empire. There are many languages."

"Would that mean because of all those languages, then, that Turkish would be understood by a fair enough number in those adjoining states, the governments?"

A long pause followed this. "Any government department in a bordering state would have people fluent in Turkish and others fluent in the languages surrounding them. It's much more complex than here: for one thing, thousands of years of history especially between Greece and Turkey, then called Anatolia."

"I would assume there is wariness?"

"That's putting it politely." Geoff half laughed.

"And Turkey is or was, in better times, our ally."

"Technically it still is. Turkey is a key to peace. Always has been, and when the Ottoman Empire was called the Sick Man of Europe and other powers began to nibble at it, politics were destabilized. Atatürk changed all that."

"So we need Turkey?"

"I think we do."

"Me, too." Jan called from the background.

"Let me switch gears for a minute. Clare Lazo was in the Navy, fluent in Russian."

"I only know Clare from beagling, but occasionally we would talk about our careers. She was in Naval Intelligence on a ship in the Gulf of Finland. I take that as her most significant assignment. I'm sure there were others. Sitting there with Russian subs gliding underneath you, I'd say Clare had a lot on her mind."

"She was discharged with honor when she didn't re-up. Forty-five, I think."

"I don't know her age but she had a good career."

"Did you ever wonder how she and Jason met?"

"No. All I know is they bought the dealership together and made bundles."

"I'm racking my brain. I think she told me she met Jason while she was in the service. He was, I don't know — why does Paris stick in my mind?"

"With luck we all got to Paris for at least a furlong." Geoff laughed.

"You've been good to give me so much of your time."

"Harry, I don't know why two people are dead at Aldie, two well-respected people and well-respected beaglers. But let me give you a piece of advice. Let this go and keep your mouth shut."

When Harry hung up the phone, she knew that Geoff and Jan also shared her suspicion and they knew far more about the world than she did. Why now and why Aldie? The other thing she felt more than she knew was that the murders had something to do with the fact that both victims excelled in two different, important languages.

Mrs. Murphy leaned on Tucker. *"She's got that look on her face."*

"Means we're in for it." Tucker groaned.

Pewter woke up. *"You two were talking about me, weren't you?"*

36

October 27, 1787
Saturday
Royal Oak's fences, sturdy, painted, set off
the lay of the land. Maryland tended toward
gentle rolls just west of Baltimore and dropping south. A beautiful state, those pastures
seemed perfect for horses. At least they were
at Royal Oak.

Ralston and William worked sunup to
sundown and they worked hard. Ard kept
an eye on them, finally putting both young
men up on two made horses. No point risking the horse or the man on a green one.

William, the better rider, preened while
Ralston, good, fumed.

Making his daily report to the Boss, Ard
said, "Mr. Finney, we could use more
crimped oats. Room up top and they'll stay
good up there."

"All right. Hay?"

"Plenty and good, too." Ard knew how to

please Cinian Finney. "Those squares you cut open over each stall, so we can pour down the oats or throw down hay, saves so much time."

A small smile crossed the craggy face. "Time is money."

"The two new hires are working out. Ralston does whatever he is asked and he's quiet with a horse. We can use him with young horses. The other one, William, I don't say that he could finish a horse, but he'd be a decent jockey. Arrogant, but a year or two of running will take care of that."

A bigger smile covered the Boss's face.

Ard nodded. "Those boys out there can get rough."

"He's tall. He'll hold his own."

"Light and slender. I'll work with him," Ard promised.

"The girl must be doing well, too, or Miss Frances would have been up here, rolling pin in hand."

They both laughed at that.

Ard left, the mist rising, for it was quite early, passing Sulli on her way to the kitchen. He noticed she had a black eye.

A bell rang. Ard stopped as Mr. Finney was summoning him back. The bell's notes, a handbell, carried. The big bell by the back of the house was only used in times of import, even crisis. That bell could be heard for miles on the days that sound carried well.

Ard trotted back up as Mr. Finney stood at the back door.

"Step inside. It's colder than I thought."

Ard did and the two men stood there for a moment as Ard could hear Mr. Finney's wife in the kitchen ordering the house cook about.

"Yes, sir."

"Do you trust these two?"

"They haven't given me a reason not to, sir."

"Can't send them back to Virginia." He figured they were runaways. "But they can go to our side of the Potomac. Won't take a day."

"Yes, sir. They're learning their way here and I can spare them. We're turning most of the horses out. We'll keep a few in light work but won't be long before the weather turns on us."

"No. Mr. Gulick up in Northern Virginia wants a Studebaker cart. Selling him mine. I'll get a letter off. Bad as the mail is, this shouldn't take forever. When I receive a reply with a date, you can send them on."

"And the horses?"

"Gulick can bring his own. They can

unhitch ours and hitch his to the cart, or just drag the cart on the ferry and Gulick's man can do it on the other side. They'll figure it out."

"It's a very good cart, sir."

"Indeed it is. I doubled my money and ordered two more." A very large smile creased his face, for Mr. Finney loved a profit. "We'll have two sturdy carts for the price of one."

"Yes, sir." Ard smiled back, and as he walked to the stables he marveled at his boss's ease in making money.

This was a gift he had not inherited, nor had he ever learned the secrets of finance, as he liked to think of it. He earned by the sweat of his brow. Then again, so did most men.

On this same brisk day, Ewing Garth paid a call to Maureen Selisse Holloway. He felt the first introduction of "the problem," as he now thought of it, should come from him.

Given the beauty of the day, the temperature now in the low fifties, the Blue Ridge vibrant with color, her own maples flaming red, Maureen suggested the two briefly walk around Big Rawly, then repair to the house for more warmth and a bit of food and drink.

A beautiful shawl wrapped around her shoulders, she slipped her arm through Ewing's. Maureen liked to walk this way with a gentleman. Women did like to feel a man's arm under his coat, and no gentleman would ever refuse a lady. The dance of politeness had its pleasures, most especially in the South.

"I hear your husband is entertaining Gerald Lawson from Charleston. The man owns half of Charleston, I believe. Has that huge plantation on the Cooper River." Ewing mentioned a former colonist made wealthy by rice, not the easiest crop either.

She smiled. "He's down there with my Jeffrey discussing not one carriage but a city carriage and a country one. Mr. Lawson has definite ideas. Jeffrey's reputation is growing."

"And well it should. His work is as good as anyone in England or France or wherever. I mention Europe because they always believe they are superior to us."

"M-m-m. Excuse me for being direct, my dear Ewing, but have you secured your holdings in France?"

He sighed. "I don't think one can secure anything in France until the government attends to its debts."

"Yes." She drew out the word. "As you

346

probably have surmised, I have moved whatever monies I had from Paris to London. My experience with the Bank of England has been excellent over the years. I do think it important to keep some funds in Europe as it is so much easier to move them from place to place, to purchase those necessities we cannot buy or manufacture here yet."

"It will come," Ewing said with finality. "But as always, you are prescient."

She stopped for a moment, sweeping her right arm toward the mountains. "These higher pastures are exposed to more wind. I sowed them with corn, as you know, but the wind blew the corn flat. So I have returned it to pasture, but I would like to grow something a bit more profitable. Unlike your extraordinary daughter, I really can't breed horses. I don't have the knowledge or the eye."

He patted her hand. "She is a wonder." Then he removed her hand from his arm for a moment, striding out on the pastures. She'd given him the perfect opening.

He knelt down, pulled up a bit of native fescue, and smelled it, inhaling the earthen sweet odor. Then he replaced it, tapping it down with his foot.

Returning to an attentive hostess, he bent

his head toward her as he took her hand. "This is good soil."

"Yes." She was expectant.

"You could again grow corn, but you would need to plant fast-growing evergreens, which would take you about five years before they would be of service to you, but they might well protect your corn from the wind."

"I see. Time-consuming and possibly costly." She placed her hand on his arm again as they renewed their stroll.

"You might consider an orchard. Again, you would need to wait at least three years before the fruits would be suitable to sell, but trees can withstand wind better and apples like this type of place. Pears and peaches need a bit more protection but, given your soil, you have choices."

She looked upward at him. "You are most helpful."

"I like farming."

They walked along, stopping at Jeffrey's shop. Mr. Lawson proved a bundle of enthusiasm, which meant he'd put in a big order and was now laying out exactly what he wanted. Jeffrey, too, was enthusiastic.

The two neighbors repaired to the house where, true to her word, Maureen had prepared a light, lovely lunch. Not too light, for it was growing colder.

"Where did you find a melon?" Ewing was astonished to find a slice of melon to freshen the repast.

"My secret."

Her female kitchen slaves glided in and out. Ewing noticed while the women, modest and becoming, performed their duties graciously, no one was truly beautiful. Clearly, Maureen would never trust a beautiful slave woman as long as she lived.

The main course, thinly sliced veal, so thin it seemed transparent, simmered in a marvelous sauce that had paprika in it.

"My dear, this is exquisite."

She beamed. "When I was in Italy I made the acquaintance of a Hungarian noble who bequeathed to me a few of the culinary secrets of his mysterious country."

"I have always wanted to visit, but my tour, after my father deemed I was educated or educated enough, stopped in Germany."

"England, France, Italy." She winked, a habit from her youth that disarmed many men.

"Yes." He noticed the silver on the hunt board gleaming, tons of it, big tureens with it. "Father overlooked Central Europe. We do, you know."

"We do. My father used to tell me Poland

was the most civilized nation in Europe in the seventeenth century when everyone was killing one another."

"My father used the Thirty Years' War as a warning to me not to indulge in, in his words, 'religious enthusiasm.' "

She chuckled lightly. "You appear to have obeyed your father."

Ewing laughed out loud. "Well — yes. You spoil me with your company and with such food. I come to you with news and with it, choices."

Her manicured eyebrows lifted. "Indeed."

"Your DoRe has asked for the hand of my Bettina."

A pause followed this information. "I see. True marriage? A Christian ceremony?"

"Yes. Of course, I will underwrite all expenses as in essence I am not exactly her father but the man in charge. With your permission, I would like to have this sacrament performed at Cloverfields. Might you allow some of your people to attend and might you and your husband also attend?"

"Of course, my dear Ewing. Jeffrey and I would be delighted. DoRe has been faithful to me."

"Yes, he has. He is a good man. But this union brings with it, oh, let's not call it problems, but rather decisions that we must make. I hope you and I can find a way to smooth the way, so to speak."

"Yes." As always, she revealed very little.

"Like any two people in love, they wish to live together."

"That can be arranged if we both make a bit of change. As DoRe is critical to my operations and Bettina an outstanding cook, neither one of us can give up our dependent." Maureen would never use the word "slave."

"That is why I am here."

"I suggest, each partner spend a month at the other partner's place. Now most times, as our plantations are close, they can travel back and forth daily. During inclement times, there will be difficulties."

"I had also considered that." He tried not to appear nervous. "What if I planted your apple orchard? My men would prepare the ground with the help from yours. I would bring you the trees and would manage the orchard for the first three years, teaching whoever you deem best how to keep an orchard. Pests, harvests, checking roots if a tree droops. There is quite a bit to it. And if you would, I would pay you for DoRe and he would come to Cloverfields."

This stunned her momentarily. "I don't see how I can do without DoRe. That worthless William ran off with the equally worthless Sulli, having stolen some funds and bits of everyday jewelry. There is no one who can train or handle horses."

"There might be another way. What if we come to terms but set DoRe's move to Cloverfields after one year of marriage? That should give him time to train someone."

"I must discuss this with my husband. It is a thorny issue."

"It is." He agreed, as he knew the dance between two good businessmen was truly beginning.

"DoRe is extremely valuable."

"I agree."

"At least twenty thousand dollars. At the very least."

"An apple orchard is extremely valuable. One must recognize that, and an apple orchard will eventually yield profits. Keeping DoRe will not."

Ewing left, kissing his hostess on the cheek, knowing this would be a long siege, praying that Jeffrey would be of some use. As he rode his sweet, bombproof, Chief, back to Cloverfields, he believed this would eventually work out, but it wasn't going to be easy.

The sun hung low in the sky. He looked up, seeing a splash of color like a rainbow.

"How beautiful," he muttered as Chief flicked his ears. "Miracles do happen."

37

May 5, 2018
Saturday

Robins hopped along the ground, mocking-birds taunted everyone from their perches, goldfinches flew about — it was an avian party. Mrs. Murphy and Pewter walked with Harry as the birds complained about their intrusion into the birds' territory.

"I have every right to be at St. Luke's," Pewter huffed.

"Oh, ignore them. They have to make a big show of it," Mrs. Murphy advised as Tucker and Pirate ambled along.

In just one month from the spring equinox, the grass had turned emerald green and the buds had opened so the color of spring green floated above the grass. Some trees, like willows, fully opened. Others took their time, but the spring green would soon turn to darker green until fall, when the leaves reached their fullest amount of chlorophyll. That's what Harry thought, anyway.

Harry passed through the quads, reaching the lone tree with the single grave. A simple wooden cross stood at the head, with no birth date or death date, as no one knew.

"Forlorn," Harry muttered.

She didn't know that the blackball on paper that had been slipped into her St. Luke's mailbox was about this grave. Given all that was happening at Aldie, she pushed the unknown murder victim to the back of her mind as best she could.

A car door closed at Reverend Jones's house. Pamela Bartlett, seeing Harry, headed in her direction, as the grave rested beyond the formal graveyard. In her late seventies, Pamela regularly attended her yoga classes four times a week. She moved with suppleness and ease, her shape that of a much younger woman. Only her shining silver hair hinted at a longer life.

Turning to see who shut the car door, Harry smiled when she beheld Pamela. She'd always liked the lady, but working with her on the Dorcas Guild enlarged that emotion.

"Mrs. Bartlett." Harry walked toward her.

"And what is our building and grounds woman doing?" Pamela extended her hand for Harry to lightly shake, then walked with her a few paces to the grave.

As Virginia women they needed to touch each other. Southerners tend to be more demonstrative physically and otherwise than, say, those north of the Mason-Dixon Line. Touch provided a reassurance that words never did.

"I wanted to see if the grass was growing on the grave."

"Doing nicely," the older woman replied. "I see you have brought your team."

"I'm the smart one." Pewter rubbed on Mrs. Bartlett's stockinged leg.

Tucker looked upward at the lovely face, deciding not to tell Pewter what she thought of her. Pirate did what Tucker did. The half-grown puppy really was learning the ropes.

"You know, they really are my team." Harry's attention returned to the grave. "This wooden cross won't last but so long given the weather. Maybe a few years. I was wondering if I could convince someone in the men's guild to perhaps carve a cross on a large stone."

"What a good idea." She looked upward as a mockingbird flew tantalizingly close. "I do hope this will prove a quiet grave."

"Me, too," Harry responded.

"I'll break your neck," Pewter threatened as

the daring fellow swooped low.

As if hearing her cat, Harry enfolded Pamela in her thoughts, for she trusted her completely. "Whoever lies here had a broken neck. The Taylors' grave, as you know, was somewhat disturbed. All these two centuries later, who knows about this murder? Pamela, it's on my mind because of the two deaths at Aldie, and it was my misfortune to see both bodies. I can't shake it. I mean, I'm not horrified. I have seen bodies before, and the deaths were fresh. But why? Why Aldie? I'm being drawn in. I can't help myself."

"Well," the silver-haired lady said, "you'd be an odd duck if you weren't affected."

"Affected. She's obsessed. I have to live with this." Pewter complained loudly.

"Pewter." Harry bent over to scratch the cat's ears, which irritated the others so Harry petted them for a moment.

"She's not shy." Pamela laughed.

"What would you do?"

"I wouldn't try to block the feelings. Never works. I'm sure you've considered why those two people died, husband and wife, at Aldie, one murdered. It's in the papers and is odd, to say the least. This murder, even though long, long ago, also casts a spell. The pearls alone would cast a spell. Janice Childe and Mags Nielsen seem under their spell."

"I wonder if either of them knows something?"

Pamela's eyes crinkled. "Do you think Mags could keep from spilling the beans?"

Harry laughed. "Well, Janice is drawn to the jewelry. Then again, who wouldn't be?"

"The killer was not."

"True, but had to be a man."

"Now what does that explain? A man would surmise the value of that necklace and the earrings. He wouldn't wish to wear them but he'd surely wish to sell them. Yet he did not."

"It's something, isn't it, to think that they lay under the ground — fabulous, fabulous jewelry — for centuries, since 1786 or so? I take the Taylors' death date as the date close to when she was tossed on their caskets."

"Why?"

"Ground would have been soft. Turned up. So digging in, throwing her down, covering up the body, tamping it down wouldn't arouse suspicion."

Pamela crossed her arms across her pale peach cashmere sweater. "You have thought about it. What have you thought about Aldie?"

"Strange that you should ask. Although

they were married and business partners, I think this has nothing to do with that profitable car dealership."

"Inheritance wasn't a motivation?"

"No. Granted, a wife or husband is always the first in the line of suspects, then comes family and friends, but I think, like this murder here, it goes back to something else."

"Fascinating."

Warming to someone interested in her ideas and not telling her to forget it, Harry went on. "He was in the foreign service, had a good career, became a communications expert, and she rose in the Navy. They met in Paris, hit it off. They were on the same wavelength. Obviously, they built a successful business together in a competitive field. But I believe this is connected to their language skills."

Pamela blinked. "What languages?"

"He was fluent in Turkish and she in Russian. I know this is important. I know it. I don't know why."

"It's a volatile part of the world," Pamela volunteered.

"Isn't every part of the world volatile eventually?"

A smile crossed Pamela's lips, a light coating of coral lipstick. "Yes, I suppose you're right. Makes me wonder if we're due." She held up her hand. "Don't get me started. Turkey and Russia. Two hereditary enemies."

"My other idea does involve the dealership, maybe a sour business deal. But their company's record is awfully good."

"I see. Back to whoever is underground in front of us. Murder, as we know. Why are people killed? Well, the old motives are dragged out. Love. Money. Revenge. Drugs, but that gets to money. What else? Well, sheer perversity and sadism, I guess, but I doubt any of our considered victims would qualify." Pamela, an educated woman, rarely strayed into her own emotions when considering a problem.

"Information. People will kill for that. We know money wasn't a motive for this woman. The jewelry would have been taken. What kind of information would someone have at the end of the eighteenth century? Our forefathers delighted in accusing one another of sexual peccadilloes. I doubt she was killed for that, even if she was a kept woman. For her I believe it was love or revenge."

"Possibly."

"This sounds damning in a way, but I don't think either Jason or Clare would arouse another human being to the heights of amorous recrimination. Not love. So I come back to money, and I don't know why, information. Clare was Naval Intelligence. She may have stumbled on something."

"Now? Her career was over." Pamela didn't argue, merely presented the idea.

"Maybe not. Russian, remember. Whatever is happening over there, they are poisoning people in other countries."

"Harry, that's a terrible thought."

Harry waved her hand somewhat dismissively. "I know. I'm out in left field. I've got to let this go. But I think I'll drive back up to Aldie, look around again. I have missed something. Then I can let go."

"Well, don't drink the water." Pamela half teased her.

Harry smiled. "Do you think we will ever know about this mystery?"

"I'm not sure, but given that the Taylors' grave was oddly disturbed, perhaps. But I don't think any of us will reason this one out. I think whoever poked around the Taylors' grave will make a mistake or simply come forward. No crime has been committed in our time."

"Speaking of coming forward —" Harry inclined her head and Pamela turned. Janice and Mags approached them, carrying a pot of unbloomed something.

"Hello," both Harry and Pamela said to their sister Dorcas Guild members.

"How about finding you two here?" Janice cradled the pot.

"We've brought marigolds, will soon open up. The big ones, orange and yellow. Thought they might brighten this grave. It's rather sad." Mags carried a hand trowel. "Harry, you don't mind if I plant these, do you? I've been nurturing them in my kitchen window."

"Of course not."

"You are in charge of building and grounds." Janice cited her title. "We want to stay on the good side of you."

"It's a lovely idea. I was here to see how the grass was doing. Good, I think, and Pamela joined me."

"What about me?" Pewter pouted.

Pamela checked her watch. "Off I go. The reverend is expecting me. Has more ideas about the homecoming. He's fallen in love with the idea."

As she left, Harry thanked Janice and Mags and she, too, walked up toward the church, as her old truck was parked in the side parking lot. As she walked, it occurred to her that Pamela, in her good-natured way, had warned her indirectly, as Geoff

Ogden had done directly.

She also remembered that May fifth was the Kentucky Derby day, and Harry walked a little faster. She wanted to watch the Run for the Roses.

38

October 29, 1787
Monday

The sprinkling of sand over wet ink, allowing it to dry, then tipping the fine-grade paper into a wastebasket focused Ewing's attention. The sound of the sand, tiny granules, moving across the paper always made him feel that he was properly working, not wasting time.

His quill, goose, of course, was perched in its stand. The ink bottle had been carefully closed. The odor from the fire infused the room. With two days remaining in October, late fall nudged toward winter. Outside a cold mist enveloped Cloverfields.

Bettina and Serena sang in the kitchen. Every now and then he could hear a pot tapped with a spoon. Even on the coldest winter day, those two women kept warm in the kitchen. Catherine and Rachel were in there, too. They wanted to talk to Bettina.

Also, Rachel was determined to see how Bettina tenderized a large loin of pork. Small pottery bowls, filled with herbs, sat in a row like little culinary soldiers.

Ewing knew his girls were in there, but he didn't know what they were doing. For the most part he believed in the gender division of labor, with particular gifts being accounted for such as Catherine's gift with horses, Rachel's with people. But men did not belong in the kitchen and he kept his distance.

The letter, concisely expressed in his quite good penmanship, concerned Bettina's manumission. He could have simply written a document in his own hand freeing his cook, but Ewing did not trust to lawyers but so much now and he had no idea what they would be like in the future. As to those men who had gathered in Philadelphia, members of Congress, he'd heard enough over time, starting with the prosecution of the war, to fear them all with the exception of Washington. He began to entertain good thoughts of Hamilton. However, wherever men gathered to discuss affairs, to make laws, a citizen should be cautious. Then again, no matter how well educated, how well meaning, no one, not one single human being, can see into the future. We can feel things, Isabelle surely did, and those things can be prescient, but to behold the whole picture and the temper of men, no.

Here he was in his late forties, he didn't care to be too precise about the date; he had observed a great deal and the trip to Europe when he was young gave him valuable insights, at least he thought it did. Exciting, new as the United States was, in many ways it had much in common with England or those nations on the Continent that he had visited.

He held up the paper again, ink dry, knowing he was doing what his wife would have wanted ultimately but wondering was he truly doing Bettina any favors? What was freedom anyway? Was it the opposite of bondage, of physical slavery? That question, hazy at first, sharpened over his lifetime. As a young man in France the money, the manners, even the way the royals walked, the nobility spoke, dazzled him. But they weren't totally free. Each one of those people had to preserve and advance the family's fortunes through the King. No one could be honest with the King and Queen or with one another. Perhaps at night before the fire with family members after yet another ghastly, expensive soiree, they could tell the truth. Still it was better than physical bondage.

Each country he visited flourished in its own way, its habits, its arts, but all endured what he felt were inhospitable governments. And what if one were the King? One needed intelligent advisers, never a certainty. One needed to pander to and be pandered to by those of great wealth, the old noble families.

Here? Well, he had believed himself a good and productive subject of George, King George III, even if he was a Hanoverian, not truly English. England had done all right but he believed that was because England had a Parliament, a real argumentative, discursive body whether King George liked it or not. In its way, that body represented the people, maybe not those on the bottom, but the ever-growing middle classes had a voice now. He thought that good.

But then King George levied more and more burdens on this colony. Not all the burdens were financial, although those were the worst. Finally, like many men of his generation, educated, of means, he believed a break with England politically necessary.

"We won," he said to himself. "We created the Articles of Confederation, frightened of nurturing a despot. They were a disaster. I pray this Constitution will hold."

He again read the paper to his lawyer

concerning proper manumission papers for Bettina and that she should be registered as a free black in court records. Since representation, the crux on which the Constitutional Convention had nearly hung itself, was so important he believed it was important that every citizen and Bettina, though not a full citizen, would be counted in some fashion if this Constitution was ratified by all the states in the time frame. He was keenly aware that the word "slave" was not in the Constitution, only the word "persons." Slave that she was, Bettina, legally, was a person. His daughters, all the women, free or slave, must be protected by their men. Every woman's status should be clear. Ewing knew that men usually only protected women that were theirs: mother, relatives, wife, daughters. It didn't trouble him that things were otherwise any more than slavery troubled him. It was the way of the world. Still, he wanted to make certain that this excellent woman who had tended and loved his wife would never be challenged. Bettina would be free.

No point in telling her until all the paperwork was done and recorded.

He turned his chair, with effort, toward the fire. His mind wandered back to representation. A true census had to be accomplished. He wondered how easily those numbers could be corrupted. According to the new document, seats in the lower chamber relied on such numbers.

Looking outside the windows, his mind felt like that cold mist. He could see the outlines. No more. Maybe that was just life. Then again, he valued clarity, logic, reliability. For a flash, he wondered if this new world was passing him by. Were younger men up to the sacrifices?

As Ewing asked himself questions, his daughters absorbed Bettina's teaching. Catherine tried. Some of it got through because she did like to delight her husband, and John, a muscular, tall man, liked to eat. He never complained about her cooking but Bettina sneaked him tidbits, for Catherine's shortcomings as well as her virtues were known to all.

"Maybe it will be an early winter." Serena, too, looked out the window.

"That's why I want that pea soup thick," Bettina told her. "You keep stirring. I'm running down to Bumbee's with the girls." She always called the daughters "the girls."

"Yes, Bettina." Since all Serena had to do was stir, she was relieved, plus she would enjoy some time alone.

The three women, wrapped in shawls, left

the house, but they hurried to Rachel's. Bettina didn't want Serena to feel anything important was being kept from her, hence the little fib about Bumbee and the weaving room. If Serena inadvertently mentioned something to Bumbee, Bettina could always say she got sidetracked, somewhat true.

Once inside, Rachel arranged chairs in front of the fire. The three, shawls hanging on pegs by the door, sat down.

"Father visited Maureen Selisse. He gave her the happy news." Catherine started the discussion. "She pretended to think all was well but, as you might imagine, she dug her heels in concerning DoRe. Right now she has put such a price on him, she knows this will delay things."

"I knew it." Bettina folded her arms across her ample bosom.

"All is not lost." Catherine looked to Rachel, better at these things.

"In fact, Bettina, Father made her an offer that will nibble away at her. He offered to put in an orchard, provide the trees, manage it for three years until the first good apple crop, and he will train a man to manage the orchard in his stead. There's a lot to it."

"Trade my man for an apple." Bettina guffawed. "Look what happened to Eve."

They all smiled, then Rachel continued. "She hid behind Jeffrey. Said she would have to talk to him but she couldn't part with such a valuable man. This will drag on, lots of back-and-forth, but in time, especially if DoRe finds a man to train there, she'll swap apples and some money for your soon-to-be husband."

"I see." Bettina tried not to get her hopes up.

After all, she had seen and hidden Moses and Ailee. She had a good idea of Maureen's character.

Rachel hopped in again. "Bettina, if you could impress DoRe with finding and training a good driving man, a man to run the stables, this will move faster."

"The carriages, remember the carriages. If he finds a handsome young fellow who will look good on one of Jeffrey's carriages, this will be easier. For Maureen, it comes down to money, money and her personal power over others," Catherine added to her sister's idea.

"I will talk to him. He's a thinking man. I'm sure this has crossed his mind."

"I'm sure it has, too, but you have the facts, for DoRe doesn't know what Father's offer was." Catherine reminded her again of Maureen's outlook.

"What price did she set on my man?" Bettina's eyes widened a bit.

"Twenty thousand dollars," Catherine forthrightly told her.

Bettina rocked back a bit in the chair. "He's priceless."

They all laughed, knowing this would take the rest of fall, most of the winter, and early spring, but Ewing, with Jeffrey's help, could make it happen.

"Now to the wedding." Rachel reached for Bettina's hand. "Spring? Or early summer? Here at Cloverfields if you wish, but then again, if you'd rather all be quiet, we understand." Rachel knew full well Bettina would want a "do."

"Before the bugs get bad." The cook laughed.

"May?" Rachel offered.

Bettina nodded her consent and Catherine beamed. "May."

While the three women at Cloverfields were thinking that 1788 would be a big year, Ralston wasn't thinking at all. He had managed to insert his member into a woman, his dream finally coming true. The pleasure exploded with such intensity, he knew he could never live without this. The desperate problem was that he had been inside Sulli.

Neither of them planned this, but William

had been batting her around. Ralston, finishing his chores early, walked in the mist, as bad in Maryland as it currently was in Virginia, down to the large pond. He wanted to plan how to reduce William in Ard's eyes, as William was doing that to him. William never missed an opportunity to point out something to Ard that he thought Ralston did wrong or didn't do at all. So far Ard hadn't paid much attention to him, but William did get the good rides and Ralston did not.

Standing at the calm pond, he heard footsteps, then turned to see Sulli. Tears ran down her face. He asked what was the matter and she poured out her misery concerning William, who hit her, didn't love her anymore, criticized everything she did. He listened, put his arm around her, offering comfort. She turned to him, holding him around the waist, resting her head on his shoulder while she cried more.

He kissed her. She kissed him back. Comfort turned to something far more exciting and they slipped through the mist to one of the empty cabins. There were many. A pallet rested on the floor. They didn't dare start a fire. They warmed up in the time-honored fashion.

She kissed him, said she had to go. He

swore he couldn't live without her. She promised he would not have to do so but she needed time.

Ralston waited a bit, then he, too, left the cabin, walking back to the bunkhouse, head full of new thoughts. They would find a way.

He, too, was planning for 1788.

Overhead, the migrating Canada geese honked to one another, a marvelous sound amplified by the mist. Sounds always seem louder when one can't see. Those beautiful geese had no sense of the future. They just knew it was time to fly. The humans below lacked such sense.

39

May 11, 2018
Friday

The broodmares, open this year, contentedly munched on the grass now containing more nutrition. Harry, knowing that March and April can fool you, even if the pastures are green, the nutrition isn't where it should be. She always supplemented her horses' food either with the best-quality hay or sweet feed or both. Horses, like people, needed a change of diet as they aged. When in work, young or old, more calories were needed, but she didn't want to give them anything that would make them hot. No corn. Stuff like that.

One foot on the bottom rail of the fence, she leaned on the top rail, watching her hoofed friends. Her old hunter, Tomahawk, a big-hearted Thoroughbred, retired now, walked over to give her a kiss. He was followed by a younger horse, given to her by

Joan Hamilton of Kalarama, named Shortro. Joan secured the horse from Shortro's owner and, knowing horses, knew the gray 15.2-hand fellow would be perfect for Harry. He needed to adjust to hunt seat. Harry loved all these creatures.

She even loved Pewter, a stretch occasionally. This morning was such a day because Pewter had opened a cabinet door that Fair, in his morning fog, left open a crack. A large plastic container of homegrown catnip, crunched up, had been hidden in that cabinet. Not anymore. Pewter's fangs and claws, with effort, tore the plastic container open. Pewter was so bombed, she lay stretched on the kitchen floor. Those glassy eyes testified to the gray cat's condition. Mrs. Murphy, late to the party, managed some catnip, but she remained functional if a bit silly.

"Is she ill?" Pirate asked Tucker.

"If she were human, she would be called 'three sheets to the wind.' " The corgi giggled. *"She'll sleep it off and pretend nothing happened."*

"Is there anything like that for dogs?" Pirate asked, a note of envy in his changing voice.

"No. Maybe the closest is Greenies, but a Greenie chewy doesn't affect your mind. Makes you happy, though."

"Let's go find Mom." The half-grown puppy headed for the kitchen door, after that the screen porch door, both of which contained animal doors.

"Right." Tucker, already dwarfed by the Irish wolfhound, bounded outside, saw Harry, and raced toward her.

"Hello, you two worthless dogs." She smiled at them.

"They are," Shortro agreed.

"You are so full of it." Tucker narrowed her eyes.

"I'm terrified." The gray Saddlebred blew air out of his nostrils, which made both dogs back up to laughter from the horses in the paddocks.

Harry laughed, as horses have a good sense of humor — she'd been the butt end of equine jokes, too.

"Come on." She turned for the barn.

A big industrial push mop leaned against the tack-room door. She cleaned out the center aisle, picked out the stalls, which weren't bad, and sprinkled some fresh shavings. Shavings, not an unreasonable expense, could still cost, so best to be prudent and not throw them around. She scrubbed out the water buckets, rehung them, then filled them with the hose attached to the faucet in the wash stall. Many people might be bored with such menial labor, but Harry enjoyed it. She could think while doing physical chores, including painting the fences, which she couldn't say she enjoyed but she could still think while doing it, painting herself mostly.

She hung the mop, brush-side up, between two nails on the wall for just that purpose. Then she walked into her tack-room office, maybe her favorite place, better than any room in the farmhouse. Plopping in the chair, she put her feet up on the desk.

"Mud." Tucker chastised her.

She looked down at her dog. "Where are those bad cats?"

"Plotzed," the dog simply said.

Harry, not knowing what her friend said, reached down with her dangling arm to scratch the smooth head while Pirate, on the other side of her, put his rough-coated head in her lap.

Closing her eyes, she took a fifteen-minute nap, wakened, reached for the phone, and dialed.

"Harry." Arlene Billeaud's alto voice sounded happy to hear Harry. "How are you?"

"Good. Just finished my barn chores, the day is radiant, and the barn swallows are back, darting everywhere."

"You know they are related to purple martins and tree swallows. I have never been able to entice purple martins to my place and I've put out the housing they like. Get the tree swallows, though. Love that iridescent dark green. Do you know that tree swallows and barn swallows can travel six hundred miles a day in search of food for their young?"

"I did. Not a real bird-watcher, I don't travel around the world, but I know what's here."

"What can I do for you?"

"Actually, Arlene, I was thinking of what I could do for you."

"Let's hear it."

"I can't get the murder of Jason and Clare's death out of my mind. Murder, I think, too."

"We don't yet know how she died."

"I know, but I am convinced the two deaths are related and unnatural."

"Okay. Why?"

"The obvious conclusion that people seem to be drawing is no one knows why he was killed, but she died of a stroke or heart attack, possibly worn down by the shock of his death and her grief. They were very close. No, I don't buy it. Nor were they killed because of their dealership, unless that's tangential. I can't think of a rival wishing to wipe them out."

"That is pretty far-fetched."

"I believe this goes back to their work days, the Navy and the foreign service."

"How can their deaths be connected to that?"

"I'm not sure, but I believe they are, and I think it involves their fluency with languages."

A silence followed this. "That's an intriguing supposition, but I'm not sure I get it."

"I'm not either. I'm rummaging around. Then there was the disappearance of Paula Devlin, another person in the foreign service and CIA."

"Harry, I'm not sure where you are going with this. I adored Paula. She was sensible. I know a lot of CIA people. The ones in Washington, in the building, if you will, and some in the field. Many retire and can be more open about their careers. Most don't talk about it. Perhaps you shouldn't either."

"Well, I am not CIA, not foreign service, not military, although I respect those careers." She took a moment. "Arlene, I believe you might be in danger."

"Me?" came the incredulous reply.

"You knew them all. You knew them stateside. Then with beagling. You knew them better over time."

"Harry, I am in no danger."

"Arlene, you could be killed. I believe it."

"No one is going to kill me."

"Humor me."

"I am."

"No, really humor me. Meet me at the Institute and let's walk through where the bodies were found, what we know, and what we don't know."

"Why don't you come to Hume? You've never been to my place. I think you'll like it. Bring your animals. We can talk here."

"No, thank you. I would like to see it, but I would like to walk through the Institute grounds with you. Maybe between the two of us, we'll hit on something."

Knowing this was a losing battle, Arlene asked, "When?"

"How about tomorrow at noon? If that doesn't work, next Wednesday."

"Sooner is better." A pause. "Have you run these ideas by Susan?"

"Not fully."

"Good. No point scaring her to death. Noon at the Institute building. If we don't find anything, will you let this go?"

"I will. I promise, but if we do figure this out, we can both go to the authorities."

"All right," came the unenthusiastic reply.

A half hour later, as Harry totaled up the barn expenses for the first two weeks of May, the phone rang.

Reverend Jones's deep voice announced, "Did you know that some members of the Dorcas Guild had an unscheduled meeting here this morning?"

"No."

"Janice called it to prepare for homecoming. In this case a true mailing, an invitation card."

"That's probably not a bad idea, but I wish they'd included Susan or myself."

"When I came into my office I found Mags and Janice going through my files! I told them never to do that without asking permission."

"Right."

He continued. "They said they were looking for an updated address book."

Harry murmured, "None of us has one, but it was rude."

After a bit more discussion, Harry hung up the phone. She felt she'd need to keep an eye on Janice and Mags. Something wasn't right, but that something was going to have to wait, for Aldie commanded her complete attention.

40

May 12, 2018
Saturday

Light fragrances filled Harry's nostrils. Finally a true spring. Mrs. Murphy, Pewter, Tucker, and Pirate sat on the Institute porch. Arlene drove in on time, for Harry, per usual was early, parking at the stone building.

Harry leaned over the porch railing. "Perfect timing."

Arlene shut the door to her Subaru Forester, looking up. "I was in the Army, remember. Zero dark forty and stuff like that."

They both laughed as Harry came down the stairs to greet her, her four friends behind her. "It's good to see you."

"It's good to see you, too, Harry, although I truly believe I am safe."

"Let's walk a bit." She started away from the Institute, passing the stables, the canary cart visible as only yellow can be. "The ground isn't soggy. Feels good."

"Does."

"My neighbor and dear friend is a deputy for the Albemarle County Sheriff's Department, Cynthia Cooper. I bedevil her. I've asked her, since she can procure information that I can't, would she keep me informed if there's a development here or with the medical examiner before anything is made public, if it is. She told me yesterday that Clare's autopsy showed she had been poisoned with tetrodotoxin. From blowfish liver, can you believe it? Just a small amount, one to two milligrams, can kill. Causes paralysis, slow at first, just a little woozy, a little numbness. Then the nerve systems begin to fail, then the throat muscles, finally asphyxiation."

"Tetrodotoxin?" Arlene looked skeptical. "How can you test for that? It can't be detected."

"So you've heard of it?" Harry watched Arlene.

Arlene dropped her head. "You were right. Two deaths, connected most likely."

"This isn't about selling cars."

"No," Arlene replied evenly.

"Let's go to where Jason was found."

They walked up the farm road, crossed

the creek burbling along, reached the top of the hill, pastures on both sides, woods at the edge of the pastures. Good bunny territory, as there was cover.

Arlene, hands on hips, looked around. "Odd, isn't it? Cavalrymen buried out here. Jason dropped here. Not that we know exactly where those men are, but sometimes I think Aldie truly is haunted."

"Me, too. You don't seem especially worried about Clare being poisoned."

"I told you. I don't think I'm going to be murdered."

"But you knew them for years." Tucker nudged closer to her as Ruffy bounded up to join them.

"In a professional capacity and not that well. Jason more than Clare because I was assigned to the State Department for a time."

"But you liked Jason and Clare?"

"I got along with them. I enjoyed hunting with them. I hunted with them at their territory, but I wouldn't say we were close, which is why I'm not worried."

Harry swept her eyes over the pleasant land, heard some birds chirping loudly.

Bud the chickadee swooped low near the dogs but not too close to the cats. *"Six eggs!"*

"Congratulations." Tucker praised the bird,

who swooped again, then headed for a bird box at the woods' edge.

The Beagle Club had put out quite a few bird boxes to encourage all manner of them.

"Saucy." Harry grinned.

"They are." Arlene also swept her eye over the area. "He was just off the road, over this little rise here." She stepped to the place that they had revisited with Clare. "I don't think he suffered."

"I'm not sure either one did, Arlene. Quick deaths. He knew who killed him. I'm convinced of that."

"Yes, me, too." Arlene inhaled the fresh odor of spring. "I wonder how many are out there. Who? When? Where?"

"We know the when," Harry posited. "Back to our time. I have racked my brain and I know this language stuff matters. So hear me out. What if they had discovered someone or someones here who were working against our country's interests? We know that Clare was CIA. As to Jason, no, but he surely had access to sensitive information as he advanced in his career. They would suspect before the rest of us. Maybe they got too close."

"No," Arlene replied emphatically.

"Well, why not?"

"Neither of those two had that kind of

courage. I know Clare was a captain in the Navy. I don't doubt she was good at what she did, but she wasn't on anyone's front line."

"She listened."

"That she did, and I don't doubt that over time she could recognize voices, as could Jason. Jason, of course, was expected to contact people in the Turkish government. He had an easy way about him. He made friends, I bet."

"The other thing I've thought about is Paula Devlin. She, too, had a sensitive career and she disappeared. Three people."

"Two were married. They ran a business. Paula wasn't tied in to them."

"But they knew her."

"We all knew one another. Paula was a bubbly person, always up for something. She knew French and German. Think I got that right. I could understand basic French conversation, you know, stuff like 'May I have a glass of water?' I'm not too good with languages."

"Me neither, except for Latin. Started in middle school. You could then and I went straight through. Helped me at Smith."

"I forget you attended Smith. That's probably why you're so smart. Let's sit on this log here. My legs are tired. I walked for miles yesterday with my Blastoff kids."

"Maybe Paula knew something or maybe she was selling secrets?"

Arlene's back stiffened. "Paula was blue chip. She would never, never do anything to jeopardize our country."

"Well, she's dead. She must have figured out something, and now Jason and Clare are dead. Maybe there's a political reason for that, too."

"No doubt."

"We should go to the sheriff's department."

"We should not." Arlene reached over to scratch Pirate's ears.

"Well, you need protection."

"I do not. You're jumping to conclusions. I am in no danger, not a bit. Your theory is interesting, but no one is going to listen to a 'what if.' "

"We should at least go to Geoff and Jan Ogden. They'll know what to do and they liked Paula."

"They will know what to do, which is to stay quiet."

"Aha. So you do think this has something to do with national secrets."

A long pause followed this. Ruffy rubbed against Arlene's leg. She felt a cool little puff of breeze.

"I do."

"I knew it. I knew it." Harry was triumphant as her animals looked up at her.

"Do you think murderers should be punished?"

"Of course I do."

"All right. In the main I agree with you, but what if someone is killed to protect our country or to even the score."

"Well — I don't know."

The animals could smell Arlene and knew that she knew something. People give off various scents. Sweat is obvious, but there are others. The one that amused the dogs and cats the most was when a human was attracted to another human. The scent changed. The other human might also be attracted but neither knew their noses were leading them to a possible union.

"I don't know if you will correctly figure this out, but you'll dog me, hound me, forgive the pun since we both hunt behind the hounds."

"You do know something. You are in danger."

"I am not in danger but yes, I do know something." She opened her arm, moving it across the meadows, as it were. "I believe Paula is out there somewhere. I know she was killed. Ruffy, her shadow, never came home, so I think Ruffy was killed with her. I mourned her for a long, long time. I still pray for her. A devoted public servant deserves our memory. A woman who loved her country, she was a spy. Not a pretty word, but she was. Her work involved risk. Her cover was good but nonetheless."

"Did she talk to you about what she'd seen and done?"

"Oh, some things. But let's consider spying for a moment. It's a ghastly game. Annually millions, possibly more, are spent on this. Money that might feed people. Even allies spy on one another. You can imagine what enemies do."

"Meddle in our elections."

Arlene shrugged. "Why is anyone surprised, really? And do we know all of what we're doing? I'm not saying it's moral, but I am saying it's necessary."

"Okay. But who do you think Jason, Clare, and perhaps Paula were close to exposing? Something or someone?"

"Jason and Clare were not. Paula was. Let's think about spying again. Our Revolutionary War. If John André had not been captured, a man of great personal charm, we would not have discovered that Benedict Arnold was a traitor, ready to hand over West Point to the British. They would have controlled the Hudson. They were rich, had a professional army and navy, and they would have hanged many of us had they won. Spying is necessary and dangerous."

"Nathan Hale, 'I regret that I have only one life to give for my country.' " Harry recalled a bit of her schooling.

"Paula died for her country."

"What?" Harry swiveled to look directly at Arlene.

"She slowly put the pieces together. The Russians wanted information about the Turks. They would pay for this. Clare could be helpful. She and Jason were not yet married, but they were getting close. She would not be selling them anything, but she could put the person she was talking to in contact with Jason. So in this way, the path was not direct, but Jason gave good information. He split the money with Clare. Over time they became even closer."

"Does that endanger us?"

"Not necessarily, although it is a violation of everything one is taught in the foreign service and in the military. However, as time went on, Clare and Jason, who Paula believed concocted this in their time together in Paris, were offered quite large sums of money, ultimately a few million, if they would give information about our country once they returned, still in service, of course."

"Like military stuff?"

"Not so much. The Russians study us more than we study ourselves. So do the Chinese and even our allies, the English, the French, the Germans. They realized the media was creating real problems, hatreds. Let me tell you something, Harry. No one turns off their TV or electronic device because they're angry. They turn it off because they're bored. Sell fear. Sell hate. People will be mesmerized, glued to the set. And the advertising budgets will soar, which is exactly what has happened. Doesn't matter if you're watching a talking head from the right or the left, the newscaster acting as though he or she is really giving you the news, those dreary talk shows on Sunday where pompous assholes, forgive my language, declaim what is happening in Washington. So-and-so of the Democratic Party will raise your taxes, destroy your wealth. So-and-so of the Republican Party will favor the rich while the poor go hungry. I could go on. But the electronic media makes so much money. Billions by now if you added it all up. Jason knew communication. He could direct our enemies to the correct formats. False news could be fed into people's computers, their phones. For him, this would be easy. As for supplying the TV types, a piece of cake. It's kind of like the corruption running all through our country. Everything is commercially driven. No one gives a damn about the people, about the country, as long as they make money. Paula did. So do I."

Harry breathed deeply. "You're telling me you killed Jason and Clare."

"Ah, Harry, Smith College turned out a truly smart woman. Then again, you were smart or they wouldn't have admitted you."

"Did you?"

"The short answer is yes. The last time I spoke with Paula, we both met in Washington, one of those expensive but really good K Street restaurants. She laid out what she had uncovered. She didn't have it all together, but she had it. She wanted the name of the Russian operative, the Turkish operative, too. She didn't want to go to her old bosses and look a fool. If she had names, she'd be listened to. She didn't need to show how much money it took to buy the dealership. That's on record. Where the money came from, well, it's clearly concealed as saved salary and investments. She also couldn't trace the rest of the funds to Switzerland, but she was certain they were

there. It's where everything winds up."
Arlene half laughed.

"I don't know if I would have figured it out correctly."

"You were on a track. You could have endangered yourself, although the Russian, whoever he or she is, I doubt would worry about it. That person is probably back in Moscow or St. Petersburg or in a fabulous dacha. I am in no danger."

"I can scratch your eyes out." Pewter puffed up. *"I am terrifying."*

"Wait," Mrs. Murphy commanded.

"Am I?"

"Let me ask you this. Would you kill for your country?"

"I, yes, I think I would, but the damage was already done. You didn't kill for your country."

"No." A long sigh followed this. "No. But Paula died for us. She was doing her duty. If she could have brought them to justice, had them arrested, we would know more and possibly be able to better safeguard America in the future."

"That's true." Harry should have been frightened but her curiosity overrode her fear.

"She was my friend. I loved her. Imagine if someone had killed Susan. Wouldn't you seek revenge if they went unpunished, were wildly successful to boot?"

"I —" Harry thought a long time. "Yes."

"She was my friend. I loved her. I even loved her little beagle. When they disappeared, I somewhat consoled myself by knowing she didn't die alone. Silly."

"Are you going to kill me?"

"No. I admire you. I like you, Harry. You don't give up. And if you turned me in, it would be your word against mine. And the law-enforcement people would have to figure out how I killed them. Well, Jason is obvious. I am hoping you will choose silence."

"Clare?"

"She had a headache. I had those pills, had them for months thinking I would eventually slip them into a drink. Instead, I handed them to her. She took them. Who would notice? Blowfish is undetectable in the bloodstream, flushes out within hours."

"It stays in the urine for up to four days. In consideration of the circumstances of Jason's death, the medical examiner's office decided to run a more extensive toxicology panel. There is a slim possibility that it was from accidental ingestion of tainted food, even though we didn't have anything on the menu like blowfish." Harry smiled wryly.

"It's like super food poisoning. Kind of like 'The Purloined Letter.' It wasn't hidden. Out in the open."

Arlene nodded. "More or less. Easily available for someone with contacts all over the world."

She stood up. "I think Paula's here. She would have readily met them here, or one of them. I don't know if Jason or Clare did the deed or if they both did. Aldie is the perfect place. Killing her on their territory wouldn't be wise, nor on hers. Here, well, it's full of ghosts. If we haven't been able to find the cavalrymen from 1863, we won't find Paula."

Harry stood up, too, looked again at the expanse. "I don't understand people."

"I understand them only too well." Arlene exhaled. "Don't sell yourself short."

Harry shrugged. "I didn't know her, of course, but she did her duty for us. I'll pray for her."

They turned to walk back to the Institute.

Ruffy smiled at his friends. *"She can be at peace. Justice is one thing. Peace is another."*

"She had a good friend," Tucker said. *"Arlene."*

"Come on, you rascals." Harry called to her friends.

Arlene smiled. "If I had made a move

toward you, I think I would have been attacked."

"Scratch your eyes out!" Pewter spat.

"Bite your legs," Tucker promised.

"Push you over," the ever-growing Irish wolfhound threatened.

"Climb up your back and claw your face while Pewter climbed up your front." Mrs. Murphy said exactly what Pewter wanted to hear.

As they took a few steps onto the farm road, Tucker turned around to see Ruffy walking with his human.

"Look," the corgi announced.

The other three watched, Ruffy's tail wagging, looking up at the human ghost.

"Love never dies," Mrs. Murphy said.

loved you," and I wish I would have been.

Dear Reader,
Pewter's message reeked of unearned self-regard. I took it out of here. Hope you are well.

Mrs. Murphy

Dear Reader,

I found my letter. See what I live with? A thief. What does Mrs. Murphy contribute to these books? Dull. The cat defines tedium.

I, on the other hand, burst with ideas and excitement.

As for human history, who cares? All they do is repeat the same stuff over and over. Only the clothes change.

Cats are far more interesting except for you-know-who.

Pewter

Dear Reader,
  Someone save me from these cats.

  Tucker

  P.S. Pirate doesn't know his ABCs yet. He can't write. But he, too, has to live with this.

THE NATIONAL BEAGLE CLUB

Founded in 1887 by farsighted and good people, the National Beagle Club benefits from continued solid leadership. If only we could send them to Congress.

I am certainly grateful to Lis Kelly, the archivist. She certainly has a task.

Liz Reeser, the assistant treasurer of the National Beagle Club, an events coordinator, and a major contributor to Hounds F4R Heroes, took a lot of time with me and made me laugh in the bargain.

Arie Rijke, M.D., Master of the Waldingfield Beagles, allows me to bedevil him. Watching him hunt his hounds, listening to tales of the past, needs of the present, has been invaluable. The other staff members of the club have also been wonderful.

Kathleen King, formerly of Ashland Bassets, whose late husband, Al Toews, was Master of Bassets, as always finds me odd tidbits of information when asked. She hunts with Oak Ridge Foxhunt Club and we have hunted behind bassets with intense pleasure.

Amy Burke Walker, Jt. MB of Holly Hill Beagles, cochair of the Triple Challenge and a member of the board of directors at the National Beagle Club, endured far too many questions from myself. We both whip-in to the Waldingfield Beagles and she whips-in to me with the Oak Ridge Foxhounds. On foot, I simply imitate her if I am able. Amy has won the Best in the Nation award two times, maybe more, for whipping-in. When she is whipping-in to me, on horseback, I know that side is covered. But I keep asking her questions and she bears it in good grace.

Hounds F4R Heroes was started by Steve Fox, ably assisted by his wife, Trish, and Matt Lafley is a cofounder. If you Google Hounds F4R Heroes, you will see if your state has such a group. This is a relatively new development and one worthy of our support.

Allow me to give thanks for the Waldingfield Beagles who left us and are now in the Happy Hunting Grounds after a life doing what they loved. I love it, too, and owe them a great deal, as I do to the people of the above-named pack. A good time is had by all.

Without Geoffrey Ogden and Jan, his wife, this novel would not have been possible. Given their long careers in service of our nation, postings overseas to sometimes dangerous places, I was astonished and sobered by their information. Geoff, among his other successes, was president of the Middleburg Hunt Club. When I talk to him I never want him to stop, whether it concerns our State Department or foxes. As for Jan, I look older, she does not. Grateful as I am for her service, I find this deeply unfair.

Finally, Joy Cummings and Harriett Love, her sister, came up with all manner of ideas about poisons. I hope to stay on their good side.

Thank you, thank you, thank you.

ACKNOWLEDGMENTS

Ideally, the eighteenth- and twenty-first-century story lines should neatly tie up at the end. You, even if this is your first Mrs. Murphy mystery, know the past impacts the future. In truth, it is never past.

There is so much happening in 1787, were I to push this into 1788, this novel would be a thousand pages. Any writer producing such heft is probably too arrogant to know to need his or her editor.

There's Sheba's jewels, which will be resolved in the next Mrs. Murphy novel, or again this would be too long.

I am indebted to Geoff and Jan Ogden.

Also to Kathleen King and her dear friend Jack Burke.

Tracy Devine, my editor, is a true literary editor. This is not to suggest I deserve her, only to suggest we both love literature and can natter on about Shakespeare, etc.

I will do as she so politely suggests.

I will also try to make production deadlines. Lisa Feuer is head of production. There's not a writer in the stable who does not benefit from her eye.

As for those eighteenth-century characters to whom I am tied, you may not know their private futures but you know what's coming in the world.

Here it is a few decades and two centuries later and we all live in the shadow of the guillotine.

All the best,
Rita Mae

ABOUT THE AUTHORS

Rita Mae Brown has written many bestsellers and received two Emmy nominations. In addition to the Mrs. Murphy series, she has authored a dog series comprised of *A Nose for Justice* and *Murder Unleashed,* and the Sister Jane foxhunting series, among many other acclaimed books. She and Sneaky Pie live with several other rescued animals.

ritamaebrownbooks.com

To inquire about booking Rita Mae Brown for a speaking engagement, please contact the Penguin Random House Speakers Bureau at speakers@penguinrandomhouse.com.

Sneaky Pie Brown, a tiger cat rescue, has written many mysteries — witness the list at the front of this novel. Having to share credit with the above-named human is a small irritant, but she manages it. Anything is better than typing, which is what "Big Brown" does for the series. Sneaky calls her human that name behind her back after the wonderful Thoroughbred racehorse. As her human is rather small, it brings giggles among the other animals. Sneaky's main character — Mrs. Murphy, a tiger cat — is a bit sweeter than Miss Pie, who can be caustic.

The employees of Thorndike Press hope
you have enjoyed this Large Print book. All
our Thorndike, Wheeler, and Kennebec
Large Print titles are designed for easy reading, and all our books are made to last.
Other Thorndike Press Large Print books
are available at your library, through se-
lected bookstores, or directly from us.

For information about titles, please call:
(800) 223-1244

or visit our website at:
gale.com/thorndike

To share your comments, please write:
Publisher
Thorndike Press
10 Water St., Suite 310
Waterville, ME 04901